1986
TOMMY

Tommy was crying, holding his head in his hands, saying over and over that he should have kissed Renaldo Calabasas that night when he had the chance.

It had been a week since Renaldo was struck by lightning. Tommy was sitting where it happened: under the charred tree in Hollow Pond Park, huddled into the base of the blackened trunk—the exact spot where they almost kissed. He wrote down his thoughts.

You are like smoke, a dark dance in the air.

No.

You are a storm cloud, weightlessly heavy.

No.

You are as mysteriously beautiful as black smoke.

No.

A crow.

No.

A raven?

Tommy crossed out his words. He was such a shitty poet. He wasn't even a smidge as good as René. And his bad poetry couldn't match what he was feeling.

But he kept writing in the book. He had to. Renaldo Calabasas was lost in the astral plane, floating somewhere in its expanse. And it was the book that told Tommy that if he wanted to find Renaldo and bring him back to Earth, he had to write down how he felt. He had to get close to him in words, and the words would be his path to him.

The book told him to write it all out.

The book. The book.

JUNE, THREE MONTHS EARLIER

Tommy stood at the bike rack watching Renaldo Calabasas unchain his clunky old banana-seat Schwinn.

René was sweating through his white button-down shirt, and Tommy could see the contours of his chest through the wet fabric.

It was Friday, the last day of school, and everyone had cleared out in an end-of-the-year frenzy, ripping up and throwing away their schoolwork and locker decorations like they were getting out of jail. The trash bins next to them were filled with spiral notebooks, crumpled papers, tattered locker posters of Van Halen and the Doors. All the wealthy juniors and seniors of Herron High had driven away in their cars to some popular person's party somewhere. Tommy wouldn't know where.

"You ready to go?" Renaldo asked, piling books into his basket before stopping suddenly. He leaned against his bike and stared up at the sky.

"What are you looking at?" Tommy asked.

"I'll come to you when the sky is cerulean blue," René said.

"What?"

"That sentence. It came to me last night after a dream. Like someone said it to me. I'm just wondering if this is what 'cerulean blue' is."

Tommy followed Renaldo's gaze. The sky was strangely dark in color, like the coldness of outer space was closer than normal. *Cerulean, cerulean,* Tommy repeated to himself.

Renaldo rummaged through the bike basket and ripped out a page from his notebook. Tommy could see that there was a poem written on it titled "Storm Omen." Even by sight, Tommy knew it would be good and that it would appear in the next *Cornucopia*—the student literary magazine they worked on. Everything René wrote made it in there.

"It's about lightning," René explained, still staring at the sky, "about this thing called *keraunoscopy*. Do you know that word?"

"No, sorry," Tommy said. He wanted to say, *Do you know how beautiful you are?* But of course he didn't.

"It means divination by lightning," said Renaldo. "I mean, isn't that the most amazing word ever? Apparently, the Etruscans believed that lightning and thunder were omens."

Tommy only had a vague idea who the Etruscans were but nodded assuredly, anyway. Renaldo was so well-read. Lightning was his latest obsession.

"Lightning on a Tuesday or Wednesday was good luck for crops. But on a Sunday meant a man would die, a whole different thing. On a Friday, it meant something foreboding was coming. I wrote this last night. Well, technically, this morning after midnight, so it was on a Friday." René talked quickly and floridly, like he always did, and Tommy ate up every word.

He scanned the page.

> I am naked, only in my skin,
> bare bark,
> listening for storms
> waiting for omens

Tommy couldn't get the naked part out of his mind.

"Come on," René said suddenly, snatching the poem back, "we have to get to the library."

Tommy watched as he folded the poem meticulously into a triangle, like he was folding a flag for a soldier, and placed the little parcel in the front pocket of his shirt. Then he hopped on his bike, and Tommy quickly strapped on his backpack full of books and grabbed his bike, too, pedaling hard to keep up.

They rolled down Freedom Avenue. Tommy let René go first so he could watch him from behind, his hair flying, white shirt billowing in the hot air. It was the beginning of June, the air was humid, and every yard they passed was dense with green lawns, sprinklers chattering away in wet stutters.

Tommy wrote poetry, too, but never as good as Renaldo's.

Except for the poetry he wrote *about* Renaldo.

About René's dark curls that cascaded down his neck.

About his strong nose and deep brown eyes that were so open and expansive, they were almost like staring into a night sky filled with stars.

About René riding his bike in his strange white pants and

white shirts that he always wore, sometimes with an equally unstylish fedora hat, his bushy hair peeking out from under it.

About his brown skin, not one freckle.

About his body that was wiry and skinny and surprisingly strong, even though he never exercised.

About his old poetry books that he was always carrying around, along with his giant hardbound notebook that he wrote in constantly.

About the callus between his left index and middle finger that had formed because he wrote so much.

About how René wasn't popular but he didn't care at all. Tommy wasn't popular, either. That was for many reasons. But the big one: His last name was Gaye. And because life was apparently one giant cruel joke, he had always known he was gay, too. Last week he even said it out loud. He shut the door to his bathroom, making sure his parents and his brother were safely downstairs, and he looked in the mirror and whispered it to himself. *I'm gay.*

He muttered it quickly in the mirror so that he wouldn't have to get close and look at his pimply skin and feel even worse about himself. But now he was with René and they were on their way to the library and school had ended and he was free, flying down Freedom Avenue, and René was on his bike in front of him. He felt jolted with life.

Just two hours ago, René had surprised him at his locker before last period.

"Hello, fine sir," he said, miming the bow of a mannered gentleman from a different age like he always did. "See you at Ziller's after sixth?"

"Yes!" Tommy answered, already regretting his enthusiasm. "I know Ms. Ziller wants to, like, say goodbye to us or something?"

"Yes. And what are you doing after?"

"Um. Nothing, I guess," Tommy answered.

"Can you join me? I want to take you to the library and show you some of my secrets there," he said. Tommy swore he winked as he spoke. It made Tommy's heart leap.

René was talking about the public library, the one behind the Kmart in the middle of town. René had discussed going there with him for months, since they met at the beginning of the semester. It was his sacred space, where he checked out poets like Anne Sexton and Langston Hughes and Christina Rossetti— always someone new—and gave them to Tommy to read. At home, Tommy would dive into each page looking for messages. (Emily Dickinson was the hardest to decipher, but at the same time, strangely the most powerful, like her words were almost supernatural visions.)

"And anyway, I have to return that Anne Sexton book you keep hogging." (He gave Tommy the poet's *Love Poems* last week. Tommy had been poring over every word trying to find messages to him: "That was the day of your tongue / your tongue that came from your lips," she wrote, and Tommy felt himself vibrate.)

"Sure," Tommy said, trying to sound calm. Inside he was shining with excitement, but he had learned to not be so expressive, ever since his brother made him feel bad about it. ("You're so . . . *expressive*," Charley said when he caught Tommy dancing in his room to the *Xanadu* soundtrack.)

"Great. Well, I better make haste to what they call 'PE,'" Renaldo said, making air quotes. "We have some sort of incomprehensible final fitness test we have to complete."

"I hate PE with all of my being," Tommy said.

"To my very essence, pure loathing," René answered, and bounded off. "See you at Ziller's!"

Ms. Ziller was their favorite teacher. She ran the poetry club and was the literary magazine supervisor. Tommy had spent a lot of time after sixth period in Ms. Ziller's room this past spring. After winter break, he saw a light purple flyer on the bulletin board saying that Poetry Club was meeting on Thursdays after school. Something about the color alone made him know it was the right place for him.

It was just the three of them every Thursday—René, Tommy, and their friend Dara—and all they did was hang out and work on *The Cornucopia* and read poems or draw. When the door was closed, Ms. Ziller was funny and talkative and like their friend and not their teacher. Dara was the artist—lately obsessed with spiders, which in turn informed René's writing to include cobwebs and entanglement. Every Thursday, René would show up with a new typed-out poem that Ms. Ziller would quickly mimeograph on thick white paper, and Tommy would hold the wet, buttery paper in his hands and read another perfect work. Then Dara would pull out her charcoal pencils and begin an illustrated reaction to it like they were a jazz duo. Tommy's friends were so talented.

Tommy had only one poem that he was proud of (but no way would he show it to anyone), called "More Than Friends."

You look at me
Brown endless eyes
As if

You were sharing something
More than enough
A more perfect union
More than friends

He crumpled it up immediately. Then tore it up. Then ripped it into smaller pieces. And then ran downstairs and put it at the bottom of the garbage can in the kitchen.

"What are you doing?" his brother, Charley, asked, suddenly behind Tommy, surprising him.

"Nothing!" Tommy answered, trying to sound calm.

Ever since he and Renaldo became friends, Tommy had a vision. Or more like a daydream. He would be in bed still half-asleep after yet another night of wild dreams that made no sense, and like a movie under his eyelids, he would see himself and René, older, maybe even as old as sixty or seventy, in a house by the ocean. Tommy was in the kitchen making something (he had no idea how to cook anything but could in this daydream). He would finish cooking and bring the food out onto the porch, and there would be the ocean, not far away, crashing in relentless shushes, and René in his chair, with a book in his lap. Then Tommy would ask if he wanted some lunch, René would say *yes* and offer to help, and Tommy would say, *No, no, keep reading.* Then, Tommy would come up to him and stroke his long hair and kiss him.

Tommy wanted to do so, badly. But even though his best friend had asked him to come to the library, and summer was starting, he wouldn't dare try to kiss Renaldo Calabasas.

And so, when the bell rang on that last day of school, Tommy walked through the trash-strewn hall to the back of the building, where Ms. Ziller's room was at the end. The sign posted on the door read:

"All that we see or seem

is but a dream within a dream."

—Edgar Allan Poe

As if she had known, Ms. Ziller opened the door before he knocked and waved him into the classroom. She was wearing a sunset-orange turtleneck and tight bell-bottom jeans—so completely out of style, they were almost cool again. Behind her, on the walls, were other quotes in bubble letters on the bulletin board from people Tommy had never heard of: *"You write in order to change the world,"* said James Baldwin, and *"Poetry . . . is the liquid voice that can wear through stone,"* by Adrienne Rich.

Tommy slipped into a seat. René was perched on the top of a desk. Dara was leaning back in a chair, wearing her usual powdered white foundation and charcoaled-out eyes, her hair spiked up and standing on end like dynamite had exploded on her face.

"René told me you're going to the library, so I don't want to take up too much of your time," Ms. Ziller said, opening and closing drawers, rummaging around in five different directions like she often did. "I have something for you guys, since I won't see you till September."

"Oh, I can't go to the library," Dara interrupted. "My parents are going out, and I have to babysit my little brothers," she explained, and Tommy felt bad for feeling thrilled that it would just be him and René.

"Well, here you go," said Ms. Ziller. She held out three slim gift-wrapped boxes. Inside each was a pen, heavy and gold, with a removable cap.

"Just a reminder from me to keep writing. All summer."

"Wow. Thank you, Ms. Ziller," said Tommy.

"Cool," said Dara.

"It has a heft to it," said René, weighing it in his hands.

"For heavy words. And light ones, too," she said, almost embarrassed by her gift. "I just want you three to keep creating this summer. And be safe." Tommy watched as tears pricked her eyelashes. She was getting emotional.

"Now go, get out of here!" Ms. Ziller composed herself and pushed the teenagers out the door.

"Have fun. I'll see you guys tomorrow," Dara said as she walked off in the opposite direction toward her locker. "We can watch this movie I rented."

Tomorrow they all had plans to hang out at Dara's. Tommy was already excited. Now he got to be alone with René. And then tomorrow, the hangout.

* * * * * * * *

Tommy and René stepped into the library. It was empty. Just a smattering of old people concentrating on their magazines. A blast of air-conditioning chilled Tommy's face, and his eyes darted around, trying to spot a bathroom so he could go to a mirror to see if his bad skin, his acne-covered skin, looked okay.

"I'll be right back!" he said.

He was glad he did—in the bathroom mirror, he saw that two whiteheads had formed on his nose. He popped them immediately. He hated mirrors. He hated his skin. Furtively, he dabbed the little spots where he was bleeding until they stopped. Someone knocked on the door and he jumped.

"Hold on! Sorry!"

He washed his face and dabbed his skin again and quickly slipped out the door, an annoyed middle-aged woman staring at him like he was in there masturbating. He felt the wetness of his skin in the air and the tiny sting of his pimples.

Tommy found René in the reference section, standing before a giant dictionary set on a wooden podium. It was the biggest dictionary Tommy had ever seen. It smelled like museums.

"Here it is," Renaldo said, introducing Tommy to it proudly, like it was his souped-up car. The pages were delicate and thin, the words so microscopic you needed a magnifying glass to see them. One dangled from the podium on a string.

"This is how I found *keraunoscopy*," Renaldo told him.

Renaldo's spectacular poetry was full of amazing words. He confidently sprinkled them into long, descriptive lines like a chef with herbs. *Caveat, brindled, encomium. The Cornucopia* was basically an excuse to publish Renaldo's work. And Dara's accompanying drawings, which were also amazing.

"So, if I ever get blocked or don't know what to write about, I come here and just close my eyes and find a word, and then *pow!*" He made a head explosion gesture. The sudden movement made Renaldo's white shirt lift up, and Tommy saw the hair leading down his stomach. "Other times I just walk through the poetry section and pick out books randomly and read a line or a stanza to try and get messages. That's called poetic divination. James Merrill did it, and so did Sylvia Plath. A lot of the great poets used to do this."

Tommy watched René glide his hands over the dictionary. He flipped through the book again.

"Augury!" he said. "Oh, I know this one. It's a sign of what will happen in the future, like an omen. It's a word from the Romans. The Romans loved omens. They even had, like, government-supported psychics called sibyls. But from what I've read, the Romans really owe their whole psychic knowledge to the Etruscans. Who were very observant about the planes."

"Planes? There were airplanes flying around?"

Renaldo laughed and rested his hand on Tommy's shoulder. Tommy felt electrified by his touch. "Not, like, airplanes. Meaning, like, areas. Planes of reality."

If he wasn't obsessing about poets, René was focused on ancient myths and magic. He often talked about spirits and other worlds like he really believed in them.

He pointed to the walls. "This," he said, pounding the floor with his fist. "This, the earth we're standing on, is just one plane. There are others!" He said this loudly, swerving his arms around.

The librarian looked up from the desk and glared disapprovingly.

René quieted down. "There isn't just life and death," he whispered. "The Etruscans, the Romans, the Mesopotamians, the Maya, all these ancient cultures thought that there were other planes—other places where we exist. They had *way* more respect for . . . elsewhere. Our culture, now, doesn't respect that. Why do we think we are so much more evolved than them?"

René tugged at his hair again and then stared at Tommy with his deep brown eyes.

"Yeah, sure, sure," Tommy answered with confused enthusiasm. "How do you get there, to this other place? I mean plane." Maybe in this other plane, René would actually kiss him. Tommy imagined it looked like one of those special episodes of afternoon soap operas where Sierra, the rich girl, and Locke, the stable boy, finally made love on a gauzy four-poster bed surrounded by a menagerie of lit candles and rose petals sprinkled on the comforter.

"Different cultures say different things," Renaldo said. Then he grabbed Tommy by the shoulders and placed him in front of the huge tome. "Your turn."

Tommy closed his eyes, flipped through the book, and moved his finger around the tissue-thin page. He opened his eyes to find his finger on *projection*.

"Cool," Renaldo said encouragingly. "*Projection*. Like a projection into the astral plane!"

"The astral plane?"

"Oh! That's what they call the other planes these days. I have to show you this book that I am obsessed with. It's about traveling to the astral plane and how to do it."

"Cool," Tommy said, not fully understanding what René meant.

René stood up, grabbing Tommy's hand. Tommy hoisted his backpack over his shoulders as they scurried through the tall stacks, down to an area that seemed like no one frequented it. It was in a corner. René crouched in front of a low shelf of books, dusty and undisturbed.

"Here it is," he said, rummaging through the shelf to find a slim volume. The cover had a swirling illustration that looked like melted stained glass. Tommy saw the title emblazoned in scarlet letters.

THE SACRED ART OF ASTRAL PROJECTION

"I check it out at least once a month. It's full of history that you won't learn at Herron," René said, scooching next to Tommy to show him the pages. "There are several different methods to project. Some are super insane, like you swallow two worms in a glass of water. The Druids were all about hanging mistletoe."

"Mistletoe? Like Christmas?"

"Yes! That's what it became. Pagan rituals of sacred passage are turned into watered-down versions in our culture."

"Oh wow, so that's why we have it around at Christmas. Like, it was some ritual before?"

"Yep. And now it's just become an excuse to make out." René laughed.

Tommy wanted so bad to say, *I wish I had some mistletoe right now*, but even just thinking it made him cringe inside. He wasn't sure how Renaldo felt. One slipup, one admission, one mistaken touch, and he could ruin everything.

René handed Tommy the book. "Now you have me obsessing about Druids," he said. "Look through it! I'm going to go find some other stuff. By the time I come back, maybe you can figure out how to astral project, too."

"Wait, you know how to do this?"

"Oh, I'm just practicing. But maybe we can help each other. Master Sebastian can teach us. He wrote the book," René said. "Read about it and maybe you can visit me tonight in our sleep. Ha!"

Renaldo Calabasas jumped up and ran excitedly down the stacks to find yet another pile of books.

I would like nothing more, Tommy thought. He sat on the floor, crossing his legs, and opened the book.

Master Sebastian. Tommy imagined him with long hair, in an

iridescent robe, with a crystal ball in front of him. *The physical body isn't the only body,* Master Sebastian explained in the introduction. Tommy read through the book for a long while. He noticed little notes in René's handwriting. He must have checked out the book a hundred times. There were exclamation points and circles around lines about the "energy body" and how time was a construct. But this was the occult section. Tommy glanced at the other titles on the shelves—about ESP and Bigfoot and space aliens. He didn't believe in those. But he wanted to believe in astral projection simply because René did.

"So, what do you think?" René said, crouching next to Tommy again. His body odor fumed off him, like he had gone through puberty since they were sitting there at the library. Tommy was intoxicated by it.

"It's pretty wild stuff," said Tommy.

"I know. And in every civilization there's always ancients who believe in this. Also that there's a multiverse with different timelines and—"

"Whoa, slow down, I'm still trying to understand what Druids are," Tommy said.

René looked at him and smiled. "Maybe you can come over to my house for dinner tonight? We can practice."

Tommy flushed with excitement. *Was he just asked on a date?*

They biked to René's even though it was uphill and on the other side of town. Tommy followed René through the streets where the houses became older and smaller. They wheeled down the end of a cul-de-sac called Imperial Court, right off Marquis Street. The cul-de-sac dropped downhill, and René's house was low and red, emerging from a deep wooded slope behind it.

Tommy walked up to the front door. To the left was a big bay window that looked into the family TV room, and beyond it, the kitchen. Tommy saw René's parents and younger brother there, in the kitchen, all talking in Spanish. Tommy had no idea what they were saying. His father was bent over a boiling pot, in an apron, stirring and tasting what was in it, and his mother, wearing a flower-printed sundress, her long black hair tied up loosely in a bun, was clanking plates onto the kitchen table. They all seemed so connected, like they enjoyed being together. René flopped his bike into the yard, and what sounded like a dozen dogs started barking.

"Cállate!" he heard René's mother say. The door opened and she stood there, two yapping dogs jumping behind her, René's younger brother peeking from behind her skirt. "Callate! Callate!"

Tommy had almost forgotten that René's family was from Argentina, which René had told him several months ago. Tommy had run home and looked in the encyclopedia to read about it.

René's mother turned and commanded the boy to grab the dogs and pull them away. "You must be Tommy," she said, opening her arms, kissing him on the cheek.

René's father peeked around the entrance to the kitchen, with a wooden spoon in his hand. "Tommy! We have heard much about you."

"It's nice to meet you, Mr. and Mrs. Calabasas," Tommy said politely.

Stepping inside, he smelled the air, rich with fried dough and vegetables and warmth. The dogs jumped on Tommy's legs and then, satisfied, ran off. René bent over a pot that his dad was stirring on the stove. He looked more juvenile. Being in his home made him seem like less of a demigod and more of a teenager.

René led Tommy around the house. It was covered with books and plants. There were charcoal drawings hanging in the foyer hall. Nudes of a woman.

"Those are my mom's self-portraits," René said, as if it wasn't at all scandalous that Tommy was seeing his mom naked. He understood then why René was so comfortable talking about nudity.

The dinner was delicious. Beef empanadas and then flan for dessert. René's parents asked him questions about his life and his own poetry as if they were genuinely interested. They spoke glowingly about *The Cornucopia* and how René's poetry was being printed in it. They were so proud.

"And your friend Dara," René's mother said, "she's such a good artist."

"Yes, she is very talented," Tommy replied.

Mrs. Calabasas leaned over to Tommy and loudly whispered, "She doesn't need all that ghost makeup! She is beautiful on her own."

"Bea," said her husband playfully, "she is expressing herself. Let her be."

René's father tapped the table. "Well, I'm sure you boys have things to do."

"Right! We have things to create," said René, who stood and cleared the dishes dutifully. "Tommy and I will clean up and then we can go to my room."

Tommy was embarrassed, afraid that this was a joke. Why were they so encouraging of them to spend time in René's bedroom? They must have thought Renaldo would never be interested in boys, much less one like Tommy. Maybe it was because René wasn't gay. *This can't be anything,* Tommy thought.

He followed René's lead, helping rinse off plates and stack them in the dishwasher. René's parents settled in the living room, reading. His younger brother played with Hot Wheels cars. The television chattered. No one paid attention while René guided Tommy up to his room.

Stepping into René's room, Tommy felt suddenly immersed in his best friend. In the past he had secretly smelled René— his clothes when he brushed past him, a whoosh of him when he made a passionate point at a Poetry Club meeting. But now those brief breezes of intimacy filled the space like a scented candle.

His bedroom faced the backyard, with a big window looking out to the trees and sloping hill. Tommy felt like he had been here before, in a dream, like this was déjà vu.

René began excitedly showing him various things he had collected: poems by H.D. and by Elizabeth Bishop and James Merrill.

"He reminds me of you," said René.

"Why?" Tommy asked.

"Oh. Just that he is sensitive to things. And he likes to write about things being . . . entangled." René suddenly grabbed his shoulder.

"Oh, and another thing about Merrill! He loved to use divination to create his words. Like Ouija boards and other channels to other planes."

Renaldo opened a bag of runes, and they tried to make a poem using the letters as a guide. The words were simple: *crow, tree, fire.* Then they tried the Ouija board to talk to spirits, only getting as far as nonsense words: *lolly, oona, pris.*

Renaldo looked up from the pile of runes and the Ouija board.

"You know, nothing we do is going be as good as that poem you wrote."

"Mine? What poem?"

"The one about leaving your body."

"Why? It's bad." He knew exactly the poem. It was in the red spiral notebook Tommy carried around full of his bad poetry (much of it about René), in his backpack now.

"No, it's not. Read it! I know you have it in your notebook," René said, nodding to Tommy's trusty backpack.

"I can't."

"Come on, poetry is meant to be read out loud," Renaldo goaded. "You know what? I'll read it." René grabbed Tommy's backpack and pulled out the notebook. Tommy lunged for it.

"Okay, okay! I'll read it," Tommy said, snatching it back and flipping quickly through the pages, careful to not show his other poems. Tommy cleared his throat.

We are just energy, just fizz.
We are far away, not hers, not his.
We meet and intertwine, not yours, not mine.

René looked at him and smiled proudly. "So good. It's like you are expressing how much we aren't locked into our bodies. How we aren't even a man or woman . . ." René stared at him. "Wow, I have never noticed how blue your eyes are," he said to Tommy. Tommy's stomach lurched.

Then René turned out the lights.

"Wait for a second," he said. "Close your eyes." And Tommy complied, sitting there and burning with anticipation. Tommy heard the thrums of guitar and keyboard. Pink Floyd.

"Keep your eyes closed and concentrate on the sound," René instructed. "I heard that they put secret messages in the music. Maybe we can detect them. Your psychic perceptions are more sensitive if the lights are off," he said.

Tommy sat there, confused. They were in René's room and it was dark and they were sitting next to each other, but they were listening to Pink Floyd. If it was the Smiths, that would be more of a signal that Renaldo *liked* him, because he heard that the lead singer was bisexual. But Pink Floyd? The scary burnouts who smoked in the back of the school wore Pink Floyd T-shirts. They didn't seem gay. What kind of signal was that?

He tried to imagine René's energy, as he had done countless times in his bed alone. But this time René was right there next to him. He was afraid that something would happen down there in his pants, and then he would be caught with proof of what he was feeling. The song continued. A bunch of noodling guitars. He didn't dare reach across the darkness to touch René.

They sat there for what seemed like ages. The record ended, and Tommy looked at the clock. It was 9:00 p.m., and he needed to go home or he would get in trouble.

"I have to go," he said, more abruptly than he wanted to sound. He rose and grabbed his bag.

"Okay. Well, we can try to astral project tonight. And then talk about it when we go to Dara's house," René said.

Tommy smiled and settled down. This wasn't his only chance with René. He had the whole summer, and a hangout at Dara's was the perfect next step.

He made it home that night dizzy with feelings. Before he

walked in the door, he parked his bike and lay on the front lawn. Nestled there in the groomed grass, looking into the sky as it darkened to a deeper blue, he felt his body expand with what he could only call promise. Maybe this was how poets felt.

He sat up, went inside, and greeted his mother. She was cleaning the dishes, an empty Stouffer's frozen pizza box on the kitchen table.

"How was your friend's?" she asked.

"Fine," he said, and then hesitating, "Can I go to Dara's tomorrow afternoon? We have a . . . a Poetry Club scrimmage."

Tommy knew that his parents would disapprove of him going over to Dara's house, a *girl's* house, even if he wasn't the least bit interested. It was easier to pretend that poetry had scrimmages— that thing his brother, Charley, was always having to go to for his dumb soccer games.

"But why? The school year's ended," his mother asked.

"Poetry Club scrimmages run all summer," Tommy lied, and then, before she could ask too many more questions, he darted up the stairs.

After Tommy brushed his teeth, he sat on his bed and thought about what René had said about seeing him tonight. Tommy closed his eyes. He tried to remember what he read in the library from *The Sacred Art of Astral Projection.* That there was a technique for taking the first step to the astral plane.

Imagine spots on a path out the door, and in your mind, put valuable objects there. They are your talismans.

Tommy decided he would place his old *Star Wars* action figures in each corner.

He mentally placed his Luke by the door, Obi-Wan in the

hall, and Princess Leia by the stairs. She was his favorite. He had learned at a very young age that boys couldn't play with dolls, so she was the closest he could get. They were all worn down, scuffed up, cherished and chipped away by a younger version of himself. When he was younger, he remembered playing with a doll and it being ripped out of his hands. But it was blurred like a lot of his childhood memories. It all seemed so long ago.

Master Sebastian said that to begin astral projecting, you had to think about someone you cared about (that was easy) and focus on that person. Tommy lay in his bed, ready to travel to Renaldo and go somewhere free of containment. Somewhere they could actually kiss, far away from any judging eyes or danger. He felt himself drifting off.

＊ ＊ ＊

Tommy jolted awake in his bed. His alarm jangled with that horrible Top 40 pop hit "We Built This City" by Starship. He lay there in bed feeling the reality of his life solidify out of the fog of sleep. He was Tommy Gaye, he had just finished ninth grade, and it was 1986.

He tried to remember his dreams. They were like they always were: absurd and hard to describe. Vibrant, intense, weird—full of strange creatures, flying whales, snake-horses, talking thumbs, hair that became gooey slime that became edible. They were always like this.

But then, suddenly, he remembered one part of his dream last night that almost made sense. He dreamed he was on a large, flat expanse, like the high-school football field but even bigger.

He felt like he was in a balloon, floating, descending through clouds, the air growing opaque until he landed like a feather. Then, he woke up.

That evening, while it was still light outside, Tommy biked to the Bauras' house. He told his mother it was much closer than it really was. Dara lived on the same side of town as René, the side with all the older, shabbier houses. He parked his bike and walked up to the cracked cement porch.

Dara opened the door as he walked up. She was wearing less makeup than usual but was still dressed somberly, in a long black coat with a black shirt under it. She motioned to him to follow her downstairs to the recreation room.

Her younger brothers were in there, loudly pelting each other with bean bags from the Toss Across game.

"Quiet! Out!" Dara said firmly. Tommy was impressed at how obediently and quickly they left.

"Look what I got," she said, and pulled out a bowl of cheddar-cheese-covered popcorn. "It's gourmet. My parents brought it back from one of the fifty thousand events they go to."

She pointed to a huge recliner and ordered Tommy to sit in it.

"Where's Renaldo?"

"He called before you got here. He says he is busy tonight. Working on some new poem about some supernatural hogwash," she said.

Tommy tried really hard not to look disappointed.

"Anyway, I am so psyched to show you this movie," Dara said, pulling out a VHS tape. "It's, like, going to change your life."

She pushed the plastic rectangle into the machine. Tommy heard a *ka-chunk* and a whir.

"It's gonna take a while to register," said Dara. He still couldn't believe movies could be contained on these things.

As they waited, Dara looked at Tommy.

"So . . . what did you do with René?" she asked, surprising him. The phrasing made Tommy feel unstable. There were so many ways for him to answer that. He really wanted, desperately, to talk about René and how he felt about him and ask Dara everything, but he couldn't. This might be a trap.

So he tried to sound casual. "We just went to the library. Then I went over to his house, and we listened to Pink Floyd in the dark."

"Ew, Pink Floyd?" Dara said to him. "That's, like, so . . . classic rock! Like something my uncle listens to. Is Renaldo secretly, like, in his thirties or something?"

Tommy laughed. "I think he thought it may be a way for us to travel to the astral plane or something?"

"Oh, gag me, is he going off about that crazy book again? *Master Sebastian!* He talked all about it last fall. He's obsessed."

Tommy couldn't hold back any longer. "I know. He won't stop talking about it."

Dara brushed popcorn off her long black skirt. "Renaldo is the most talented person I know . . . but he is also a little—"

"A little what?" Tommy interrupted, and then immediately regretted sounding so eager.

"Like he is on another planet sometimes. Just a little fragile," she said. She busied herself with her bangs, twisted them into dark spikes like icicles on her forehead. "I worry that he gets too deep into all that occult stuff. Like it's making him, like, overly focus on stuff. He can get a little *too* invested sometimes," she said carefully. "Last fall before we met you? He was so obsessed with the concept of time, he didn't sleep, and then he got sick. He was out for a week. Just be careful with him."

Tommy felt his face burn.

The movie came on. It was called *The Hunger*, and starred Catherine Deneuve and David Bowie as vampires seducing people, and Susan Sarandon as their next victim. Halfway through, there was a scene where Susan Sarandon and Catherine Deneuve started making out, two women touching each other. Tommy couldn't believe that something like this was in a movie. He and Dara remained silent. He looked behind him to make sure Dara's brothers weren't coming down the stairs.

They kept watching the movie. It was sensual and soft focused and scary. New York City seemed so dangerous and seductive. And David Bowie was . . . beautiful.

"Bowie is so beautiful," Dara said, as if on cue.

Tommy didn't dare agree.

Soon he found himself dozing off, and when he woke up, the TV was blaring a Lollipop Crunch commercial. Dara was in the chair next to him curled into a fetal position, sleeping peacefully.

He had to get back home. He promised his mom he'd be there by 9:00 p.m., and it was 8:30. Tommy didn't want to wake Dara, so he left her a note and quietly walked upstairs and out the door.

When he got home, he could hear his mother arguing on the phone with his father.

"I understand, Walter. It's fine. But we are going to see my sister. And you are coming. Have a great night at . . . *work*."

She hung up the phone angrily. Tommy heard her sigh. He pretended to have just walked in.

"You're back!" she said, with rehearsed brightness. "How was your poetry scrimmage?"

"Fine!" he said cheerily.

He ran up to his room and shut the door. He wanted to call René but thought he would just write another poem about him instead. But right before he put pen to paper, his mother knocked on the door, making him jump out of bed. She walked into his room and told him to think about packing tonight. With Tommy's father working so much, she had put her foot down and insisted they all needed a family vacation. In two days, they would be driving ten-plus hours to Ohio to visit his aunt Susan. For almost three months.

He didn't even get to say goodbye to Dara or René. He called their houses, but there was no answer. He left a message on the Bauras' and Calabasases' answering machines, letting them know he would be gone until the end of August. His dreams of a summer riding bikes with René and maybe possibly holding hands with René would have to wait.

And wait. And wait.

He bought *The Hunger* soundtrack and listened to it on his Walkman constantly, writing more poems about René, trying as hard as he could to pour himself into concealed objects like flowers and branches.

When he got to Ohio, Tommy wanted to call René and check up on him but couldn't because that would be a long-distance call, and his parents would be angry at him for spending the money on his aunt's phone. He wondered if René was maybe reaching out to him. He wished for a signal or a sign and looked for it in everything: the weather, the color of a car passing by, even what the next commercial on TV might announce.

The weeks seemed like they spanned decades. Tommy played with his cousins and cleared dishes and slept with his snoring brother on couches in Uncle Ross's office den, surrounded by stamp collections and old books about maritime history. There was not one book of poetry in the entire house. Tommy would lie there and think about René, and worry about him, and fantasize about saving him, and he would, night after night, turn to a vision of them on a porch, the ocean roaring in the distance, René reading, Tommy kissing his head.

The days moved on and on in monotony: breakfast, pool, dinner, Charley's snores, only broken up by his florid, bizarre dreams of flying absurdities and looming figures.

August rolled on. Tommy felt the air begin to thin and saw the yellowed edges of tree leaves begin to appear. Finally, during his last week there, his aunt took him to the library in town, because it was next to her dry cleaner.

"We don't have much time!" she said from the chugging car.

Tommy ran into it, rushing to the poetry section. Hoping for a sign or signal, he thought he would attempt that "poetic divination" that René had talked about. Quickly he looked for his divine message, reached out for a book, opened it, and pointed at a line:

> Divulging it would rest my Heart
> But it would ravage theirs—

Emily Dickinson, once again, freaking him out. He chose again. Anna Akhmatova, who René had mentioned before. The book was worn down and old. He closed his eyes and pointed.

> Because it is unbearably painful
> For the soul to love silently.

He let out a sigh trapped inside him for weeks.
He chose again, Stanley Kunitz:

> The universe expanding, thinning out,
> Our worlds flying, oh flying, fast apart.

He hated that message, and grabbed a thick tome to his left above him. He opened it, closed his eyes, trying his best to feel like he had powers of premonition, and pointed his finger to a page. William Blake, one of René's favorites:

> O ROSE, thou art sick!
> The invisible worm
> That flies in the night,
> In the howling storm,
>
> Has found out thy bed
> Of crimson joy,
> And his dark secret love
> Does thy life destroy.

"Tommy!" someone screeched.

As if he had been caught by police, he furtively shoved the book back onto the shelf. His aunt walked up. "Tommy, I've been honking outside. We have to go!"

LATE AUGUST

The day he got back, he called Dara as soon as he could. His heart sang when she answered. As droll as she tried to be, Tommy could tell she was happy to talk to him, too.

"Have you seen René?" she asked.

"No, how is he?" Tommy asked as calmly as he could.

"He's not feeling well," she answered. "He's been in bed sleeping every time I call. His mom tries to sound like it's not a big deal."

Tommy felt nauseous. He went upstairs and lay in his bed thinking about everything he had ever said to René. It began to rain a chilly late summer rain. He went for a walk by the creek, throwing bark into the sewer pipe runoff. He came back wet. His mother stood there holding the phone.

"Oh, there you are. It's your friend, Ray Naldo? He called three times and I told him you—"

Tommy snatched the phone out of her hands. "Hello? René? I tried calling your house but—"

"I'm at the library, come meet me?" René asked abruptly. It was as if he hadn't left for three months.

Tommy obeyed all too willingly. He biked there, still in his wet jacket. He threw his bike on the rack and sped through the front doors. The same woman was at the circulation desk, bent over the big computer, barely noticing as he walked in. He didn't have time to check his skin in the bathroom mirror.

He found René on the floor, in front of the occult section, right where he was the last time they were here together. In front of René were a dozen books, scattered around in a semicircle. René was picking through them and then writing down notes in his big journal.

"Hey there, weirdo," Tommy said, trying to sound as casual and playful as Dara.

René jumped. "Oh! You startled me," he said.

Tommy sat himself across from René, the jumble of books between them. He didn't *look* sick. In fact, he looked just fine, poring over the books, not bothering to ask how Tommy's visit at his aunt's went.

Tommy tried to extend his legs so that there was the possibility of their feet touching. But René was too twitchy for something that subtle. He kept picking up books and setting them down, scribbling in his journal as he did so.

"What are you working on?"

"It's hard to explain," René said, surprisingly short with him. Tommy watched him pick up *The Sacred Art of Astral Projection* book and furiously flip through its pages.

"Well, if it helps, I haven't had much luck projecting," Tommy said. "I think Master Sebastian might be pulling our leg." He chuckled.

René looked up and into his eyes. Tommy hadn't seen this look before. It was like René had experienced something that he couldn't talk about. Like he had sex maybe? Tommy thought that was it, and then he thought about how stupid he was for thinking he and René would ever go anywhere. He prepared himself to hear how René had found a nice girl over the summer while he was gone. He tried to appear casual as he brushed his hand over his face to see if there were any blemishes he had to deal with.

"I'm in the middle of something very important, and I want to explain it to you, but it's so . . . big . . . Tommy, I—" René exhaled, in distress. "It's like what I write is becoming my dreams and what I dream is becoming what I write . . . It's in this loop. I go to sleep and all these images and thoughts fill my head. I am going farther and farther somewhere in my dreams, and I wake up frozen! You know those dreams where you are lying in your bed and can't move your body? That's what I wake up like but I'm not awake yet and then I DO wake up and . . ." René stopped talking. "Sorry," he said.

"No don't be sorry, I didn't—"

René gasped suddenly, staring out at something far away.

"What? Are you okay?"

"Did you hear that?"

"Hear what?"

"A voice, someone calling."

"A voice?"

"Nothing. Nothing."

René slumped down across from Tommy in the aisle. Now Tommy saw how exhausted he looked. His forehead was more furrowed, his eyes more darting, his skin paler, grayed. It was like a thought had entered his head that was changing his face, his skin. Maybe he was sick, after all.

SEPTEMBER

The first day of school was always the worst for Tommy. His name would be called out loud at roll call, and he would hear giggles scatter through class like titters from a flock of birds. ("His last name's Gay!") Not only that, but he had to endure it six times a day for each class, as each group got to think they were the first person who ever found it funny.

In the frenzy of the first day, Tommy hadn't seen Renaldo or Dara. Ms. Ziller was too busy with her classes and wouldn't start Poetry Club until next week. He kept thinking he would run into his friends, but he didn't. He thought about René's strange behavior in the library, and worried about him endlessly. On Wednesday, Tommy got up the nerve to call René, but he didn't pick up. Instead Tommy waited and waited, aching for his phone to ring until he fell asleep.

When the week ended with no phone call and no sign of Dara

or René, Tommy sat on his back porch, sullenly eating a bowl of Grape-Nuts. He had put on a grubby pair of shorts and a T-shirt he hated—his "Calligraphy Camp!" T-shirt from three years ago when he was obsessed with cursive and begged his mom to take him to classes (his brother called him a fairy). He couldn't call Dara and René today because his parents had given him a chore—sanding the rust off the porch iron railing. He was supposed to have completed the task right when he returned from their summer trip, but of course, he hadn't.

Tommy stood up and grabbed the sanding drill and goggles. Sanding the railing meant that all these little shards of rust sprayed onto him, covering his arms and face. Part of him worried this would exacerbate his acne, which was really bad right now, maybe due to the humidity or the fact that he had started school again.

He had no idea why his skin was so bad. But it was all he thought about. Except for being gay. He thought a lot about that, too. And he thought, also, that they were bound together somehow—his skin and his sexuality. Like all the feelings he couldn't say aloud were coming out through his pores.

Through his goggles, he saw his mom waving to him. She opened the screen door, looking cheery but confused. "Ray Naldo is here to see you."

"Renaldo? He's here?" Tommy said.

"Well, yes, I—"

René appeared behind her.

"Thank you, Mrs. Gaye," he said. "I can see Tommy is at work, so this will only take a minute. I'll show myself outside."

He was wearing his usual outfit of white pants and a white

shirt. He bowed to Tommy's mother in his courtly way. His mother was charmed by that, a gesture that his father probably had not performed since he got down on his knee to propose. (It was even hard to imagine his stiff, unemotional dad doing this.) She smiled and let him through, closing the screen door behind her in puzzlement.

Renaldo walked over to him, and Tommy wished he could stop time and go to the bathroom and wipe his face and check his skin and be wearing something less childish than a calligraphy camp T-shirt.

"Hi," Tommy said. The closer he got, the more he noticed René's ashen complexion and disheveled hair, like he hadn't slept well. He coughed and sniffled.

"Are you okay?" Tommy asked.

Renaldo let out a sarcastic laugh. He reached out and placed his hand on Tommy's shoulder.

"That is actually a very cogent question," he said. Tommy noticed there was a sooty stain on the front of his shirt.

"Can you come to my house tonight around nine?" Renaldo asked. "Don't say hello to my parents. Just come around back and let me know. I have to tell you something."

He looked at Tommy with seriousness, then squeezed his shoulder and walked around the side of the house to leave.

René wants to see me, Tommy thought. *This is finally the time.* He would finally kiss Renaldo, the love of his life, the person he had been writing and thinking about all summer, ever since they became friends last spring.

Nine p.m. was late. Tommy would have to think of the right excuse.

That night, the wet Virginia air was still thick. "Close," as his mom always said. "Be sure to bring an extra shirt, it's still so close out."

She repeated this when Tommy lied and told her he was going to the country club pool for a late-night swim. Saying he was going to the country club was always a good lie. He could have told her he was going to smoke five doobies there, and she would still have said okay as long as it ended with the words "at the country club."

Tommy's mom would have freaked out about how far he was going on his bike, too. Finally, he turned down Imperial Court. It seemed so much farther away later at night. Tommy parked his bike quietly. He knew he had to be as silent as possible. His heart thumped. This felt so wrong, so personal and private, like the things that the popular kids in school did.

When he got to the house, Tommy peered through the bay window into the living room. Mr. and Mrs. Calabasas were watching TV, the light flickering over their faces. He felt guilty not saying hello to them. But then again, this must be how first kisses happened, behind prying parental eyes. He walked around to the backyard. He stepped under René's window, which was about two feet above his head. There was a string dangling from the windowsill, with a note taped to it: *Pull this string to tell me you're here.*

Tommy pulled it and felt a tug on the other side.

"Ow! Oh! Hey!" Renaldo showed up above him leaning out the window, with the other end of the string looped around a thatch of his dark hair.

"Tommy? Tommy!" He reached his hand through the open

window and grabbed Tommy's hand like he had been at sea for days, bobbing in a lifeboat.

Tommy sensed that Renaldo might still be unwell. His skin was even more ashen, his face oilier and sallow. He started coughing, as if there was fluid in his lungs.

"Excuse me," he said, and blew his nose into a white hankie that he pulled from his pants pocket.

Tommy should have told him to get some rest. But he couldn't, not now. Renaldo was all he wanted, and he didn't care how sick he looked. It was almost embarrassing how much he wanted him. He thought about slipping his fingers inside the loose fabric between the buttons of his poly-blend shirt and touching his hairy stomach.

Renaldo clambered outside, brushing against the flimsy aluminum of the storm window, jumping down onto the mound of grass beside Tommy. Renaldo's white outfit was smudged with dirt and food.

He touched Tommy like he was a stuffed animal, squeezing his arms, prodding him as if to make sure he was real.

"Oh, thank God," he said, panting like a dog. "I've been up since Friday. Well, not up exactly. I've been asleep . . . but . . . traveling." He spoke with a strange, conspiratorial energy.

Renaldo sniffled again and blew his nose.

"Oh!" he gasped suddenly. "I forgot something."

He jumped halfway up through the window again, with surprising agility, lunging his arms back in, legs dangling out the sill, then landed back down on the ground and clutched his big notebook with papers sticking out of it, along with the book on astral projection.

He grabbed Tommy by the back of the neck. He squeezed and brought his face close. "I have to tell you something. I feel like you are the only one who will understand."

There was something grave in his tone. Whatever Renaldo Calabasas had to show him was serious. Tommy hoped it was that he felt horrible that he was gay, too, that he was similarly scared and full of shame and terrified of being found out and could only say it aloud somewhere there was no one else around to hear it, like the forest.

They quietly stepped through the dew-wet lawn to the front of the house and grabbed their bikes. Tommy looked back at René's house, his parents still sitting there, innocently watching a weather report and Zack Masters, the weatherman, gesticulating over blue blobs of clouds.

"Follow me," René whispered, hopping on his bike and pedaling furiously. He sped out of the cul-de-sac, and Tommy quickly climbed on his bike to catch up.

The air was getting cooler, like summer was changing into autumn before their eyes. *The trees were like broccoli, the trees were like bouquets, the trees were like an embrace*—Tommy tried to find the right words to describe things as he flew down Colonial Street, René pumping his pedals in front of him. It was happening. René was going to show him something, something wonderful, and then they would declare their love, and at last be together. The clouds sped by quickly overhead. They raced through the suburbs, Tommy following as René took odd shortcuts through side streets. Tommy realized they were on the other side of town, where the newer apartment complexes were being built. Big apartment buildings with little balconies and useless bay windows, erected like bright toy blocks over the red dirt of clear-cut forests. They passed by a new school, as fresh-bricked and monolithic as a megachurch, so much bigger than Herron High School. The dark woods where Tommy wandered as a kid were now being cleared and fitted with cement foundations and sewers. The developments had even fancier, more aspirational names like Coventry Mansions and Willow Estates. Everything seemed to be getting bigger, poised for a wave of humans that hadn't yet arrived.

Renaldo made a sudden left. A flat, grassy area emerged in the misty air. It was a new park, fresh with mulch and gravel and bright wooden benches. Hollow Pond Park, it was called. The sign hadn't been battered by the elements yet, and the wooden fence and playground were brightly painted and shiny. Tommy imagined future young families with their children playing here, all with fresh faces and clear skin and uncomplicated desires. They would grow up and attend the new school and live productive lives where no one was gay or had a zit or cried at night in their room listening to Pat Benatar's song "Don't Let It Show" on their Walkman in their bed and then had to pretend to be laughing and not sobbing when their mom barged in to give them their clean underwear.

Renaldo jumped off his bike. He motioned for Tommy to follow him and then ran out into the dark expanse of the park. Tommy scooted off his ten-speed, laid it delicately on top of Renaldo's battered banana-seat bike, and followed him across the field. It was easy to spot him, in his white clothes, like a ghost bouncing across the grass, through the mist. But then René dove into the dark forest and the shadows swallowed him up.

"René?" Tommy whispered. "Where are you?"

"I'm here!" Renaldo called.

Tommy chased after his voice, emerging in a park. René ran up a hill, up to a giant willow tree, its leaves descending around it like a shaken wig, and entered through them like curtains. Tommy scurried up the hill and parted the leaves. Inside the brushing branches was a small circle of mossy earth around the tree trunk. Moonlight beaming through the clouds made mottled light patterns on the ground. Tommy searched for René, finding him huddled on the other side of the trunk, tucked into a recess in its surface like a shallow cave. René was crouched there, arms wrapped around his legs.

"Come sit here," Renaldo said, patting the root right beside him, staring out at the field through the patchwork of branches. Tommy sat down and followed Renaldo's gaze. In front of them were spots as bright as Renaldo's dirty shirt, hundreds of little stipples of white.

"African violets," Renaldo said. "Apparently, they have been here for a hundred years."

"Really? How did you find that out? At the library?"

"Someone . . . told me," Renaldo said. "Oh, hold on," he added, opening his book and pulling out five long black feathers, which he arranged in a semicircle in front of them. "This is supposed to help direct the energy to us." His voice was shaking. He buried his face in his hands and whimpered. This was not going as Tommy had hoped.

"René, are you okay?" Tommy asked gently.

Renaldo lifted his face to look at him, eyes filling with tears.

The sky grumbled with summer thunder, and suddenly

Renaldo yelped. He tugged Tommy toward him for protection from something Tommy couldn't see.

"René?" Tommy said, now worried. "What's going on?"

Renaldo chose his words carefully. "I've been having . . . visits," he said. "This . . . person . . . who wants me to come here, under this tree, and sit with him. He—I think it's a he—says he has something for me. And all these signs are lining up. The thunder. The feathers."

Tommy nodded, trying to understand.

Renaldo buried his face in his hands, letting out a wail. He coughed snotty globs (Tommy didn't care if he was sick—this was his moment, or it would be soon) and then composed himself again.

"I think someone, something, is trying to reach to me from somewhere . . . else."

"Like, um, Master Sebastian?" Tommy felt funny asking this. A person from a book was calling him?

"Yes! Yes, I think it might be him."

Tommy felt a pit grow in his stomach. Renaldo was as unwell as Dara had warned. He was conflating things. "Supernatural hogwash," as Dara called it—René was taking it seriously. It wasn't a game to him.

"It started a few weeks ago when you were away. I tried to ignore it. I would feel someone behind me or calling me, and I would turn around and no one would be there. I thought I was just making things up. Then, when school started, I started having dreams I was walking in the hall and someone would tap on my shoulder, and I would turn and then wake up. And then, last night, I—"

Renaldo rubbed his eyes.

"Last night I woke up in my bed. I heard a noise on the other side of the door, and I got up and thought maybe it was you. That maybe it worked! But when I opened the door, it wasn't the hallway of my house. I mean, it was, but it was all different. Like my house, but all old and dusty, like it was abandoned. It was really dark. There was someone looking at me, through the window, in the shadows. It told me it was so glad that I came, and that it wanted to see me again, here, in this park. It said, 'Watch for signs I am coming.' It said it needs me. Tommy, it has the weirdest voice. Like these awful wet lungs full of mucus. It told me it *needs* me."

He started crying. "Do you think I'm crazy?"

"No! Of course not," Tommy said, but he wasn't so sure.

The horizon blinked with lightning. Renaldo stopped talking. He breathed heavily.

Another rumble of thunder growled far away.

Renaldo laid his head in Tommy's lap. Tommy froze, his heart beating. He reached down and began stroking Renaldo's long hair, smoothing his curls off his face.

"It's okay," Tommy reassured him. "We're going to figure this out."

René shut his eyes and curled closer to Tommy, grabbing his other hand and pulling it to his chest. Soon, Renaldo was asleep. Tommy held him, staying still as long as he could, his legs getting pins and needles because he didn't want to jostle Renaldo awake.

It finally started to rain, and the petals of the African violets began to shake under the droplets.

Tommy had fantasized about this night all summer long. The

night he and Renaldo would finally share their feelings for each other—in a place where no one could hear them and everyone at school would have no idea. He had been waiting and waiting for this night when they would be alone in the dark, and he would be able to kiss Renaldo and feel the warmth coming off his wiry body. But now, with Renaldo's sobbing head in his lap, Tommy realized his night was not going at all as planned.

Soon, Tommy dozed off. He woke up, or rather dreamed he woke up, sitting there under the tree. Renaldo was there, but soon a shadow of René began to emerge from his physical body, as if there was a hook pulling his soul out of him. Tommy called Renaldo's name, but no sound came out of him. He heard a screeching above his head. A huge bird was perched above him in the tree, and its black beak was somehow curled down, winding like a trail of ink into René's body.

"Don't move!" he heard someone say, far off. A figure came running toward him. It was a girl, around his age. She had strange skin, like she was covered in birthmarks that made her look striped, and her hair was cropped short in a flattop. She was wearing tight, stretchy pants that looked like underwear or a leotard. Tommy was confused. He had never seen someone like her in this neighborhood. She moved swiftly, running across the field of African violets with surprising speed, like a powerful track-and-field athlete. She had something in her hand—a Frisbee, but bigger, like a flat football—and she threw it toward Tommy. The Frisbee arced up toward the bird and struck it.

Tommy snapped awake. His body shook Renaldo awake, too. He sat up, groggy and confused, as if he had just taken a long flight.

He wasn't sure how much time had passed, but he knew he had to get home before his parents woke up.

"You should leave," Renaldo said, as if reading his thoughts. "I don't want you to get in trouble because of me."

"No, I don't care. I want to—"

"I care," said René, looking at him with sad, tired eyes. "I'll follow you soon."

Tommy wasn't sure if he should believe Renaldo. He wanted to be at the tree, stroking his hair.

Then Renaldo came close to Tommy and put his arms around him, giving Tommy a hug. He still seemed groggy. He grumbled in Tommy's shoulder. "You are . . ."

"What?" Tommy asked. "I'm . . . what?"

"You are . . . such a . . . good person, Tommy."

They stood there, and Tommy felt René's warm breath sigh out of him. Then René separated from him.

"I'll call you tomorrow," Renaldo promised.

"Please do," Tommy said, and then immediately regretted how squeaky and desperate he sounded.

Finally, he got up, untangled his bike from Renaldo's, and began riding home. He was steeped in his frustrated desire and regret. He could not stop thinking about that dream of the girl running toward him with the Frisbee. The bird above him spreading its oily black feathers.

Tommy snuck back into the house, his parents and brother asleep, thank God, and he lay in his bed, replaying the night in his head until he fell asleep.

He woke up shockingly late. It was Sunday, around 2:00 p.m. He stumbled to the bathroom. In the mirror, he saw that he had broken out even worse than before, a big red zit forming right between his eyes. No wonder Renaldo had wanted him to go home.

Rain still pelted the bathroom window. He looked outside and saw the street so dark with storm clouds that the new automatic streetlights had switched on. The gutters were overflowing with water. Trudging downstairs, he walked in on his mom and brother in the kitchen.

"Well, look who decided to join the living," his mom said sharply. "I thought maybe you were sick. Anyway, I've been busy calling the country club members because it looks like our Sunday fundraiser is canceled."

"Yeah, and my game," Charley grumbled, wearing his soccer uniform and shin pads like he believed it would still happen.

"The news says this is some sort of freak tropical storm, with dangerous lightning and flash flood warnings."

"Yeah, it sucks. We were going to ream those damn Spartans."

"Charley."

"What? I'm missing the game. I'm allowed to say whatever the hell I want."

"Charley!"

Tommy stared at Charley, fascinated by how much he cared about sports and teams and screaming and high-fiving and scores. He marveled at how little they had in common now, how Charley would have been disgusted to see his brother and Renaldo holding each other under that tree last night. He desperately wanted to call René, make sure he got home okay.

Suddenly lightning cracked, like it was right over their heads. The kitchen was filled with blinding stark-white light, and then the entire house went dark.

*   *   *   *   *   *

When Tommy woke up for school the next morning, that same song, "We Built This City," was playing. He remembered his dream. In it, strange voices kept saying, *Follow me, follow me.* And Tommy, in his dream, would try to move but felt like he was glued in place.

In a daze, he crept out of bed and got ready, avoiding the mirror in the bathroom (he didn't want to see any new eruptions he would have to deal with). He race-walked to school so he could get there early and be able to grab his things and slip into class before the hallways got too full.

At his locker, he heard two Penguin Cheer girls at the other end of the hall. In the emptiness, their voices echoed, and he could only pick up phrases. "Lightning . . . the storm . . . fire department."

He quickly opened his locker to get his first three periods' books and then shut it. He was about to turn when Dara walked up, her face bare. Her hair was pulled back, her skin almost ruddy, like she had been rubbing it.

"Tommy," she said, "did you hear what happened?"

"About the thunderstorm yesterday? Did your lights go out, too? I think it happened to everyone but—"

"Tommy. Renaldo was struck by lightning. He's in the hospital."

Tommy laughed at first. Then he saw Dara wasn't joking. The bell rang.

"I'll see you after sixth," she said firmly.

Tommy shuffled to history class, confused. Next to him was the big football jock Mike Grady, barely awake, his large muscular forearm plopped on the desk. He was popular, too, but Mike Grady was always too sleepy and too tired to make fun of Tommy.

Mr. Roman started droning on about the Blitz of England in World War II. The amount of artillery fired, the war plans. Mr. Roman never talked about people, about how it was to live in London at the time, hungry families, how it must have felt to be living in fear of another bombing. He just talked about tactics and war plans.

An announcement came over the PA system. The principal's voice crackled over the loudspeakers.

"As many of you know, last night's storm caused a blackout as well as damage across our community," the principal began. "Unfortunately, it also harmed one of our students, Renaldo Calabasas, who is now in the ICU."

Tommy's heart plummeted into his stomach.

"His parents are at the hospital and say he is stable but in a coma. Let's all come together as Herron Penguins and show Renaldo and his family support in this difficult time."

Tommy felt dizzy. He looked around, thinking all eyes were on him. His face flushed again. His skin, his horrible, sensitive skin showing everything he wanted to conceal. The rain was still pelting the classroom windows. He knew instantly that René must have stayed in the park Saturday night and didn't go home right after Tommy left, like he promised. Maybe he even spent the night. And then someone must have found him, found his parents, and in a panic they had taken him to the hospital. He saw

René in his mind, alone, wet, and in trouble. He wanted to scream out René's name but muttered it, quietly.

"Tommy? Do you have something to share?" said Mr. Roman.

"No. I'm fine," said Tommy, curling into himself.

The rest of the day was agonizing. Tommy wasn't sure what he should do. He grabbed his books out of his locker, and when he closed it, someone yanked his arm.

"Come on," Dara said, dragging him forward. "Ms. Ziller is gonna drive us to the hospital." She took him over to the pay phone and handed him two dimes. "Tell your mom you'll be home by dinner."

Tommy obeyed. But inside, he really didn't want to go to the hospital, didn't want to be near the person that made his heart scream. It was like heading toward a car crash and knowing what would happen. But Dara's grip was strong, like she knew what was better for Tommy than he did.

Ms. Ziller was waiting in the parking lot, her brown-topped Duster chugging. She motioned to them to duck inside the car. Dara and Tommy got in. It smelled like cigarettes and adulthood. Ms. Ziller quickly brushed the crumbs and wrappers off the seat and onto the floor. Tommy noticed the ashtray, crammed and dusty with cigarettes.

"Sorry it's so messy. This is Jenna . . . my roommate's car. She smokes too much and should quit," she said.

They drove twenty minutes across the flat pasture to the new hospital. Occasionally, they noticed more construction.

"It's wild how many houses are being built now," said Ms. Ziller. "I'm old enough to remember when this was all just pig farms and Civil War battlefields."

They neared the hospital. The building was bright white, and sprang out of the forest like an intrusion. They parked and walked into the lobby. Ms. Ziller found out what floor Renaldo was on, and Tommy felt outside of himself, like this wasn't really the truth of what was happening, like he was in a movie version of his life.

The elevator opened on the sixth floor, and they walked to room D645. In the hallway, framed in bright light, stood Mr. and Mrs. Calabasas. Mrs. Calabasas immediately came up to Tommy and hugged him. Tommy felt shocked by it, by the grief she shared with him.

"I'm . . . so sorry." It was all he could say as she sobbed into his shoulder.

"Can we get you anything?" Dara said, approaching them.

Mrs. Calabasas said *no* with a gasp, gulping her air so she didn't cry. René's younger brother, looking determined, furiously scratched a crayon over a coloring book. Tommy watched Ms. Ziller bend down and compliment his drawing, using her cheery teacher voice.

They were outside the door to Renaldo's room. And even the light from the window was enough for Tommy to feel a dagger in his heart. He peered into the window to see him but could only see the edge of the bed. He didn't want to ask about Renaldo, about how he was, if he was burned or dying.

Mrs. Calabasas stood at the door. "We are told no one in the room, for sanitate . . . sani—"

"They want us to keep the room clean," René's father gently interjected. "To prevent infection in case there are internal burns. But you can stand in the doorway? I know he would want to see you," he said.

Tommy could have sworn Mr. Calabasas looked directly at him when he said it. He opened the heavy door, and the three of them gathered in the doorframe, careful not to step into the room. Tommy heard the repetitive whoosh of the respirator, the faint chirps and whirs of various machines.

There was René. He looked, Tommy thought, oddly comfortable, restful, and to Tommy's relief, unmarked by burns from the lightning. His beautiful face was arced back, almost concentrated on a point in the heavens, as if he was on the beach and angling his chin toward the sun.

"Hey, weirdo," Dara whispered.

Tommy's mind was racing. He felt as though his entire being was trying to find ways to distract himself from what he was looking at so that he wouldn't burst into tears, so that he wouldn't reveal all he felt in front of everyone. He began to shake, but then Ms. Ziller lightly touched his shoulder and pulled the three of them back through the doorway.

"We will of course continue with *The Cornucopia*, and publish his work," said Ms. Ziller to the Calabasas family.

Mrs. Calabasas cried again. "It's all burned up."

She pointed to a pile of blackened ash on a steel tray outside the door. Dara and Ms. Ziller walked over to it. There was Renaldo's legendary journal—what was left of it—black tatters, curled and crumbled.

"Oh my lord, all that work, destroyed," Ms. Ziller said, poking at the mass of ash.

"Cinders and soot," said Mr. Calabasas.

After more hugs and goodbyes, Dara, Ms. Ziller, and Tommy finally left the hospital, stepping silently through the hallway and across the parking lot. Driving back, Ms. Ziller was rigid at the wheel. She jutted her hand in front of Tommy in the seat and opened the glove compartment. Three packs of menthols were there.

"I'm, um," she said sheepishly, "just going to have one."

That night, when Tommy came home, his family's eyes were glazed over the television, absorbed by a military show, men in helmets yelling things he couldn't decipher.

"Tommy, there's a plate for you," said his mother, getting up from the couch.

He took the plate and sat down in the kitchen, less because he was hungry and more because he knew he probably should eat. His mother stood in her plush terry-cloth robe and peeked her head into the kitchen.

"I'm sorry to hear about your friend," she sympathized. "How is he?"

"He's stable, I guess. He's still, um, in a coma."

"Oh, that's terrible. Well, you are a good friend for visiting him," she said.

He looked at her and could tell she had absolutely no idea what it meant that it was *Renaldo Calabasas*, the boy he had written poem after ridiculous poem about this summer, the boy he was in love with. But he knew he had to say something to make her leave him alone.

"We are all rooting for him. He'll be okay," he said unconvincingly. He had to stop talking or he would cry in front of his mother and brother, and that was the last thing he wanted to do.

"Yes! Yes," his mother answered, visibly relieved that he gave her a sensible, plucky response. She left to return to the TV.

A commercial came on for Lollipop Crunch. The mascot, Lolly, a perky animated character with lollipops for hair, was dancing around a candy-colored bowl of sugary cereal. "It's a lollipop cereal bowl of surprise!" he said, his lollipop hair jangling and bouncing. "Come along, come along. Come a lolly long, no lollygagging! Teehee!"

"Lollipop-flavored cereal?" said his mother to no one.

Tommy ducked his head into the fridge for more food. He was hungrier than he thought.

The local news chattered on, about a couple who were murdered in Williamsburg, Virginia, a mass grave found in Cambodia, a capsized boat full of refugees that drowned off the coast of South Carolina, trying to make it to the United States from El Salvador. Then a report on gay men dying of some strange disease in New York City and San Francisco.

"The CDC is calling it AIDS. Acquired immunodeficiency syndrome," said the reporter. Tommy peeked from behind the fridge door, turkey and potatoes in his mouth, looking at the TV screen to see a very thin man lying in a hospital bed, surrounded by a doctor and nurse and tubes. He looked emaciated, his face gripped in a delirious pain. Tommy was afraid to look, for fear that he would be caught by his family.

"Gross!" said Charley from the TV room.

And then, as if on cue, the news anchor shifted tone. "Now, for our local news, Southfield students band together for their fellow student Renaldo Calabasas, who is in a coma after being struck by lightning."

Tommy bolted out of the kitchen and up to his room. He couldn't hear any more. He lay in bed, and turned his face, his horrible, zitty face, into the pillow and sobbed. He screamed into the pillow with all his breath. His tears and spit made the pillow wet, but he didn't care. He cried and cried, and somewhere in between the sobbing heaves, he felt himself drift off.

Tommy woke up with a snort. He was in Renaldo's bedroom. He wasn't awake—he was dreaming. He sat on Renaldo's bed and picked up the pillow and smelled it. It had Renaldo's signature scent—the mix of Dove soap and Pert shampoo.

Tommy looked at the door. He felt something entreating him to open it.

"Hello? Renaldo?" he called, walking over. Hesitantly, he opened the door and peered out.

He smelled dust. It made him cough. It wasn't the Calabasases' hallway in front of him. Or rather, it was, but as if it were abandoned. The walls were covered with graffiti and the couch was knocked over and dismantled. The coffee table and chairs, where just the other day Tommy had seen René's parents sitting watching TV, were covered in dust, wallpaper torn away, television screen kicked in and shattered. But then Tommy noticed something odd. There, resting on the arm of the one upright chair, was the book. *The Sacred Art of Astral Projection*, sitting there like someone had just leafed through it. The corner of the cover was ripped off, as if someone had wrested it out of a possessive grip. Tommy reached for it.

His mother knocked on his door, jolting him out of his dream.

"Thomas, you're going to be late for school!"

He didn't know where he was, but then he heard his brother brushing his teeth. It was morning. Tuesday.

"Sorry, okay!" Tommy called.

He got out of bed. When Charley was done in the bathroom, Tommy looked in the mirror and saw his face and tried to not think about his skin or about how René was in a coma. He was just a normal boy going to school. He could convince himself of this.

Fortunately, he made it to school early again, the clunky blue doors shut behind him as he walked into the main Trophy Hall, mercifully empty of bullies. But before he turned to his locker, he ran into Renaldo—a two-dimensional, flat version. A poster, almost life-size, was before him. It was René's yearbook photo (looking beautiful as usual—now everyone knew) blown up, with the words "Pray for Renaldo" over his head. He quickly looked around the Trophy Hall. There were posters of Renaldo everywhere. René's face and fake yearbook smile, hair tamed in a side part. Tommy stood there for minutes, until the hall began filling with students. A group of girls who had never noticed him before rushed by wearing T-shirts that said "Remember Renaldo." One of them handed him a flyer, which Tommy accepted, speechless. On it was Renaldo's face.

"We're holding a silent vigil for Renaldo between third and fourth period. Hope you can make it!" she said before bouncing off.

Soon, a makeshift shrine erupted around René's locker—candles and flowers and tiny teddy bears, along with more girls sitting there like he was a dead rock star.

The day was long and blurry. Tommy experienced it like he was moving through clouds. His grief was now eclipsed by

Renaldo's burgeoning fame. It was like he couldn't have a private feeling about the boy he had obsessed over all summer. Now everyone did.

He was so puzzled that even gym class didn't stress him out. The sport this week was basketball, and he stood there while boys moved around him dribbling the orange ball, trying to win something that Tommy just could not comprehend.

Finally, sixth period ended and he made his way to Poetry Club. He walked in to see Dara standing there, waving a flyer. Ms. Ziller was at her desk.

"... and the *vigil*, are they fucking—"

"Dara, you know I can't support that language."

"Gosh DARN IT, do they even know who he is? His coma became cool!" Dara slammed the flyer down on the desk. "Why did he go to that park? Why was he even there?"

She looked at Tommy, knowing he had some information.

"He—he, well, he told me that—" Tommy stammered.

"It's okay, Tommy," Ms. Ziller said. "No one is blaming you."

"He was distraught," Tommy said, stumbling into the desk next to Dara.

"He's always distraught," said Dara.

"No, I mean, he was saying some scary stuff. Like about how someone was telling him to go to the park."

"Who?"

"Someone in his dreams? He was having dreams about someone telling him to go there. But he told me he was going home. He promised."

Dara reached out and touched his thigh. "Why don't we go to the park and see for ourselves?"

The afternoon was bright and cloudless. The storm had swept the sky clean. Tommy couldn't retrace how he and René got to that tree. In the daylight, it all just seemed like blocks and blocks of suburban houses on streets like Royal Estate Way and Empire Boulevard. It took Ms. Ziller a few attempts and a couple stops to ask people out on their front lawns, but they finally found it. There, down a newly paved street, amid unearthed dirt and tractors and sewage pipes was a new hand-printed sign: "Hollow Pond Park," yellow-painted letters embossed into brick-red wood.

"There it is!" Tommy said.

"Wow, wasn't this all forest before?" said Dara, stepping out of the car and adjusting her long coat.

"I think I remember hiking around here as a kid," said Ms. Ziller. "Like, when this was all woods."

They watched as Tommy quickly strode ahead. They tried to keep up. He dove into a thicket of trees and they followed, until they reached a field. Up the hill, they saw the charred husk of a tree.

"That's it," said Tommy, choking up. "I mean, I think that's it."

He had to hold back his words because he once again felt like he was about to cry. He didn't want to say anything about the night they shared together.

Dara tugged at him. "Come on."

As they approached, Tommy saw for the first time where he had been two nights before. Like seeing a theater during the day, it was less enchanting. The field of African violets was smaller, sparser, and the trees surrounding them were less lush than he remembered. The ground was mangy, adolescent.

They walked up to the tree. Under it was a black circle of charred earth, as if some great magnifying glass from above had sent down a searing beam.

"Look at this. More of them," Ms. Ziller said as she bent down to pick up another black feather, like the ones that Renaldo had collected over the past months. They were spread out in a circle, along with stones and twigs, in an elaborate pattern. Tommy remembered René placing feathers there that night, but this was more intricate.

He walked through the pattern to where they had sat two nights ago. Like one of those new Xerox machines had created it, there was the image of someone's seat cast into the soot, burn marks emanating from it. Next to it was a charred square, where Tommy imagined René's journal sat when the lightning struck. It was gone, obliterated, all those words from Renaldo's brilliant mind. He wanted to sob but tried to steady himself. Dara came up beside him.

"It's okay," she said. "Why don't you tell us what happened the other night here?" she said.

"How did you know we came here?" Tommy asked, surprised.

"Because. A month or so ago, René told me how much he liked this place and that he wanted to share it with you," she said kindly, before adding, "He likes you."

Tommy felt his heart sing and ache at the same time. He wished he knew what Dara meant by *like*. But it was not the right time to ask. He looked at the tree for an answer, as if it would tell him.

"Um," Tommy began, "he was pretty upset. He had been having bad dreams. He said he was being, like, visited by something. I think he was reading a book and it gave him nightmares. And then he must have come back here because someone in his dreams was telling him to come here. He was so upset, but I didn't think it would end up that he—he's . . . oh God, I don't know!"

He felt like he was going to be sick. Dara folded him into her arms. It took all his strength not to burst into tears in front of her and Ms. Ziller.

Dara let go of him. "Look at that," she said, pointing to a tatter of paper lodged in the root of the tree.

Dara snatched it. It was just a corner. The paper was thick. "It's laminated. Like—like a library book, the way they are protected from, like, stains and spaghetti sauce."

"It's from the library," Tommy said, feeling a chill run through his body. He remembered the dream, seeing the book with the corner missing.

"The school library?" Ms. Ziller said, blowing out smoke. She somehow had lit a cigarette without them seeing her do it.

"No, the one by the Kmart, the public one. He's been checking out a lot of stuff, but one book . . ." Tommy stopped himself.

"What is it?" Dara asked.

"We have to go there. To the library."

"Why? To see what he has checked out?"

Tommy wouldn't answer, but he was insistent.

"Can we please go there?"

"Oh no. Deb works there," Ms. Ziller said.

"Who is Deb?"

Ms. Ziller didn't seem to hear. "Well, I guess I was bound to see her sometime," she said, wrinkling her nose. "This will be fun. You guys don't have to be home for another hour, right?"

They entered the library. As usual, there were just a handful of people there, mostly old people, flipping through magazines. Ms. Ziller went right up to the front desk. A tense woman with a short haircut and glasses looked up.

"Hi, Deb," Ms. Ziller said.

"Sally? What are you doing here?"

Dara and Tommy watched them.

"Yeah, um, weird, right?" Ms. Ziller said with odd animation. "I'm here, well, *we're* here for one of my students."

"There is definitely something going on with them," Dara whispered.

Tommy nodded, but he was focused on the book. He hoped it would be back there, on the shelf, somehow. It wasn't at the tree, and for some reason, Tommy wanted to believe it hadn't burned up with René, that his dream was just nonsense. He didn't want any of this to be true. He felt a prickle on the back of his neck, like someone was watching him. He turned and saw a young girl at one of the reading tables, sitting at the end of it. Her eyes were almond-shaped and the strangest shade of hazel. She was pale, almost scarily so, like the blood had run out of her. Her hair was down her shoulders in a roughly brushed tangle.

Ms. Ziller kept talking to the librarian. "So, you may know about the tragedy . . . ," she said. "We just wanted to see what books Renaldo may have checked out so we can do our part and return them. Penguins stick together!"

"Well, I understand that, sure, but our guidelines state we

can't give out any information about a library member. Also, we just moved over to this computerized system. I'm not even sure I would have the records."

Ms. Ziller laughed and stuttered, "No! Of course, of course, of course. It's just that his parents personally asked me to retrieve any books and to just square things away because they are at the hospital and have no idea what the . . . outcome will be."

Tommy noticed Ms. Ziller's voice was now breathless. Deb, the librarian, bent down and typed into the keyboard in front of her.

"I just want to see what Renaldo took out this past weekend so I can return them," Ms. Ziller explained. "If that helps you find it on the, um, computer thingie."

Tommy turned to look around for the girl. She wasn't there. But then he saw the big dictionary, spread out. It was on the same page as before, *P*, and there was his word, *projection*. He knew exactly what book Renaldo had checked out; he just didn't want to say it out loud. Hesitantly, he walked over to the spot he sat with René, the 606.11 section of the Dewey decimal system, in the dusty back right corner of the library.

"Where are you going?" asked Dara, following him.

"I know the last book he checked out," said Ms. Ziller triumphantly. "It's 133.95 . . ."

Tommy was already there. On the spare shelf of occult titles, between Alien Life and Crystals, was a narrow gap, where a book had been.

"The title is *The Sacred Art of Astral—*"

"*Projection*," Tommy finished. "*Astral Projection*. It's not here."

Tommy was afraid to sleep that night, and barely did. He felt restless, and when he drifted off to sleep, it seemed like just seconds. In his dreams, he was flying low over the ground. Something was urgent and he was late and wouldn't make it. He glided over the streets, slowly dodging stumpy remnants of trees and old rusty mailboxes. The streets were old and crumbling. Neglected, with no cars or bicycles. He felt a whoosh of air as a huge, violently loud cargo truck barreled past him from behind, almost running him over. He watched it pass, realizing it wasn't on the ground, but floating—shooting over him like a hovercraft in *Star Wars*. He seemed to be in a different time. Some kind of future place?

He kept flying over charred, trashed terrain until he arrived at a familiar spot. Hollow Pond Park. But it was different. Barren. The lush trees of the forest were dried into straw and bare limbs. But the tree—where René had sat—was still there, burnt and hulking, like a blackened block of stone.

Then he saw that girl. The one who looked striped from his dreams. She was tossing that weird Frisbee around the charred tree. Clouds came swiftly, and there were cracks of thunder and lightning. Fat drops fell, and Tommy watched the girl duck into the crevice in the base of the tree—where he and René had sat last weekend. She was grasping a stack of papers under her arm. The cover was familiar—it was the astral projection book with the corner missing. Above his head, he heard a bird screeching. Then the dream faded.

He woke feeling cloudy, clobbered. He coughed up phlegm and blew his nose. He didn't remember much except a feeling like someone was calling out for him, but he couldn't hear them and was only now realizing it.

He made it to school in the same funk, bumping into Billy Major, who said, with cocky spite, "Look out, pizza-face gay. Ha, Pizza Gay! Get it?"

Tommy quietly went to his locker. He heard the popular girls talking next to him—Linda Lissel, Carla Austin, and Stacey Divine.

"Did you hear?" Linda said. "Renaldo is better. He's returning to school tomorrow."

"It's a miracle. Our vigil must have worked."

"Rain called me last night," said Stacey Divine, beaming. Being a messenger burnished her popularity even more.

"Rain?"

"Yeah. He goes by Rain now. He told me to call him that. He prefers it. He's coming back today after lunch."

"Gosh, we'll have to organize a rally."

Tommy was dazed. *Rain?* And why would he call Stacey Divine?

After lunch, Tommy and Dara met to walk to the main lobby of the school for the rally. The large atrium was lined with glass cases full of old trophies commemorating football jocks from years past. The crowds were converging. Kids were wearing "René Returns" T-shirts and holding up banners with poor renderings of his face and corkscrew hair. Scrawled across the banners were the words: "Welcome Back, Survivor, Hero, and Penguin!"

Dara pointed and laughed. "Gag me. Weirdo is going to hate this shit."

Tommy and Dara couldn't get close to the entrance. But from far away, they heard squeals and cheers. The crowd parted and Renaldo stood there. He looked different. Taller. His hair was shorter, and he was wearing jeans and a rugby shirt like popular seniors did.

Everyone applauded and cheered. He held up his hands in a gesture to silence the crowd, and they all dutifully quieted down.

"Hello," he said in a throaty, strange voice, like he had gone away for a semester in Europe while he was comatose. "I want to thank you deeply for all the cards and well-wishes these past few days." Suddenly he coughed violently, pulling out a handkerchief. "Please excuse me. I'm still recovering."

People clapped.

"As I was saying, words cannot express my gratitude."

"Words cannot express?" Dara whispered.

"Even though I've been at this school for a while, I don't think I've had the pleasure of really getting to know many of you. But coming back to Herron High after such a horrific accident has changed my perspective. I look forward to participating in, um"—Renaldo looked down at a piece of paper—"extracurricular activities, such as student council or a sport of some variety. I'm so lucky to have had such wonderful guidance from my friend Stacey Divine as well as many others who have lifted my spirits as I convalesced. I am so proud to be a Penguin today!"

The audience cheered again, and he walked through the crowd, with Stacey Divine and Welsh Walsh flanking him.

He passed by Tommy and Dara, who stood and waved.

"Hey, weirdo!" said Dara, smiling.

Renaldo blinked at her. "Weirdo? That's not very nice," he said.

He continued walking with his new friends.

"What the fuck?" Dara fumed. She tried to march over to him, but Tommy grabbed her tunic top.

"Dara, it's not a big deal. He's still recovering. Maybe he's just—"

"No, that's fucked."

"Hey! Renaldo," she yelled.

He stopped by the principal's office, and the crowd around him did as well.

"It's me, Dara. And your friend Tommy."

Renaldo looked at them quizzically. Tommy watched him gaze at them with a superior kind of goodwill, like he was royalty and they were common folk.

His eyes had changed. They were lighter, hazel. It was like the lightning had struck his irises and blanched them from dark brown to a green Tommy had never seen before.

"Oh! Of course! Hi, Dara. Hi, Tommy. It's nice to see you. I hope to see you again."

He quickly turned away.

"Did he really just do that?" Dara said.

Renaldo kept walking. As they reached the first set of lockers, Tommy could overhear Stacey telling him about the party they were having at Luke Smoshe's house this weekend. Dara was about to lunge forward again, but Tommy grabbed her by the arm to stop her. "Dara, don't!"

She wrenched herself free, and Tommy grabbed her with both his hands firmly. It surprised her.

"Don't even try to talk to him," Tommy said. "It's no use. I don't think, um, that's even Renaldo."

"What do you mean? Of course it is. He just became an asshole. A weird, apparently popular asshole."

"No. I think . . ." Tommy took a deep breath, trying to make sense of the situation. "Well, this is going to sound unhinged, but I think something happened to him. Like he traveled somewhere and got . . . affected by it."

"Traveled where?"

"To the, um . . . to the . . ."

"Come on, tell me."

"To the astral plane," Tommy said, now sure of his theory.

Dara sighed. "Tommy. I'm so sorry to say this, but"—she rested her hand on his arm—"all that talk from René was just his fantasies. Like I said, René is . . . fragile. I'm almost not surprised he's decided to blow us off."

"But you didn't see him that night! He was so scared."

Suddenly there was a whoop down the echoey hall. Dara and Tommy looked up to see a group of popular guys lifting René up as if he had won the Olympics.

"Well, look at him now," said Dara.

2044
PRIS

Pris was dreaming, but she sat up from her bed. She slid off the mattress and stood in her room. She knew she was not awake because she looked down and saw herself curled in a fetal position with her pillow bunched up around her stomach. Pris noticed how she looked so small, so childish, with her snoring, crooked face, and Dora the Explorer T-shirt (it was her uncle Myles's) all bunched up around her waist. *Do I always look like a child when I sleep?* she thought as she stared down at herself.

Then she turned away from her sleeping body. She floated across her room and opened her bedroom door. There, across the hall, was a mirror—a big, full-length mirror in an ornate frame. This was definitely a dream, because there wasn't a mirror there in her actual apartment where she and Uncle Myles lived, just a hybrid air plant. Uncle Myles would never have such a mirror, especially one that didn't provide access to his biometric data and mineral levels on its screen—not to mention a way for him to talk to Cammie, his new holo-girlfriend. Everything in their place was "enmeshed."

She walked up to the mirror, and like she knew how to do this, she stepped into it.

She found herself amid gnarled grass and dead roots. She kept walking in that confident way you do in dreams, no hesitation, just the strange trust that you know where to go as if you always knew.

She was walking way outside of the Glade—where she lived—into the area where no one lived anymore. On the exit ramps and overpasses, the huge cargo trucks above her kept swooshing by. Off across the bumpy terrain, she saw the dead tree of Hell Park. The tree was blackened with soot, in the center of the brown expanse of dirt. That damn tree.

That's where she met Taya, and where everything unraveled. *Crap, why is this dream bringing me here?* she asked to no one. *Fuck this dream. Like my subconscious needs to remind me that everyone in school thinks I am a stalker.*

Suddenly she saw the dirty ground transform. Flowers grew around her feet, white petals everywhere, and in place of the dead tree was a beautiful, huge, lush willow, its leaves tumbling down around it like tousled hair. Was this the same park?

She felt a strong wind brush past her. Thunder rumbled far off. She looked down and saw that she was wearing the high school disk team uniform, disk suddenly in hand. This was definitely a dream, and an embarrassing one, because there was no way she would be on the disk team now, not after what she did.

Lightning cracked, brightening the ground around her, and

she heard someone yelp like they were hurt.

At the bottom of the tree she saw two figures. Two boys. One was beautiful and angular, his head in the lap of the other, who looked down at the boy with loving concern. They seemed sweet. Their hair was all floppy and their clothes baggy. They had their shirt collars buttoned up to the top button like she saw in those vintage videos Uncle Myles loved to watch on the holoscreen.

Under the tree, the one sitting up looked down at the other. He took his hand and gently smoothed down the other boy's thick black hair. *Oh, I see, they're queer boys,* she thought. *Sweet.*

There was a shivering cry. A bird, a huge crow, landed on the tree above the boys. The crow flapped above them and leaned down and pointed its shiny black beak at the couple. Pris watched in fascination as the beak began to stretch, to elongate, delicately descending out of the air and curling downward like a drop of ink into water. It grew in a mass, solidifying into a writhing, undulating black scarf that hovered over the boys. She saw the tendril of it wriggle itself down toward the dark-haired, stormy boy lying there. The crow let out a bloodcurdling cry, but the boys didn't seem to notice.

Pris had watched enough old movies on her holospecs to know this was not a good thing. Without hesitation, she grabbed her disk. The other boy looked up at her. She noticed his skin had bumps all over it. She heard Uncle Myles call them *zits.* Something people had before home benzoyl-laser washes.

"Don't move!" she said to him, and threw her disk at the crow. The disk hit it and the bird splattered, like the way she had clobbered that piñata at her best friend Jayde's quinceañera. She'd always had good aim.

Then there was a flash of lightning.

Pris woke up. Her arm shook. Her alarm was Tinging.

What a vivid dream.

She walked to the bathroom. She could hear Uncle Myles and his girlfriend, Cammie, downstairs preparing breakfast and getting ready for work. He was a Data Hub manager—six months from retirement at age eighty. He also had a new subsidized insurance that covered Regularity Therapy, to help him with the deep-seated trauma he experienced as a nurse during the first waves of the Virus, over two decades ago.

Pris felt a Ting on her wrist. She waved on a video chat with Jayde.

"Hey!" Jayde exclaimed. "I can't believe it's Friday. Our first day back in person!"

School had been in lockdown since a new variant of the Virus had been found in the next district. Luckily no one had died, but as usual, all students at Herron had to be scanned and then tested this morning before they entered the school.

"Are you doing the spirit colors? Here's what I am wearing," Jayde said, extending the frame so that it revealed them in a tight-fitting catsuit.

"Where did you even get that?"

"I designed it myself. And then I watched, like, a million vids of how to 3D print and assemble."

"Wow, I am really impressed," Pris said. She wanted to be supportive to Jayde even when she didn't really want to be a part of this effort, because Pris knew what Jayde really wanted—to be noticed by older men.

"So what are you wearing?" Jayde demanded.

"I don't care," said Pris.

It was Penguin Spirit Day. The school was supposed to wear black and white to show spirit for the school athletic teams—all the disk and soccer players. It was 2044, and apparently stupid school spirit still mattered. She knew Jayde wanted to go so that they could take photos of themselves in sexy outfits for their Ting profiles. Pris wasn't going to go wearing black and white again to school, because last year when she did, anonymous people on Ting said she looked like a striped beach ball in a tuxedo—it was better to try and not be noticed.

"I do! I just want to anneal my persona," Jayde said. *Anneal.* Pris had to look it up quickly. *Verb: to strengthen or harden.* Jayde's immense vocabulary was something they couldn't hide, no matter how *modelicious* they tried to be.

"You know those new twins in our class?" Jayde now asked, changing the subject.

"Yeah. I mean, not personally," said Pris. Jayde was talking about Benz and Knip, the two new boys who moved from the Pacific District.

"Well, I told them about the Murder House, and they want to go there after class."

Pris hesitated. You weren't supposed to be near strangers for longer than twenty-two minutes to prevent some unforeseen surge of a new variant.

"Jayde, if we get caught . . ."

"Oh, come on. You know you want to go."

They were right. Pris was drawn to that house. She wasn't sure she believed all the legends about it. But still, she had always wanted to explore. The house was in the abandoned old suburbs—

the rows of burned and ruined homes on the outskirts of their district. A murder happened there decades ago. What happened at the Murder House was completely mythical at this point. There wasn't anything about it when you searched the Hub. Nothing came up. All they had were the legends they heard from a friend's friend's mother's grandmother that a terrible, twisted murder happened there.

"Fine," Pris relented, "but we'll have to make it quick."

Jayde clapped their hands in excitement. Pris knew that Jayde had their own reasons for going. Benz and Knip were both tall and angular. They were beautiful and effortlessly fashionable in their draped trench coats and long bangs. The boys were Jayde's discovery, like they were a model scout. Going to the Murder House—something totally wild and unlike anything anyone else would dare to do in the school—would make Jayde memorable to them. The twins would think of Jayde (*and I guess me too*, Pris thought) as cooler than anyone else. Or they would think back on those first weeks in their new school when they met Jayde and her, one of the least-liked people in Herron, who tried to impress them.

Jayde was spending a lot of time socializing. Lately, when Pris was Tinging Jayde, they weren't really listening. They were waiting for someone to message them, Pris could tell. On her screen Jayde had that smile in their eyes.

"I've been talking a lot with this very successful real estate agent assistant on Ting," Jayde had confessed when they were walking home last week. "His name is Nomed. Like, look at him. Isn't he hotness defined?" They swiped up a photo of a guy, maybe in college, in the seat of a swank, sleek hover sedan.

"Jayde, he's, like, twenty-five!"

"No! He's twenty. And super, super kind and nice."

"Have you . . . met?"

"No. Not yet. He's gentle. He just likes to talk and hear about my life. He likes to see me living fully." Pris noticed they sounded exactly like the Ting superstar Contessa. Trying to be humble while enjoying their celebrity.

Pris saw where this was going. Jayde would ask Pris to take their picture together so they could post it on their profile. That way this older guy could see them, without Jayde having to send it to him, which would alert the Appropriate Age filters in the school.

"You can't *not* wear something spirited on Spirit Day," Jayde reminded her, taking Pris out of her memories as they circled back to their school day. "Find something cute to wear."

"Uh-huh," Pris said noncommittally. Then she ended the Ting call.

Pris pulled back the covers. She and Jayde had been friends since they were five, when they attended the Glade nursery school. They grew up together. Between surges, they ran through the huge sewer pipes outside of the Glade, making dams or playing store with old plastic bottle tops (Jayde lived next to the Plastics Collection and Eradication Facility).

That changed last year, when Jayde grew a few inches and started dressing differently. Jayde's favorite celebrity was Contessa, who was trans and a Ting presenter, as well as a pop star and entrepreneur and thought leader. Her mantra, "Be the be," had become a clothing line and a self-realization seminar at the same time. It inspired Jayde to try and become a successful trans queer thought leader, too. And lately all Jayde talked about was how many new winks and waves and pinches they've received on Ting.

It wasn't so long ago that Pris and Jayde were hanging out in Jayde's room, writing. They wrote poetry together. Jayde would throw out words, and Pris couldn't tell if they were real or invented. Pris's lines felt stumpy and smaller in comparison to Jayde's—full of big words and large ideas, but Jayde was encouraging. Creating art with your best friend? It was the best time of Pris's life.

Jayde had an obsession with words, which led them to poetry, "Where words can do anything you want them to!" Jayde said to Pris one afternoon last year. "Like, you can even make up words if you want. Like, listen to this one old, old poet I found: *'Selfyeast of spirit a dull dough sours.' Selfyeast!* Isn't that incredible?" Jayde said, and Pris looked at them in awe of their magnificent mind. They would scribble away, until one or the other of their parents would Ting them to come home. Jayde was brilliant, but also they were becoming tall and angular and elegant. Her best friend was one of the most beautiful people she knew.

Pris looked in the mirror: She was squat, her orange hair matted. And then there was her skin. Her striped skin. Uncle Myles said that it was a genetic thing. A form of vitiligo, a pigment issue that some people had, but along with acne, port-wine stains, and other skin conditions, the anomaly had been eliminated years ago. Why she specifically had it in this day and age was even more puzzling. And her skin wasn't elegantly splotchy (like the modeling legend Winnie Marlow). It was head-to-toe striped, like a warped version of a crosswalk sign on the hoverway.

She never realized it was something strange until fifth grade, that time that kids start separating into groups and people realize they are different from one another. Pris was singled out. And she was called names in Ting messages: Black and White, Crosswalk, Half-n-Half. They always came to it as if they were the first people who had ever thought of these insults, like they were brilliant creative minds.

Pris tried to get ready without looking at her reflection. Right there, she composed a poem:

Mirrors
Are terrible things
You can see what's behind you
Ahead of you.

When she finished in the bathroom, she grabbed her laptop from her dresser and quickly typed it out. She decided to print it. No way was she going to keep her writing on her Mat now, not after what happened with her poems, with Taya.

"Pris! You're going to be late for school," Uncle Myles shouted from downstairs.

"I'm coming, jeez!" Pris answered as she waited for the printer—an ancient, clunky orb—to produce a sheet of paper with words on it. She flicked a frame and chose one of the last options on the menu, *print.* She watched the ancient machine spit out a page. She might have been the only Penguin then using a printer. No one did this anymore except for a few millennials and Gen Xers like Uncle Myles or even the rare Boomers, who were nearly one hundred years old but preserved by nutrient infusions and mitochondria replacement therapy.

"Priscilla! Hurry up, you don't have much time," Uncle Myles said.

She grabbed the paper and stuffed it into her spiral-bound notebook (where she had been writing her thoughts now instead of the Mat), and also her disk—she didn't go anywhere without it.

She ran downstairs and sat in front of her Completia Meal Box and quickly ate the beetmeat tofrittata. She looked up and caught her uncle kissing Cammie in front of the dish vaporizer. They drew apart quickly.

Pris didn't like Cammie. She was too—what was the word that Uncle Myles used all the time?—basic. She had voluminous hair and giant anime eyes and a tiny waist and wore high heels paired with skin-tight miniskirts.

Cammie was his virtual girlfriend. Uncle Myles had spent two days filling out the complicated form. But with the new government stimulus checks to combat the War on Loneliness plus his new Virus Veterans insurance, Uncle Myles could finally afford it.

Apparently, she was the best-reviewed model for a virtual companion on the market. She was as "real" as they made them these days. For example, she even had a job—as the executive editor at a Hub news vertical.

Uncle Myles was spending a lot of his time with her, when Pris wasn't around. Of course, Pris wanted Uncle Myles to be happy, but she worried that Cammie wasn't good enough for him. Uncle Myles was caring and smart and, well, fragile. All her life, Pris knew from as early as she could remember that she needed to watch out for him. He had done so much for her—making sure she did her homework and brushed her teeth and got to bed early.

He was her mother when she didn't have one. But he was lonely, she knew, and he needed company. In a way, he was preparing for when she would grow up and move out.

Pris tucked her disk into her backpack. Her first day back at school in person since everything happened.

* * * * * *

Two months ago, Pris was down at Hell Park. Between quarantines, she would go there often and throw her disk back and forth against the Black Tree. Tossing the disk helped her think clearly, and she usually brought her Mat so she could type out her thoughts as they came to her. It was there she finally discovered the right technique to get the disk to return to her like an eager dog. And it was there, right before the latest lockdown, that she met Taya and ruined her chance at everything. She had been tossing her disk around the Black Tree late one night when she heard a voice.

"Not bad," someone had said behind her.

It was Taya, captain of the disk team at school. Her long hair was pulled back, and she was in her varsity uniform—practice must have gone late.

"What are you doing here?" Pris asked.

"Me? Like you, throwing. It's hard to find a wide-open place to really chuck it," Taya said as she flung it far across Hell Park with precision. Pris watched her long, sinewy arm as she threw. Her dark skin was glowing with sweat. Taya turned to her as if she knew she was watching.

"Your turn," she said, smiling.

Pris threw her disk as well, not as far, but with a steady arc.

"Nice thrust."

For an hour, they tossed their disks together, Taya giving Pris pointers on proper stance.

"Stabilize your shoulders," she said, coming behind Pris and firmly squeezing her arms in place. Pris could smell Taya's skin and hair—a sweet coconut scent.

Then Taya got a Ting. "Oh. I have to go. Team strategy meeting." She punched in her code for a hover cab, which came in seconds. The escalator unspooled beside her and she stepped up. As it ascended, Taya turned her face to Pris and looked her up and down.

"You're strong. You should try out for the team," she said as she climbed in the hover cab. "A lot of good players graduate next year, and we need some new blood."

Pris watched the vehicle streak away. She felt out of breath. It was the first time someone had touched her who wasn't her uncle or Jayde. She felt wobbly, full of energy. She went home and wrote about Taya. Wrote all kinds of dumb words about Taya's brown eyes.

The only brackish pools that she would ever drink from.
No.
Earthy eyes like two oak trees.
No.
Eyes as deep brown as polished mahogany.

She wrote and wrote line after line about Taya. She couldn't help herself. She had spent months describing sunsets and the way the moon peeked from between the holo-billboards out her window, but now she could attach her words to Taya, who became planetary. The words kept coming.

The next day, Pris was at the warm-up station, juicing up her Mat and subcutaneous device.

"Devrees. Hey," she heard behind her, and saw Taya walking by with her varsity disk friends. She was with the other popular Serenas like Jett Diablo and Fleek Watson, and she still said hello. It made Pris feel like she was floating the rest of the day.

She walked across the school atrium, a cavernous space that she usually avoided so no one would Ting her a mean name. She found the holoscreen with the sign-up code for disk tryouts the following week. She quickly added her profile to the list.

She made it to biology, where they were having their Basics in Genetics module. Everyone had taken samples of their saliva to study ancestry. Then each student entered a data key, and a holo-projection beamed into the center of the classroom, displaying a treetop waving in the wind with the student's name on a leaf. The projection widened, and you could see all the other leaves of the tree and the names of ancestors sprinkled out on branches, thickening to a wide trunk on which another student's family existed, on and on, so you could see how you were all connected. It was supposed to be a first introduction to genetics.

Jayde found out their father's father's father's father had owned a ranch in the Southwest Health District, in a state that used to be called New Mexico. The genetic technology had even progressed so that the formerly impossible—tracking down enslaved ancestors—was possible.

It was Pris's turn. She entered her data key. The hologram tree grew in front of them, but remained bare. Her leaf hung there on a branch, all by itself. The image blinked, hesitating. It was as if the genetic material of her parents, her ancestors, wasn't even there.

"Strange. There must be a glitch in the system," said Mx. Powell.

"Or she's a zero!" someone said. Everyone laughed, and the teacher commanded them to be quiet. Pris felt lost. Another thing for everyone to name call her—*Highway Stripe, Zero*—she could already imagine the Ting posts.

She made it to history class just in time. Mr. Richards was already talking. "We have a lot to cover today!"

Mr. Richards was old, probably seventy or so, and everyone thought he was eccentric because he tended to rant and get very passionate. Pris liked him, though. She felt like everyone around her didn't react in real time but said what they felt into their devices and Tings. He, at least, spoke how he thought out loud.

"History repeats until humankind learns its lesson!" he said all the time, holding out his arms in this weird way, like he was embracing a whale.

On that day, they were presenting their summer project proposal. They each had to choose a subject that they would work on over the summer—a deeper dive into a moment in history they had covered that year, from American enslavement of African people to the Spanish flu to the AIDS crisis. (He was very adamant about that one—how this other virus killed millions of people, how no one helped the communities affected until they created a resistance effort.)

"If it bothers you that you are reading over the summer, bring it up with the school board and tell them they need to spend more time on these subjects in the annual curriculum! I can only pick so many battles. It took me years to get them to spend one DAY talking about AIDS! Apparently it is too 'upsetting' for you," he said, rolling his eyes.

Pris was nervous. She still wasn't sure what she wanted to research this summer. She couldn't decide. She prayed Mr. Richards wouldn't call on her. *Maybe if you had given it some thought instead of obsessing over Taya last night you wouldn't be in this mess,* her inner voice said.

"Jett, why don't you start," Mr. Richards said. Jett pulled out their Mat and swiped their report up on the wall. "My summer project will be about the Brown Paper Bag Test. After slavery was abolished in eighteen . . . um . . ."

"Eighteen sixty-five, go on," said Mr. Richards.

"Um. Well, there was still discrimination, and lots of Black people were judged on the darkness of their skin. In fact, some societies and clubs wouldn't allow entry unless you passed a test. It was based on the paper bag, which was this common, like, bag that everyone had that was a light brown color. So if you were lighter, you were allowed into the society, and if you were darker, you weren't."

"That's an interesting point," said Mr. Richards. "So, as we have seen in other moments in history, suppression of people is often based on clear demarcations between 'us' and 'other,' right? But then there end up being all these complicated work-arounds to justify the oppression. Continue, Jett."

"Well, I read that in some states in the South, like in Mississippi, there were even, like, um, levels of color. Some were called octoroons, meaning they were an eighth Black."

"Yes! So your skin tone had to land somewhere on either side of white or black, which as we know are socially constructed," Mr. Richards chimed in passionately.

"What if you're both?" someone said behind Pris. The class

tittered with giggles. Pris felt her stomach drop.

"What's so funny?" Mr. Richards said. Then it dawned on him. Pris felt eyes looking at her.

"Okay, that's enough," said Mr. Richards. He looked exasperated. "The rest of you, please place your homework assignments on the wall."

Barely looking, Pris quickly brushed her homework up on the screen.

The others in the class kept laughing. Pris turned around angrily and was about to tell them off when she saw everyone looking at the wall and pointing. Pris had swiped the wrong file. Up on the screen were her poems.

> You are tied to me
> Your eyes electrifying
> Glistening sweaty skin
> Something I want 2 dive in.
> You smell vast like oceans,
> Foam of my emotions

She scrambled to her Mat and threw up her homework. The bell rang.

"Okay, remember tomorrow we will have a quiz! A crowdsourced quiz on the culture of enslavement!" Mr. Richards said. Pris quickly gathered her Mat and jacket and ran out before everyone else. She couldn't think as she raced down the halls and tucked herself into the warm-up station to plug in her Mat.

Jayde rushed up to her. "Girl, your diary is all over the school!"

"I know."

"Don't worry, I blocked it. I think I got most of the screenshots."

She knew that Jayde's attempts to block the information were futile. Other students would have captured it and Tinged the whole school by now. She looked at her Ting. They were full of anonymous messages. Jayde put their hand on Pris's shoulder.

"They're immature," Jayde declared. "Fuck them."

Pris flinched and brushed off Jayde's hand. If she allowed any sympathy from them, she would start to cry there on the spot.

"I'm fine," she said.

"Sure," they sighed. "Well, I'll Ting you after school. Okay?"

Jayde walked off and Pris stood there at her warm-up station, wanting to die.

> Did you see what Crosswalk was writing?

> It sounds like she has a crush.

> A messed-up, obsessive crush.

> Striped freak.

> Did you hear what happened in genetics?

> Black and White is a ZERO.

The anonymous Tings piled up in her inbox.

She tried to ignore them and just breathe, but then one

message came through with a red flag icon. It was from the school office.

Please report immediately to the administration offices. Your teachers have been informed, it said.

Minutes later, Pris waved her hand over the entrance cone, and the doors to the Herron school administration offices opened up. No one was there. It was silent. The virtual receptionist blinked, awaking. It scanned her retina and told her to go down the hall to room CC.

She walked past the translucent office doors where she imagined school officials were busy working, but she couldn't hear anyone in any room.

She came up to room CC. She knocked and entered. A young man in a crisp pantsuit waved hello to her.

"Hi there, I'm Angel Jaleel. I'll be your behavioral adjudicator today. Please have a seat," the man said. Pris sat down, and the counselor quickly observed her and began writing, looking at her with a tight smile.

"So, as you know, your diary was released out on the Hub."

"I know. I didn't mean for that to happen. It was an accident."

"Yes. We have wiped many if not all the copies and re-Tings. But what I am here today to address is some of the language. It flagged our behavioral sensors."

"Okay."

"As you know, we take Disturbance Potential seriously. Using our target algorithm, it seems the language you have been using in your schoolwork spiked recently with florid adjectives and even a few unnecessary adverbs. We just need to make sure it isn't a potential sign of a future problem or incident."

"But what I wrote wasn't meant for—"

"I think what might be best is if we set up some Language Management seminars for you," said Angel Jaleel, tapping away on his Mat.

There was a knock on the door. Mr. Richards entered.

"Hi there, Mr. Jaleel," he said, in a syrupy tone that Pris hadn't heard from him before. "Thank you so much for taking the helm on this matter." He placed his hand on the back of Pris's chair. "But I think I can take it from here. Since it happened in my classroom."

Angel Jaleel bristled. "Well, as the district deputy behavioral statistical engineer—"

"I'm so appreciative of your role," said Mr. Richards, "but I think it's best if I contact her parents since I know her so well, and make sure to schedule any seminars she might need to attend." Mr. Richards swiftly moved Pris out of the room and into the hall. "We wouldn't want to cause a destructive interference equation in the demographic, would we?"

Mr. Jaleel stiffened. He adjusted the files in his large-format Mat. "Well, if you're sure!" he said.

But they were both out of sight.

"Thank Goddess that's dealt with," Mr. Richards growled under his breath, Pris having to speed up to stay next to him. "I swear I don't know which is worse. This constant algorithmic language monitoring you kids have to deal with, or what I went through when I was your age, which was basically the opposite. Adults looking the other way while you were slammed into lockers and called *faggot*."

Pris blushed as he said that word. Mr. Richards exhaled,

coming down from his heated anger. "I'm sorry. I shouldn't have said that."

They made it back to his classroom. Mr. Richards pulled up a chair on the other side of his desk and asked Pris to sit down. She could see his skin, from up close, was rougher than she had noticed before.

"Pris, I'm so sorry. I should have put a stop to the name-calling immediately."

Pris looked down at her Mat.

"Look. I know you think I'm just some old guy, but I've been there. I've been called names, too. It's almost comforting to see how cruel kids still can be to one another," he said. Then he smiled and rapped his desk with his knuckles. "But hey, I didn't know you wrote poetry!"

"Poetry? Those were just, like, dumb thoughts."

"No. They are not dumb." Mr. Richards was suddenly very serious. He sighed. "Your work is bright, has energy. But sometimes as a writer, you get fixated on a subject. A muse. And muses are a two-way street. Since the beginning of civilization, they have been both a blessing and a curse. They are hard to let go of," Mr. Richards said, drifting off. "Anyway, that's not important. What *is* important is that you keep writing, young lady! How about I send you some poets to check out? I think you would love Natalie Diaz. Or Audre Lorde! Or Brenda Shaughnessy! Or Essex Hemphill! There are so many greats to read."

Pris took a funicular home and browsed the list of poets. She grabbed a few poems from the Hub to read on her Mat.

One popped up, that old, old man named Gerard Manley Hopkins that Jayde liked.

My own heart let me more have pity on; let
Me live to my sad self hereafter kind,
Charitable; not live this tormented mind
With this tormented mind tormenting yet.

These poets—they understood tormented minds and trampled hearts. Her wrist buzzed with an anonymous message: **Zero!**

This was the worst day ever. Pris leaned her head against the smooth, cool bubble window. She had always assumed that when she reached the legal age of eighteen, she would be able to find her birth parents. Uncle Myles never said she wouldn't be able to. He told her he had seen her mother at the hospital. But was he lying? Why didn't she have any data about her ancestors like everyone else? She *was* a zero; she had no past, and now, shunned by half the school, she had no future. Pris stepped out of the hovercar and walked into the gateway of the Glade in a cloud of thought.

Back in their apartment, Uncle Myles was sitting at the table, Cammie next to him. They smiled at her.

"How was school?" Cammie asked as she floated next to Uncle Myles. Pris felt stung with anger.

"My genetics test came back with no trace of anyone," said Pris, not even bothering to mention the Taya poem debacle and the torrent of Tings still rolling in. She watched Uncle Myles stiffen. "Why don't I have any ancestors?"

The color ran from his face. She was afraid he was going to collapse again.

"Oh dear. I forgot that they would be doing that godforsaken genetics module," he said, burying his face in his hands. He looked weary, like he had been expecting this question for years and had been building up so much resistance to it that it exhausted him.

"Pris. It was just fifteen of us nurses in the NICU, and so many people were dying. And you were there, all alone."

"But what about my parents?"

"I don't even know if they knew who brought you in."

"But you said I could search for them when I turned eighteen—"

Uncle Myles interrupted her with a painful sigh.

"It was so chaotic, there was so much death, and there you were, and I held you and told them I would take you home and . . . I'm so sorry . . . I . . ." And then he started shaking again.

Cammie, hovering over him with a look of concern on her face, pulled up his vitals onto a cartoon clipboard.

"His insulin levels are extremely low," she said.

Pris ran to get him his injection.

The next day, the whole region went into yet another lockdown because of a new Virus variant.

✦　✦　·　✦　✦　·　✦　✦

That was two months ago. Over that time, Pris tried to wrap her mind around how truly orphaned she was. Between throwing the disk around and helping Uncle Myles with housework, she spent the time writing in her notebook, parentless, a hater of mirrors and school spirit.

Now, today, the area was officially out of lockdown, and Pris was returning to physical school for the first time since everything happened. She hoped people would have moved on from calling her Crosswalk or Zero.

She had made it downstairs in time to quickly snarf down the Completia meal and for Uncle Myles to call a hovercar and shove her onto the dock in front of their unit. A black escalator up to the door clattered down, and Pris stepped up on it and sat in the back seat.

"Wait for me!" Cammie said, running up next to Pris.

"You're coming, too?" said Pris.

"I sure am! Myles . . . I mean . . ." Pris watched while Cammie's face buffered with logic algorithms. "Your uncle . . . has to attend to his annual checkup this morning. So I'll just drop you on my way to my Inner Fitness class."

She slipped next to Pris.

"I can go by myself."

"I know you can," she answered cheerily. "But you know your uncle. He worries about you."

Pris held out her wrist while Cammie waited politely, watching Pris with a joyous interest as Pris was quickly stabbed with a needle. The screens went green and the hovercar spewed out of their house's dock and into the air. Somehow Cammie's holobody sat next to her, streamed from the holoscreens inside the hovercar.

The craft ascended, the old overpasses curling around the ground below like lace. Pris looked down at the mismatched jumble of buildings of the Glade and to the other Contained Communities scattering across the landscape like spilled toy blocks.

Between them, she could see remnants of a world where people used to drive instead of hover, a life without protocols and skin tests. *This is what the world was like before the Virus,* Pris thought. Harder, less protected, full of possibility. Somewhere out there was her history, her mother, her father, buried like some lost object in a massive landfill.

She spotted an odd little triangle of land, partially shadowed under the crisscross pattern of elevated highway. Hell Park. She could make out the long bumpy field that sloped up to a tangle of dead trees, including the big blackened stump where she threw around her disk. From above she could see an emanation from it, crags in the earth formed out of it, as if a meteor or lightning had landed there long ago.

"Your uncle and I both are working late tonight, so just take a hovercar straight home after school. There are some frozen PowerPizzas that just need to be zapped," Cammie said as she was swiping the air around her, answering dozens of messages. Pris couldn't tell if she actually had things to do or was pretending she did.

Finally, Pris saw Herron High School. The car hovered over a circle in its curved metal roof. The doorway opened, revealing a tiny pod, steaming with disinfectant. It was worn down, scuffed, with a plastic seat and flickering screens. It was one of the older Virus screener pods that smelled like rust and a bathroom that hadn't been cleaned. *Just my luck*, thought Pris.

Pris put her legs over the side of the exit chute, in her protective suit, and stepped on the circular surface. The funicular door opened, and a chute curled down out of it. It slid her gently into the pod.

Pris put on the tester goggles and tester earbuds and nose probes that were laid out in front of her. They were wet and fuming with sanitizer.

The probe dug deep into her sinus. They would make her nostrils burn all day. The tester pulled back into its slots, already hissing with heat, churning in suds behind glass.

"Please close your eyes," said a computerized voice, so loud it made Pris jump, even though she had done this numerous times. She shut her eyes as a radiant blue light glided over her body. When it reached her waist, it stopped. She opened her eyes and saw the light had turned an amber blinking color over her book bag. "Unapproved object in receptacle. Please open for further scanning." Pris opened her bag, and a tiny drone, the size of a dragonfly, was dispatched from above. It flew directly into the bag and emerged again, clutching her spiral notebook—where she had written things down instead of her Mat.

"Oh, um, that's just my, um, book of ideas and stuff," Pris said, embarrassed.

"No talking please," said a tired, more human voice over the speaker.

The dragonfly drone gingerly held Pris's diary as another blue light swept over it. Pris was embarrassed and felt exposed. Would the scanner pick her out again? She thought of all her poetry and words in that book. She waited in anticipation for the CONTAMINANT FREE sign to appear.

Finally, a green plus sign appeared, and Pris exhaled. The chamber screen opened into Pris's high school. She landed in the vast atrium. Within seconds someone knocked into her, spilling her books out of her hands, her spiral notebook of poetry sliding across the floor.

"Oops, sorry," they said sarcastically. She didn't even have enough time to figure out who it was and didn't care because she just needed to scramble across the atrium and get that notebook.

After grabbing it, she walked quickly through the atrium to her locker. She was trying to not be seen. The atrium was a gathering point, like a rush in a river, of all the different clamorous crowds of students—the Cools and the Serenas and the Organics and the Wonks. Pris didn't fit into any of these.

This was the last month of school before summer, and she just needed to endure a few more weeks of mean looks, and then she would be able to walk to Hell Park and be alone, toss her disk, and write poems.

Pris walked down the hall, being sure to stay on her side of the center line, because they weren't allowed to touch one another, to prevent possible spread. She waited for the comments to appear on her Ting feed.

"Well, if it isn't the striped *zero*."

She felt her before she saw her. Taya. She didn't even look Pris's way—as if she wasn't even there. Pris felt stabbed with embarrassment but kept her composure as she kept walking down the hall. Throughout the rest of the day, she endured everyone whooping in the hallways for Spirit Day, dressed in school colors. Pris watched them, almost anthropologically, observing how every group still cared, still clung to the notion of "spirit," whatever that meant.

At the end of her last period, right as the bell rang, Jayde Tinged her wrist. Pris waved them on.

> Where are you? Come to entrance A2.

Pris was nervous going to A2. That was the side entrance to school where all the cool Queers hung out.

Pris made it to the door and waved it open. Outside was Jayde, along with Benz and Knip, the cute twin brothers who just got here a month ago from the Pacific District.

Jayde was in the middle of a very intense story that seemed to consume the twins' attention, so they barely acknowledged Pris was in the room.

"... and apparently this huge, terrible murder happened there. And since then, it's been abandoned, and some say haunted. Like seriously, people walk by and see figures in the windows."

"Oh, come on."

"No! It's, like, something at least five people have witnessed. I mean, you know that place has to have major ghosts. A family all dead," said Jayde to the boys. Their eyes widened in surprise. "Someone went crazy and stabbed them and ripped out the family's guts and smeared them all over the interior, and blood apparently is still dried in drips down the walls."

"Pris has been there, right?" asked Benz.

"Yes, we both have," answered Jayde.

The boys turned to Pris, searching her face for validation.

Pris nodded, but there wasn't much of a story. They both went there last summer when there was a week between lockdowns. They took their hover scooters across the neighborhood. The house was there, at the end of a dilapidated cul-de-sac, windows dark. They stood there looking at it, and then, suddenly, there was a crack of lightning and thunder nearby. They both screamed and quickly turned home, soaked to the skin with rainwater. That was their visit.

"Let's go. You have your sedan right?" Jayde asked, turning to the twins.

"Yeah," said Benz.

"Great. Ting your prison guards and tell them that because of the lockdown lift, you are going to Pizza Slab with your new friends to talk about history class or school spirit or some other bullshit."

The boys did this dutifully. Jayde glared at Pris with eyes that demanded she play along.

✦   •   ✳   ✦   •   ✦   ✦

They piled into the twins' hover sedan, and Knip punched in the location. The car shuddered off the ground and began its programmed trajectory.

The sky grumbled. *Here it comes*, Pris thought. They were about to be deluged with rain. The boys didn't really notice the shift, but Pris could smell it—that metallic odor of a storm, the leaves turning downward.

They scooted above the houses and cargo ways. The clouds kept coming, darkening the sky, speeding up a sunset that was still two hours away from now.

The twins' hover sedan descended onto the cul-de-sac and landed in front of the Murder House. They all looked at it through the tinted windows. It was small, peeking out over a slope behind it, the neglected yard around it unmanicured and gnarled with brush. Everything was brown, including the house, like nothing could live there.

"Let's go," said Jayde, jumping out.

The twins and Pris followed behind. Another wet breeze surged through the air.

"You can even see the living room from here," Jayde said, pointing to the window by the front door.

"Wow. Look at that couch! This is like a museum," said Benz.

A sign on the front door screamed NO TRESPASSING in bold red letters.

Peering inside, Pris noticed the dismantled couch, two legs missing, and a big reclining chair overturned on its side. There was trash everywhere. It had been ransacked over the years, it seemed, by dozens of other trespassing kids looking for a thrill. Graffiti tags dripped from the walls—names, epithets, the usual. But that didn't keep Jayde from creating a mood.

"It feels … chilly, right? The energy. You can tell that something happened here," they said, grabbing Knip's arm.

Jayde tried the door handles.

"Jayde! We aren't supposed to," said Pris.

Jayde looked at Pris and rolled their eyes. They pointed to the abandoned streets around the house. The pavement was cracked with weeds, the houses all empty of cars, the lawns all unattended. "Look around. No one's here. This whole neighborhood must have been abandoned during Peak Virus."

They tried the handle. "It's locked, anyway. Guess we have to go around back!"

Jayde scurried around the side of the house. The twins followed. Pris hesitated. She stared out at the rows of dried-up yards and ramshackle houses. After the first devastating waves of the Virus and the Fires, it was rare to find neighborhoods like this still intact. Maybe this was like the house the parents she would never know lived in.

"Pris!" she heard Jayde call out.

She walked around the back and saw Jayde's legs hanging out of the house, with Benz pushing their feet.

"Aah!" Jayde screamed. There was a thump. The others froze.

Jayde's head emerged from the window, laughing. "Oh my god, I just landed on an end table! It was so slippery. Anyway, I'm fine."

Jayde reached out their hand. Benz grabbed the windowsill and jumped, easily hoisting himself inside.

Knip turned to Pris. "May I offer to help you up?" he asked gallantly, even though he was at least three inches shorter than her and at least thirty pounds lighter.

"No, I got it," she replied, watching him bow to her and then jump up and into the open window.

Pris heard a rumble of thunder from miles away. She stood there below the others, mustering up her courage. With a running start she jumped and threw her hands up on the sill. The sharp edge dug into her hands, but she pulled herself up and over, leaping into the space in one movement.

"Wow, that was great!" said Knip.

Pris dusted herself off.

"Pris is trying out for disk team," said Jayde.

"I am not," Pris snapped, and then privately, to herself, she muttered, "*anymore.*"

"Yes, you are!" Jayde insisted, like her coach.

Pris examined the bedroom. She felt she knew this room. Or rather, the room reminded her of her own. The walls were dark and stained, like an old book left out in the rain. There was a small bed to one side. The mattress had been shredded, covered with plastic cups from fast food joints. It was in the same place as hers, across from the door. A desk, scuffed, and also tagged with graffiti, leaned against the wall.

Benz opened the closet. "Whew. It smells like something died in there."

"I wonder if they left a body behind," said Jayde, wiggling their eyebrows.

"Jayde!" Pris scolded. Outside, the thunder got closer.

She stepped out into the hall. The wallpaper was peeling, and when she inspected it more closely, she swore she saw a shadowy figure emerge, leering at her. She immediately jolted backward, yelping. The others turned to see what was wrong.

But it was just her, reflected in a dirty old mirror that she hadn't noticed was there. She had seen a similar mirror in her dream. Pris felt a shiver surge through her body.

"You really thought there was something there, huh?" Benz laughed.

Pris glared at him.

"Um, I mean, I don't blame you."

Jayde grabbed Knip's hand flirtatiously and pushed past Pris. "Let's go see if there are bloodstains!"

"This is just like that show *Slaughter Sleuths*."

They went running through the house, kicking up dust and cackling.

"Guys!" Pris whisper-yelled. "Murders happened here. Even if it was sixty years ago, have some respect for the dead," she said, more serious than she intended.

Everyone stopped speaking. It was so quiet, even the air seemed to have a story. A beam of sunlight filled the living room. It shone across the space, exposing the dust mites, making the furniture glow. Then, she noticed a book, spread over the armrest of a recliner, as if someone had just been reading it. She walked over to it. The cover was torn.

"*The Art of As—*"

"*The Art of Ass!*" Jayde proclaimed, walking up behind Pris and leaning over to snatch the book from her hands. They coughed from the dust. "Jeez, this book must have been sitting here for a long time," they said, waving the air and trying to brush the silt out of their hair. "Huh, I thought it was going to be some kind of antique erotica or something. *How to Artfully Worship Ass.*"

The twins laughed.

"It's actually a goofy New Age book," Jayde said.

Pris watched her best friend try not to care, but she knew Jayde was fascinated. They flipped through the pages and a piece of paper slipped out, folded in a triangle. It swooped and landed on the dusty coffee table. Jayde didn't notice, but Pris did and picked it up, unfolding it.

STORM OMEN, a POEM BY RENÉ CALABASAS.
(a PLAY ON THE WORD KERAUNOSCOPY)
FOR T. G.

I am naked, only in my skin,
bare bark,
listening for storms
waiting for omens

Pris heard a tap on the roof, then another. Soon, rain started pouring from the sky.

The twins approached the window, looking nervous.

"We should get home," said Benz.

"Fine," Jayde replied. "But I'm taking this."

They took the book and stuffed it under their jacket. Pris held on to the paper, tucking it into her pocket so it wouldn't get wet.

When she got back from the Murder House, Pris ran upstairs before Uncle Myles could see her so wet and bedraggled. She changed into sweats, sat on her bed and pulled out the poem. Whatever happened to this René Calabasas in the Murder House must have been a long, long time ago—but surely she would find something. You can find anything about anyone on the Hub. She started to type, but something made her hesitate. A voice inside her, saying: *That is not the way to find out.*

Laying on her bed, drowsiness came over her like a cloud.

Pris sat up. *I'm dreaming again,* she thought. She looked behind her and saw herself lying there, sprawled out on top of her bed, her Mat on her stomach. *I look like crap when I sleep.*

She walked across the floor of her room and stopped at her door. She opened it and realized her non-body was opening a door, not her. Down the hall, she saw that mirror hanging there, crooked—the one in the Murder House. Inside the mirror, there was a woman sitting in a large wicker chair on a screened-in porch in front of a bright yellow house. The sills of the windows and the lip of the roof were decorated in swirling wooden accents, like a gingerbread house. It was sunset there, and shafts of light beamed across the room, casting the woman in shadows. The woman saw her and motioned for her to come in, as if the mirror were a screen door. Pris hesitated, but the woman motioned again, impatiently.

Pris walked over, carefully, like the floorboards were going to give way under her. The wood creaked. The woman stood up, but the shadows across her stayed as she moved. Pris realized, with sudden clarity and surprise, that she was also striped. She glared at Pris with fierce, fiery eyes. She was armed—like a warrior from another time—wearing, heavy colorful necklaces, holding a long scythe. She wouldn't take her eyes off Pris. She beckoned Pris to walk through the mirror, this time more urgently. Pris took a breath, closed her eyes, and walked into the mirror.

She opened her eyes. Pris looked around and realized she was standing on the creaky porch. She felt a breeze and breathed in the briny, vegetal odor of beaches. The woman smiled. She nodded over to the door in front of Pris that led into the house. Pris opened it and saw plush parlor chairs and couches and carpets—all colored in mustards and other shades of golden yellow, all a little threadbare, like they had been there for years. The walls were full of mirrors of various lengths and sizes, framed in no discernible format, some with filigree carvings, some in hard black metal like they were from a cold office.

The woman walked into the room with her. She leaned her long scythe on her shoulder nodded again. Then she turned and walked out to the porch. And opened the screen door onto the beach.

"Wait!" Pris called. "Where are you going?"

The woman raised her hand as if to say goodbye. The screen door, creaking slowly at first, then gathering force, slammed closed behind her.

Pris woke with a gasp. She sat up and felt like she had been hit by hundreds of pillows. She was late for school again, but Uncle Myles wasn't barging in to chastise her. Pris scrambled out of bed and quickly got ready, digging around for her usual uniform of black pants and a dull-colored shirt.

She walked downstairs. Uncle Myles was moving around the kitchen slowly.

"I feel so out of sorts today," he said as he staggered and reached for the beverage materializer. Cammie made gestures to help him with her ineffective virtual arms.

The hovercar for school approached, and Cammie joined Pris again for the ride.

In the hovercar, even Cammie looked tired. Her forehead was furrowed with wrinkles.

They both rode silently.

When they got outside the school, she put her arm around the back of Pris's chair. "Are you too old to give your aunt Cammie a hug goodbye?" Pris cringed as she hugged the empty space where Cammie was floating.

Pris just made it through the contamination check to first period. Afterward she quickly walked to Jayde's locker.

Jayde looked pale and not well. They blew their nose and coughed up some phlegm, something Pris had never seen Jayde do in all the years of knowing them. They were always so healthy. Jayde placed the book from the Murder House in their locker.

"Can I look at that tonight?" Pris asked.

Jayde shrugged. "Yeah, sure, knock yourself out. It's totally garbled. Full of all these hilarious rituals you are supposed to do to ready yourself for the *astral plane* and stuff. I tried one of the chants and just fell right asleep. I had a terrible dream, though," they added. "I was being chased by some scary entity through, like, an air duct or something. It kept saying it was coming for me."

"I had weird dreams, too, and woke up feeling awful."

"Well, we both know you aren't much of a morning person," Jayde said, running their hand over their face and neck, looking in the mirror inside their locker. "Ugh, I look like crap."

"No, you don't."

"I do. I think being stuck out in the rain yesterday made me a little sick. And I am supposed to have a date with Nomed tonight. I can't cancel."

"Can't you tell him you will meet him some other time?"

"Girl, you have to act fast when it comes to love," Jayde said, like they knew what they were talking about. "Strike while the iron's hot, so to speak. Whatever an iron is."

"When are you meeting him?"

"Tonight at nine."

"Where? At Hell Park?"

"Why, do you wanna chaperone me?"

"Well, yeah. I want him to see there is someone looking out for you. Who else is going to?"

Jayde smiled, the softness of their childhood back in their eyes.

"Okay. Meet me at, like, eight thirty at Hell Park?"

"Okay, I'll have to figure out an excuse, but I'll be there."

"Tell Uncle Myles and his virtual girlfriend that I need help with my homework. Your uncle loves me," Jayde said, laughing, which turned into another hacking cough.

A student glared at them from across the hall.

"It's not the Virus!" Jayde yelled. "I already went through the contamination chamber."

Jayde turned back to Pris. "I still don't know what to wear tonight."

Pris waved on the weather alert blinking on her wrist. "Well, bring a hover-cover. Looks like there's a chance for another storm."

After school, Pris walked to the contamination check chamber. She pulled the book out of her bag. Without even opening it, she sensed some strange attraction to it—the same way she felt about the Murder House, like she was an animal sensing something about it with some other sense than the ones she knew. *The Sacred Art of As*—the corner, ripped off like someone was clutching it as it was torn from their grasp. She opened the book and glanced at the first chapter.

Within this book lies the secret to traveling into higher planes than this physical world. You will learn interdimensional travel and welcome your inner power.

Harnessing your power to travel outside your physical body takes practice, but if you use this tome as your guide, you will discover many different methods: through dreams, chanting, breathing, and even mirrors.

Mirrors. Pris felt a little lurch of panic inside. She hated mirrors. That mirror at the Murder House. And the ones in that house in her dreams.

She slid the book in her bag and sat in the contamination chamber. The drone glided over her body and her book bag. She worried the astral projection book would show up, and she was already thinking of an excuse to tell the drone police, because it would assuredly detect a foreign object. But the green eye scanned over it as if it weren't even there.

That evening, after a dinner with her uncle and Cammie, Pris mentioned, as casually as she could, that Jayde needed help with their history report due tomorrow and she needed to meet them. That was easy because Jayde was right. Her uncle did love them. He still saw Jayde as this innocent little scrappy nerd that Pris had known since they were five.

"Okay, just be sure to check the contamination levels outside before you go," said Uncle Myles. He pulled up a Hub report. "Looks like there are no virus alerts coming down the pike tonight. Just stay within—"

"I know, I know. Stay within the Health District. Don't worry—I'm just going to spend the night at Jayde's. The Border is miles away, and I don't even have a car."

"And be sure to wear sunscreen. Because your skin is sensitive," her uncle said, almost as if he knew Pris was lying about where she was going.

"Myles," said Cammie, floating above them, resting her vaporous hand on his shoulder. "Let her be a teenager."

Jayde Tinged her.

See you in a bit! And can you do me a favor and bring that weird book? Nomed was super interested in seeing it from a design perspective because he also dabbles in antique books

Pris sighed. Ok, sure thing! she wrote with fake enthusiasm.

She looked down at the book. She decided to print a copy, quickly. She had seen Uncle Myles do this with his Hub manuals. She turned on her detection camera and held the book in front of it, flipping quickly through each page.

Complete, said the computer. Then she connected to the old 3D printer and set it on *print*, and out spat a bound copy of the book, same size, same soft cover. Instead of a torn edge, the printer created a shiny corner of black ink. She grabbed it quickly and dropped both the book and the copy into her side satchel. Then she remembered. She plucked out the poem, folded neatly in a triangle, and slipped it into her new copy. Then she tucked her disk into the front pocket. Jayde had begged her to stop carrying around her satchel, but Pris refused to go anywhere without it. She yelled goodbye and shut the door behind her.

Pris decided to walk to Hell Park instead of hover there. She needed the time to think. She turned down Sierra and crossed Topiary Boulevard and stepped out of the massive gates that sealed off the Glade and into the surrounding neighborhood.

Every time she left the Glade, she remembered how tall and overpowering the buildings were around her at home. The sky was so big, suddenly. Few people were on the street, hover sedans streaking by quickly, full of deliveries. Out here, the terrain was wide open. The houses looked battered by the wind. The ground was dry, crumbled, with charcoal clods, remnants of the Fires, like the earth was a big, stale chocolate-chip cookie. The wind was fresher out here. She felt exposed. She could see how, years ago, people in this raw, windy world could get exposed to the Virus, and its many mutations and resurgences. People like her parents.

She looked up to see the sky glimmering with a half dozen addirigibles, displaying products and apps and systems and cures. They lit up the sky with their colors and urges—*"Set Yourself Up for Success with Fiduciary Frappuccino," "Kiss the Future of Taste with Plant-*

Based Tender Skins." The dirigibles floated by with surprising speed. She was far enough away from the Glade now that she could see them all descending like pollinating bees until they rose up and off to the next pod village.

The streets were empty, with rows of old houses or even just foundations where houses used to be, squares of cement like the ghost of a structure that used to be there. They hadn't reached the section in Twentieth-Century History about what had happened, how the Virus swept through the world and changed economies and cultures, but Pris knew this was what was left of how people lived before.

Another ad-dirigible floated overhead with a grating jingle: "*Come along, come along, crunchy colors, tasty song, come along, come along, Lollipop Crunch!*" She watched a hologram of the strange, overexcited lollipop man mascot dance over the floating signage, joyful for no one. She hated that song; it got stuck in her head all the time.

As Pris walked to Hell Park, she kept reading about astral travel while dodging the occasional pothole and delivery bot. Jayde wasn't there yet.

I'm coming! Needed to wash dishes 😊, they Tinged. Pris knew they were lying—they were still at home, primping. They wouldn't say it, but Jayde was expecting tonight to be big. This older guy was taking them to a club. Jayde seemed to be getting more and more mature before Pris's eyes. They were growing into themselves, becoming beautiful. It made Pris feel lonely. She wondered if Jayde would still be her friend after tonight.

Pris made it to the park and walked up to the old, hulking dead tree. She threw her disk back and forth around it, deep in thought. She thought about Taya; the last time she was with her was here at this tree. How much hope for the future she felt then. Not now.

She listened to the storm clouds approaching.

She heard thunder. What day was it? Friday. She pulled out the poem.

JAYDE

In their room with the door shut, Jayde pulled a baggy black hoodie over their outfit. They wanted to leave quickly, with no trace of themselves—not even a sillage of their departure. *Sillage* was a word they just learned—the odor of you, left in the room after you leave.

"I'm just hanging out with Pris tonight," Jayde told their parents, trying to achieve exactly the right tone of effortlessness and casualness like it was just another day.

Jayde was also trying hard to achieve the same effortlessness with product in their hair. It was alchemical—the right amount of balm and conditioner and holding nanotech, and their hair had the healthy, juicy look they were going for, but one tiny overstep and it looked like they had been disembogued from a muddy river.

Disembogue, Jayde discovered, meant to flow or come forth from a river or channel. They just loved that word. They loved words in general. They used to spend hours writing poems, showing them to Pris. Jayde called them poem-songs because they were more sound than meaning:

Satiny silk dresses in etched leather,
beams of light through the conifers,
leaves blending together

Sometimes they sat for hours on Ting's little-known vocab app, VOCAPP, just looking up words. But not as often, now that they were constantly checking in on the social hub to find out how many players were up for the final round of *Poly House* or who was winning on *The Leak*. Jayde knew they needed to burnish their image for their burgeoning career path.

There was a time—just last year—when Pris and Jayde would spend hours in their room writing rhymes. But Jayde, even then, had bigger dreams of writing real songs, lyrics that mattered, hits that would make them a superstar. They had so much they wanted to share with the world.

They decided to check on their Goss app to see if there were updates. That's when they saw the news. Contessa was dead. It was something terrible—a murder-suicide by her boyfriend. Jayde felt their stomach drop. There were already virtual vigils and songs and tributes being put together, and Jayde had just heard about it fifteen seconds ago.

Contessa was Jayde's role model. She was the first trans Latinx trillionaire who made her money her own way, through her music, fashion line, and entertainment company. Maybe that's why they slept so poorly last night. Their body was sensing the death of Contessa.

Jayde's hair balm froze in their hand. They didn't know what to do. Contessa's death gripped at their chest, and the grief was beginning to inhabit their whole body. They glanced at their hair in the full-length mirror hanging on the back of their bedroom door. They decided, right then, that to get through this date, they would have to push these feelings down. They would have to swallow them whole. *Just to get through the date,* they repeated to themselves. *Just stay poised,* they insisted. This was the night that everything might change for them. They had to think about their own future.

Jayde had never really spoken to Nomed in person or even in hologram, but their relationship felt real. He got them. *Knew* them.

"I like your insides," he once said. He had met Contessa, too. At a party. "I know it sounds like I'm exaggerating, but you have the same ineluctable thing that Contessa embodies." *Ineluctable.* That was what clinched it for Jayde—Nomed was using big words, just like Jayde, but with confidence and poise. *"I know that what we have together is right,"* he had Tinged them.

He said he wanted to take them far out of town, to a beautiful waterfront dance club. Apparently, Contessa was supposed to be there. Jayde imagined they would finally see a landscape that seemed undisturbed by the Virus, or the Fires, or any of the Collapse that happened afterward. It would just be the two of them and Jayde's role model. But now Contessa was gone.

Underneath the hoodie, Jayde had put together the perfect outfit: a structured bra to make them look like a real adult—not like a high schooler Nomed would have to feel embarrassed about being seen with.

Jayde called up his photo again, as they had done dozens of times. They felt this huge gust of emotion every time they looked at Nomed. He was so handsome, kind, and worldly. Holovids of him blowing out birthday candles, bouldering on a simulation of Old Utah, and their favorite, participating in the Shirtless for Toddlers with Virus Variant #F14 Campaign.

He was going places; he was pre-med and had a vision for himself. Jayde could see how easily their life would fit in with his.

Pris Tinged: **Where are you?**

Fitfully, Jayde responded. **Sorry, almost there! Had to wash dishes** 😳

Jayde hated lying but had grown used to it with Pris. Pris was their best friend, but Jayde was feeling like Pris wasn't mature enough for the vision that was forming of their life, the one Jayde wanted. Jayde wanted more than throwing a disk around and waiting for school to end before they could be an adult. Pris was childish. Jayde had to admit it.

Jayde of course would never stop being her friend. But maybe they were diverging in their destinies. Maybe Jayde was meant to be with an older man and live more globally. Maybe Pris was meant to be here, with her disk and medium-size dreams.

Last night's nightmare lingered. Jayde had fallen asleep and then quickly shot up in bed. They were awake but not awake, asleep but perched on the edge of their bed. They stood and walked to their bedroom door. It felt like something was beckoning to them on the other side, saying their name. They opened the door and felt someone embracing them, affectionately, warmly. It was like a hot blanket had enveloped their body. *Soon,* it said in their ear, *soon.* The voice sent ecstatic shivers down their body, all the hairs standing on end as if they were near a huge electrical source.

Then they woke up, heart pounding, feeling stuffy and congested, clobbered like they were jet-lagged from a trip around the world. They had a runny nose and a gross, phlegmy cough, and were about to call Nomed and ask for a rain check, but luckily they ran a Virus test and it all started clearing up by the end of school. Still, the nightmare stuck with them. As did Contessa's death. Jayde refused to believe it was an augury.

Now Jayde shouted *goodbye* to their parents.

"Stay safe," they heard their mother say as they shut the door behind them.

They hopped on their glider and streaked out of the cul-de-sac and through the neighborhood. Jayde had told their parents that they were spending the night at Pris's. It was an easy excuse but risky because they hadn't slept over at each other's house for at least a year. It seemed so infantile now. When Jayde told their parents, they even put on a bit of a baby voice as if to say, "Golly gee, we can't wait to play nice wholesome vintage video games!"

Pris told Uncle Myles she was going over to Jayde's as well, so they had a kind of double-blind night ahead of them. Jayde wasn't sure what Pris would do with hers other than just throw that disk around the tree.

Jayde swept through the gate of their enclosed community and out into the dry, crumbled landscape. The sky was grumbling, clouds converging far off on the horizon. Pris was right about a storm approaching, but Jayde would be safe in Nomed's hovercar by the time it arrived. To their right, on the other side of the old ruins of the highway, Jayde saw the Glade, Pris's complex.

Jayde's mixed community was much smaller and newer, more state-of-the-art. The Glade looked, from the outside, like the ugly hulking backside of factories. But inside the Glade were shopping malls and restaurants and markets and parks, along with residential dwellings. Everything had been recently reopened after another lockdown, and Jayde could see the glimmering lights of activity emanating from the tall buildings. They liked visiting Pris there, when they were younger—there were television rooms and candy kiosks and all sorts of colorful bustle, but that was when they were a child. Now it was time to be an adult.

Jayde's glider passed over rocky, dismantled roads, and the streets became rougher as they reached the old cargo ways that bisected the edge of town, where Hell Park was nestled underneath.

There was Pris, throwing her disk around the tree. She really was good with that thing. Jayde felt terrible about what happened, how Pris had been humiliated just as she was beginning to have feelings for someone and admit her attraction to women. Being on the disk team would have helped both their social standings. But then Pris had to "accidentally" post her diary. It was obvious, at least to Jayde, that her poems were about Taya—they noticed Pris stealing looks at her in the halls of school. In some ways, Jayde wondered if the "accident" was a form of self-sabotage. Pris was always undercutting herself.

Jayde parked their glider, folded it up into a sack, and put it in their backpack (Jayde didn't want Nomed to see they were riding a glider—too juvenile). They took off their long hoodie, walked to the other side of the Black Tree, and made a dramatic entrance in their floral-printed bra and flared pants.

"Hey! How do I look?"

"Like you are going to a seedy pod motel, to tell you the truth."

"This is *synthetic silk*." Jayde sniffed. "And anyway, we are going to a four-star dance club on the coast."

"I don't think that's such a good idea," Pris said. She sounded like Jayde's mother. "What do you know about this guy? How can you trust him?"

"It's not that dark, Pris! We're just having dinner and then going dancing."

"He's basically a stranger."

"Nomed is *not* a stranger." Jayde shook their wrist and tapped it onto the back of Pris's arm. "Look. Here are my directionals. You can trace me so you will know where I am, okay?"

As Jayde tapped, a blue car descended from above. It hovered close to the two of them. A man's face appeared on the windshield, a projection of the interior.

"Hey there, babe," the projection said.

"Hi," Jayde said, glowing. "This is Pris."

"Hello!" the face said enthusiastically. "I've heard so much about you. It's great to meet you in person. I'd come out and say hello, but I'm all strapped in here and decontaminated."

"That's cool," Pris said. Jayde could tell she was still cautious.

Jayde held out their wrist as a thin robotic arm unfolded from the car door like a praying mantis. It pricked Jayde's skin. NO CONTAMINATION it read on the car window.

"Get in, darling," said the face on the screen.

Jayde turned to Pris. "Swear you won't tell anyone."

"Swear you won't be killed."

"I'll Ting you tomorrow morning."

Jayde gave Pris a long hug. They were about to become a different person. And, in a way, they were saying goodbye to Pris. At least a version of themselves was.

+   +   .   +   +   .   +   .

Jayde slid into the car. It was dark inside, and Nomed kept facing forward. Jayde couldn't make out his features too well. The pair shot up into the sky with such velocity, Jayde didn't even really have time to gather their bearings. They looked down as Hell Park, the Glade, and all the tracts of houses quickly shrank into the size of dollhouses and then into tiny dots. Jayde tried to find their house. It should have been next to the Glade, but they couldn't spot it. They felt a little tinge of fear, that they were so far from home they couldn't even see it anymore.

The car sped toward the horizon. Jayde looked out at the wide, open earth in front of them. Their fear subsided. This was exactly as Jayde had imagined. They were going somewhere exotic and wild, outside of Jayde's prison of life with the same people, the same school, the same schedule. Jayde breathed deeply. The dream, Contessa, and now this—their heart tugged. They felt sorrowful and joyful at once. This day was preternatural, kinetic. Maybe they were living an augury as it was happening. Their true destiny was unfolding.

Nomed hadn't spoken, but Jayde thought he was just being silently mysterious. Jayde reached out to touch his hand. At first it seemed like the hand of a hardworking man, but then Jayde felt flakes of skin, like Nomed had bad eczema. It was rough and cold. Jayde glanced down and saw that his hand was purple, the skin mottled and blistered, falling off into Jayde's palm like fried chicken crust.

Jayde slowly turned to look at him. He remained in profile. But his eye seemed turned toward Jayde. It looked like his nose was bleeding, like there was a long cut down his face.

Advertising dirigibles floated by announcing New Delight Home Delivery, Pumpkin Time Eye Baths, and that old children's cereal with its annoying jingle. The light beamed in, and Jayde finally saw Nomed for what he was.

Lightning struck.

The storm was here.

1986
SALLY

Sally Ziller had been having dreams about Edward for weeks. But last night's was the most vivid. In the dream, she was in a yellow house, ornately decorated, with all sorts of curlicue detail. It was furnished from another time, with wide wooden bannisters and chintzy overstuffed chairs. There were mirrors everywhere, crowding the walls. She walked to the screened-in porch, and stepping on creaky floorboards, she saw Edward standing there. He looked strong, like he had just come from his aerobics class. Like he wasn't sick. She watched him gather his backpack, that ratty thing he used all three years of grad school, and hoist it over his shoulder.

"Something big is coming," he said to her.

"What . . . what do you mean?"

"Listen. Listen to your kids. Don't doubt them," he said. He opened the screen door and turned to her, smiling. "Goodbye, sweet cheeks."

"Don't go!" she shouted.

Silently, Edward walked out into the hot, sunny day, the rickety door slamming behind him.

Sally woke up with a loud snort. Jenna, sleeping next to her, grunted in her disturbed slumber.

Just yesterday, she got a call that Edward was in the hospital with pneumonia. His roommate told her that he hadn't been feeling well since August, and it had been getting worse. Of course, his parents wouldn't be going to San Francisco to see him. They were disgusted by his way of life. But he had friends to look after him and visit, thankfully. She regretted not flying to San Francisco to see him in August, but he had been feeling so much better before this week. It all changed so quickly.

So many men Sally knew were sick. Chris, Blane, Jim—most of them she knew through Edward. All of them gay. She feared the worst.

She didn't believe this thing would get Edward. Edward was tall and broad and strong. He hadn't been sick a day in his life. When she first saw him in pedagogy class at their school for a master's in childhood education, he looked like one of the strapping actors in *Seven Brides for Seven Brothers*.

Somehow, he knew that she was gay, too. With her long hair and prairie skirts, she usually went through life "passing," people assuming she was straight.

"I have a sense you are a friend of Dorothy, too," he said when they came out to each other. It was an afternoon lunch on campus.

"I don't know anyone named Dorothy," she said.

Edward laughed loudly, and everyone in the university courtyard turned to look at them.

"Honey. Dorothy. *Wizard of Oz*. It's a code word for gay."

He said it because he was like that—ready to declare himself and change the world. Sally stuttered and nodded. She tried to say it out loud, and she wasn't even sure if she did.

All she could remember was Edward saying, "Listen, I just knew. We queers can spot one another."

The minute he said *queer*, Sally's eyes darted around the courtyard, praying no one else heard. If only her fiery Baptist father saw her now. It had been five years since she'd left home, and she could still make herself shudder thinking about him and his angry sermons about sinners and the hell where they belonged.

Ed moved out to San Francisco right after they graduated. Sally was sad about it, but Edward said, point-blank, "You have Jenna, the hottest butch on the East Coast. You don't need me."

The last time she saw him was a year ago, May, at his goodbye party. He walked in wearing a headdress of silver lamé, meticulously constructed. He looked like Cher from her *Take Me Home* album.

In September, they took their first teaching jobs. They both swore to protect their students—especially their gay students. When she got her position as a language arts teacher at Herron, her first idea was to start a poetry club. *Poetry itself is gay*, she thought. Or at least, it embraced sensitivity. Poetry welcomed feeling. Everything else in the school was so competitive. Even the band was angrily directed at achievement. She watched the kids in their varsity jackets and first-chair band badges walking mightily through the halls—as obsessed with their station as nobility in Versailles. She wanted to create a place where kids could be themselves with no judgment, no pressure. They would learn to express themselves through simile and metaphor and voice.

And Shakespeare's sonnets. And Cavafy. And Sappho. And Adrienne Rich. And Walt Whitman. "A secretly queer place," Ed called it.

Of course she wouldn't explain her under-agenda to the faculty. Not to Mrs. George, the straightlaced principal. And especially not to Mr. Roman, head of the history department, who viewed history as some kind of male-centered battle of the gods.

All she could do was put a dreamy Edgar Allan Poe quote on her door and cross her fingers.

Not a week after she posted about Poetry Club, Renaldo walked in her door. He was energetic and unapologetic and creative. She felt like she struck gold on the first try.

"You would love him," she told Edward. "I'm not sure he knows he is queer, but I think he is."

"Ha," Ed had said. "But don't say that to anyone else, Sal, or you'll be fired."

By January, Dara and Tommy were in her club. Dara, who was furious and dressed like she was going to a funeral. She had a wonderful artistic skill, drawing spiders and webs in meticulous detail. And Tommy—with his broken-out face and wounded posture, just needing someone to support him. He walked into the club meeting like a cast-off toy. It was nice to see René looking after him.

Tommy's poetry was opening up as he attended the club. Sally saw through the metaphors about tree limbs intertwined and nesting doves. He wanted to "crack open" and "blossom." She saw that every poem was about René. She saw them become friends and how much they enjoyed spending time together, along with Dara. Maybe she could, quietly, nurture their relationship, give them space to connect.

As winter turned to spring, she was worried they would move on, but the three of them kept showing up. Renaldo even had some new poets he discovered he wanted to share with her—ones even she didn't know, like Carolyn Forché, W. S. Merwin, and Lucille Clifton. The three of them sat in silence as Renaldo read some lines. He said he had a new poem he was working on about thunder.

"It's about divination, looking for something new, hoping that something will turn out the way you want it to so much that you look to the sky for answers," he told her.

By the end of school, as the summer approached, René's interests had turned toward the occult. Normally, Sally wouldn't be concerned—it's common, they said in education school, for kids at this age to begin exploring supernatural myths and superstitions. Only Renaldo didn't do anything lightly. He came into her classroom after school with sheets of paper fluttering out of his book, and he would talk, floridly, about how there was "like, the Polynesian belief in the Tupapau, and in Kenya, it's the shaitani." He explained that "they think that a ghost can linger in our world. Instead of going to heaven or hell, they linger and sometimes can invade the body."

His poetry became more like rituals or incantations, where he was calling out to spirits, for them to come to him. Sally worried that not only was he wasting his talents on esoterica, but that he may have been taking his curious mind down a wrong path. But then summer started, and she wasn't able to see them every day. She couldn't reach out—that would be against school policy. Instead, she just gifted them pens, waited, and hoped that her three kids would come back in the fall, and that she could find more kids to bring into their queer safe space.

It all changed so fast.

By the end of summer, Edward was telling a different story. He would talk on the phone, trying to not sound terrified, about how people were getting sick and no one knew who would come next. He said that the *Chronicle's* obituary section had become longer than the "Help Wanted" section.

School started, but policy dictated that she wasn't allowed to resume an extracurricular until a week later. Sally tried to find her kids just to see if they were okay. She spotted Tommy and Dara at one point. Dara, in her long cape-like overcoat, and Tommy hunched over, red-faced and careful.

It took her a while to find René, but finally she saw him, crouched in the corner of the library, curled over a book. She tried to act casual and said *hello*. René looked off. He seemed paler, as if he hadn't gone out in the sun all summer. Sally didn't even want to allow it to enter her mind: *Was he sick, too? But how could he have the gay cancer if he was a virgin?* Maybe Sally didn't know anything about him. But René didn't seem sickly or emaciated, just erratic, like he wasn't sleeping well.

"Is everything all right? You seem tired," Sally asked carefully.

"I'm fine," René said. "Just been having some intense dreams lately."

"Well, write them down," Sally suggested. "It's always good to get things out of you. It's healthy."

René packed up his bag swiftly. "I have to go now," he said

politely, as if he had an appointment he needed to attend.

"You don't even have to show anyone."

René adjusted his bag on his shoulders, clutching his huge book of writing.

"What if your dreams become visitations?" he asked abruptly, leaving the library before she could answer.

Sally couldn't stop thinking about him. She was on the balcony of the apartment that night, Jenna asleep (she had to get up early for her job at the health department), sneaking a cigarette (Jenna would yell at her), and she looked to the sky for answers. She saw thunder coming, rumbling, then the crack of lightning and rain. She decided to take it as a sign that things were being washed away. And when it rained all weekend with furious storms, she took it as a sign that a fever was burning through, and on Monday when the sky was clear and the air clean-smelling and fresh, she took it as a sign of rebirth.

It was when she got to school and was told there was a special faculty meeting in the lounge, and found out about Renaldo, that she realized she had made a series of personal myths about rain, about storms, about everything. Signs. There were no such things. René and Edward were in hospital beds on either coast, two of the most beautiful people she had ever known.

She was in shock. She found Dara and told her to get Tommy and meet her in the parking lot after school. Praying no other teacher would see her, she quickly swept them into her car and drove them to the hospital to see René, and then to the site of his accident and to the library . . . all to understand or retrace his steps, as if that even mattered, but she allowed herself to think it did. She even confronted Deb, the nice librarian, who she had broken up with awkwardly to date Jenna in the middle of grad school.

When Renaldo miraculously recovered, she couldn't believe her eyes. It was like he was healthier than he had been before. Taller, in different clothing, and, she would almost say, a new person. He gave his speech, proud and cocky. She watched as Tommy and Dara stood dumbfounded across the atrium.

Sally returned to her classroom in a daze. It was like Renaldo had chosen to change himself instead of deal with the challenge of being his true identity. She had failed them. The nursery she had started had been poisoned while they were still seedlings. The gay cancer or GRID or AIDS or whatever they were calling it now was also killing future queers, scaring them into suppression before they could become who they were supposed to be.

Outside, kids crossed the courtyard as they changed periods. She remembered Edward giving her a statistic that at least one in thirty people was a homosexual.

"It may be one in ten, but that's being too hopeful, I think," he said.

Ever since she heard that, she would walk into a crowded room and think, *Statistically, there* has *to be someone here like me*, but then realize that she was the one in thirty. Every classroom she taught in, *she* was the statistic.

Sally spotted René in the courtyard. He walked across it with Welsh Walsh, the strapping football player with model good looks. The way René brazenly had his arm around Welsh's shoulder angered her. She was mad that he could shift his friendship so quickly, ignoring Tommy and Dara. And her.

The phone rang. It was Jenna.

"He's dead," Jenna said. "Edward. He died last night."

Sally sat there, at her desk in room C122, after school, and laughed. She couldn't believe how absurd this was. Edward was her age, twenty-five, and was the healthiest person she knew.

"His friend Frank just called here asking for you. I told him you were at school and that you would get in touch," Jenna said. "It's that virus. It got him."

She waited for Jenna to give her some kind words, but Jenna was cold, the way she always was in times of crisis—unable to show emotion because she had to be strong. Sally hung up the phone abruptly.

She buried her face in her hands and wailed, muffling it so no one walking by the classroom would hear her.

There was a knock on the door. It made her heart leap.

"Just a minute!" she said like she had swallowed a frog. She tried to compose herself, putting on her glasses to shield her puffy eyes.

She opened the door to find Mr. and Mrs. Calabasas standing there.

TOMMY

The bell rang. His face burning, Tommy ducked into history class and sat at his desk, refusing to look up. He was still processing what had just happened—seeing René ignore him, hanging out with Stacey Divine and Welsh Walsh as if he had become popular overnight. Even his eyes had changed. He couldn't stop thinking about his best friend's strange, suddenly greenish-hazel eyes. He felt like he had been stabbed with a knife.

His teacher, Mr. Roman, a short, wiry man with a slow, torpid energy, droned on and on. Every lesson seemed boring, like history had never really happened, or if it did, all that was left were endless paragraphs about bank bonds and presidents.

That week, they were learning about the events leading up to World War II, and Mr. Roman had told them to read the corresponding chapter in their huge four-pound tome, *World History at a Glance.*

"So, as you read in your chapter, the Spanish Civil War was a precursor to World War II. What are the three factors that led to the larger conflict?"

No one answered, of course.

Mr. Roman sighed. "Well, we know that there were vast . . . What were there vast amounts of?"

Tommy ducked into his desk and tried to make himself invisible so he wasn't called on. He hadn't read the assignment because he was too obsessed with René's new personality.

"Stacey?"

"Um, grain?" Stacey Divine answered.

Someone exhaled in disgust in the back.

Mr. Roman looked up. "Yes, I should have introduced you. Everyone, please welcome a new student to Herron, Miss . . ." Mr. Roman looked down at his roll book. "Oona Loos—?" He hesitated.

"Lustrada. Oona Lustrada," someone said, in a rasp, as if her vocal cords were damaged. Her voice sounded familiar.

Tommy turned around. It was that strange girl he saw at the library. She was wearing the same old outfit. Plaid skirt with a black woolly sweater, the shirt underneath brown, like it had been dyed in dark tea. She looked sickly, her face tinged green. When she spoke, he saw that she had gray teeth, like those of a skeleton. But her eyes were a strange, otherworldly color of hazel, bright and glowing.

"After the Spanish Civil War, there was a lot of income inequality," Oona explained. "The landowners had teamed up with the church, who owned even more land, to try and put a stop to the democratic reforms being instated by the new Republic." She had an accent Tommy couldn't place. From some other place, some other time.

"That's right, and so—"

"But it's imbecilic to reduce the civil war to simply a cause of World War II. Do you know how many people died? How hard it was to live then? In Madrid, we had no food because Franco had sold us out, starving us into submission. I mean, *they* had no food—"

Mr. Roman stood there speechless. The class turned to look at this odd, pale girl named Oona Lustrada and collectively glared. They just wanted the class to end so they could leave school for the weekend. Mike Grady, Tommy's seatmate, already had his Walkman on.

Oona looked around the room. Her eyes settled on Tommy. He quickly turned away. She formed her face into a grin and waved away the air with her mottled hand. "Sorry. My, um, grandparents were—*are* Spanish, and they told me a lot of stuff." Then she coughed violently, clearing her throat. "Sorry. Allergies."

The class went on, soporifically. (Tommy just learned that word from René. Along with *keraunoscopy*, *effulgent*, and *unctuous*. Where was the René he knew?)

Mr. Roman let the class out early. Tommy darted into the hall. There were ten minutes before the end of school, a Friday, and Tommy needed to get to his locker before everyone else so he could avoid being called names.

He was about to head home when something stopped him. It was like his body took over. The body that had held René and stroked his hair. He found himself walking toward Renaldo's locker, on the other side of the school.

He would confront him. He would ask for the truth. He would demand to know why he was ignoring him.

The bell rang, and students poured out into the halls. Weekend-giddy, they scurried around him.

He saw René with Welsh Walsh, walking away from his locker. They chatted, and Renaldo punched him in the shoulder affectionately, in the way maybe gladiators did in Rome. (René would know exactly what gladiators did then.) Tommy saw Welsh grab onto the back of René's neck and pull him close. They were being affectionate, but in that sporty way that guys can be when they are jocks. It was everything Tommy wanted to do with René but couldn't because he couldn't throw a football or make a basket. Hot waves of desire and sadness burned through him.

He thought of all the poems he had written about René— how he was languid black smoke, how he was nestling doves, how he was carved shadows. He wasn't any of that. He was just a liar.

He walked through the exit doors to his bike and jangled the chain to unlock it. All the cool kids were hanging around their cars. One car revved its engine loudly. Tommy looked up and heard someone from the back seat yell, "Ew! It's Gay! Don't give me AIDS, Gay!" and drive off. Tommy could swear he saw the back of René's head in the car, too.

No. He couldn't be the one who said it. *No.*

He stood there, as if splashed with icy water, shivering. The car drove off to whatever pool party of beer and sex and pleasure and kegs and watermelon soaked in vodka was happening.

Tommy should have kissed him that night at the tree, or any

night, or every night this summer, but now René was with Welsh, a pairing that just a few days ago would have been incomprehensible, but now, because Tommy's entire world was upside down, it was happening right in front of him.

He had to get out of here. He jumped on his bike and rode off, hoping no one could see his tears.

DARA

"Freak," said Billy Major as he walked by.

"Eat me," retorted Dara. She was at her locker, getting together her books for the weekend.

Billy Major turned around. "What did you say?"

"I said: *Eat. Me.*" Dara felt the flare of blood in her face. Billy began walking toward her, his sweaty, block-shaped linebacker head getting right up in hers. All year he had been yelling in the halls and screaming in the parking lot. Dara tried not to shake in fear.

"Billy, come on, we'll be late for Luke's," said his girlfriend, Tracy Shaw, her chestnut hair meticulously brushed and cascading over her Penguin Varsity Cheer Squad uniform. Billy Major turned and roughly pulled her to him.

"Spic," he said as he walked away. "Lowrider."

Dara laughed. He couldn't even get his insults right.

When she was younger, she didn't remember anyone calling her spic or lowrider. But that was because kids didn't learn words like that until later in grade school, and then they spread through the classroom like a cough.

Popularity was a virus. Somehow it had infected her best friend.

Weirdo isn't weird anymore, she thought. René was plastic now. One less artist. One less weirdo.

Dara walked out along the edge of the school, where the asphalt gave way to the woods. She decided she would walk through the forest to get home. She felt more comfortable there. The air was dry, crisp dead leaves crunching under her shoes. She listened to the insects hidden in the foliage. She felt a tickle. A spider had crawled up her arm. She gently scooped it into her hands and put it back on the forest floor. She was never that scared of spiders.

Dara remembered the day she decided to be weird. It was at a trip to the supermarket. Her mother had filled the cart with a week's worth of pork and cabbage and stiff apples and oranges, as well as more herbs and greens and root vegetables that no one else in the store seemed to buy. A line was forming behind them.

A man exhaled as her mom tried to quickly load her items onto the conveyor belt. "Dog-eater," he whispered.

Her mother didn't flinch.

"No wonder it's taking so long."

Dara had turned to look at him. He had an old ratty cap on with the words "The Infantry Regiment" on it. He had that look in his eye like something had been shaken out of him.

"I was stationed there before we went over to 'Nam. A bunch of dog-eaters," he said to no one, but also everyone.

Dara didn't remember her mother's reaction.

Not long after that incident in the supermarket, Dara noticed classmates began asking her where she was from, more and more often. As if they needed desperately to know if she was Mexican or Indian, and they would not rest until they could place her. When she said that she was from the Philippines, they would usually nod, but she could tell they had no idea where that was. She barely remembered herself. Her family moved here when she was five. Her dad, mom, and younger brothers. Batangas, her hometown, was blurry, obscured as if cobwebs had been layered over every street. Maybe she didn't want to remember.

Instead of weathering probing questions and battering, racist insults, Dara decided to give them something else to talk about: her black eyeliner and long dresses, her obsession with spiders, her death glare that kept her classmates at an arm's distance. Let them stare at her. Go ahead, be confused.

And everyone was. Everyone except Renaldo. She remembered crouching at the foot of her locker that first week of ninth grade, drawing again—a spider dangling from a complicated web.

"Hey!" said someone above her with friendly excitement. "You're really good. Such a cool drawing."

It was a handsome boy dressed in all white like he was an intern from heaven.

"I'm Renaldo. René for short," he said, unfazed by her goth attire. "I'd love to see more. I write poems—maybe we could collaborate?"

"Um, sure," Dara replied.

"But I don't want you to feel like that always has to be how we collaborate," he said to her with more concern than anyone had shown her. "I could write an ekphrastic poem if you wanted to do that!"

"A what?"

"Ekphrastic. It's, like, a response in verse to a work of art. Like 'Ode on a Grecian Urn.' Like, you could draw something, and I can respond in verse."

In just one minute, René shook her out of her clouded mood like he was a sunrise burning off fog.

He convinced her to join *The Cornucopia* as an illustrator. Poetry Club met on Tuesdays and Thursdays after school in Ms. Ziller's room, the language arts teacher who was nice and nervous and wore head-to-toe polyester like it was still 1978. Poetry Club, Dara discovered, was just Renaldo and her. René always presenting some new brilliant poem and asking her to illustrate it. Her drawings expanded to mysterious women, who looked like they were dressed in long gowns made of spiderwebs. She couldn't stop drawing them. She showed him the witch princesses she was drawing, and he gasped. "Wow, Dara. You are so good. Your technique is fantastic!"

He began captioning each drawing. *I have an acre of frost around me. I am uncrossable tundra.*

They would sit there in Ms. Ziller's room for what seemed like hours, drawing and talking. René introduced Dara to writers he knew she would obsess over, like Edgar Allan Poe, Emily Dickinson, Sylvia Plath.

"I think you would like them not just for their verse but for their aesthetics," he explained. She didn't know what the word *aesthetic* meant, but René was great at explaining.

Soon, Dara's drawings became less hardened and more elegant. Her witches wore long gowns and tight bodices with lace in ochres and scarlets. Behind them she would draw multicolored backgrounds resembling stained glass. Ms. Ziller let them reign over the magazine.

And even though she was a girl and he was a boy, Dara didn't feel like they were at risk of making out or having to even talk about dating or anything like that. René seemed like her—not obsessed like so many of her classmates with finding a person of the opposite sex to hold hands with in the hall and ask to the Sweetheart Dance.

It didn't stop everyone else from thinking they were going out.

"Look at the freaks in love," she heard someone say when she and René walked out of the building one day after school. But René didn't even seem to hear them, and just continued reciting his favorite Poe poem.

* * * * * *

Eventually, Dara invited Renaldo over to her house. It was the first time Dara had a friend over since years ago when she was friends with Lisa Klimpton down the street and they played obsessively (and maybe a little sexually) with their Barbies. Now Lisa ignored her in the halls.

Even though René and Dara weren't going anywhere, Dara chose her favorite black shift dress to wear. Her parents were going out again (they were always going to social events, now that Dara was old enough to watch over her two younger brothers), but they allowed René to come over because Dara said they were going to work on the literary magazine. That excuse seemed to work with her parents, who didn't see René as a threat. It helped that René was exceedingly polite.

When he arrived, Dara discovered him in the kitchen with her mother, talking.

"Your mother was just describing where you were born, in Batangas? Am I saying that correctly?"

"Yes," Dara's mother said, smiling. "Dara doesn't remember. Or doesn't want to," she added.

"Let's go downstairs," Dara said, pulling René out of the kitchen, glaring at her mother. She led him down to their rec room. She had a video of *Gremlins* and couldn't wait to watch it with him.

"Sorry. She has been bugging me all week," Dara said as they marched down the basement steps.

"I wonder if she can tell me about the Anito."

"The what?"

"Well, I was reading how in the Philippines, just like everywhere else, there's a belief in spirits, and that they can cross over from the other world into ours. Some are demons that can possess you. Do you know about that?"

"Can we please just watch the movie?" Dara snapped.

She watched René sink in his seat, looking reprimanded. She felt bad about it the entire time that they sat in silence and watched the movie. As the sky darkened, Renaldo stood up.

"I better go now. I'm still on curfew. I spent the night outside and didn't come home last weekend. I was just sitting under a tree like Robert Louis Stevenson!" he protested.

Dara walked him outside. The night was surprisingly warm for November. The wind was picking up, though, like winter was making itself known.

"Are you sure you are okay to bike home?"

"Yeah, it's fine. I'm good."

René mounted his bike, with his bag precariously balanced on his back.

"Dara, I'm sorry. I didn't mean to ask about mystical stuff like that." He paused. "I didn't want to exoticize your mother. I feel like I did that all wrong. I'm just so interested in how so many cultures talk about the spirit world."

Exoticize. Leave it to Renaldo to use the perfect word in his apology, she thought.

"No, it's okay. I just don't want to talk about that weird stuff."

"It's cool, not weird."

"Well, you are weird, weirdo," Dara said.

René smiled. "By the way, that movie was terrible." He smiled and rode off.

Dara watched him pedal down the street. René was special. He had access to a different way of seeing the world. It wasn't like she didn't kind of also believe in all those arcane, occult ideas he kept chattering about. She also felt penned in by this world, where people judged her for her color, for her appearance, where everyone was striving toward the same mainstream social status. There had to be something more. She wanted to believe in other worlds, alternative dimensions like René did, but at the same time, here she was, here they all were, stuck in the muddy suburbs.

Now, Dara stood at the entrance of the path outside the school.

She walked into the forest and felt the trees and leaves enfold her. The insects were humming, a crescendo into a loud buzz. Dara was struck with the vibrating intensity of the hidden creatures that surrounded her. The insects' hums became vowels. She felt the sound penetrate her ears.

René, the hum said. *René, René, where is Renaayyy?*

Suddenly she knew she had to go back to the school. She would find René and confront him, shake him out of his new boring existence. She needed him back the way he was.

She knew he had biology at sixth period, and that it let out early on Fridays. She race-walked across the school to the hallway where René's locker was. She planned on confronting him face-to-face, with no one around. She marched around the corner of the hall, and there he was, opening his locker.

His appearance made Dara hesitate. She took a step back so she was pushed against the corner wall. She watched Renaldo pull out a mirror—a hand mirror, oval, with a wood handle. Strangely antique, like he had stolen it from a museum. René looked at himself adoringly, as if his face was new and he was seeing it for the first time. He grinned and scrunched his nose. Then he lifted up his shirt and flexed his abdominals, making a pouty face.

"You are so beautiful. I am so lucky," he said.

Dara watched him as he explored his body, running his hands over his stomach, chest, and arms worshipfully. He stretched out his arm and looked at his veins in fascination. Then, suddenly, almost erotically, he dug his fingers into his skin. Dara watched his eyes flutter, in a mix of pain and ecstasy as his nails buried into his forearm so deeply that blood formed under his fingers.

"Calabadass!" someone said, making Dara jump. Welsh Walsh walked by her, as if she didn't exist, barreling through the hall. She watched René abruptly put away the mirror and roll down his sleeve, smiling. Welsh came up and gave René a strangely affectionate hug, like two football players covering up their desire with sportsmanship.

"Let's bolt. There's a party at Luke's. I'll take you in my Camaro," said Welsh, jangling his keys. They high-fived.

Dara was incredulous as she watched them leave, arm in arm, kicking open the exit doors and laughing.

Dara stumbled back. Tommy was right. That wasn't René at all. Maybe he was overtaken by someone, something. She couldn't believe she was thinking it, but maybe René was possessed. She had to find Tommy.

She rushed to Ms. Ziller's room, hoping he would be there. Without knocking, she walked in. Ms. Ziller was sitting on her desk. Crammed into two student chairs were Mr. and Mrs. Calabasas. They turned to look at her, with concerned looks on their faces.

"Dara, what did I say about knocking first?"

"Sorry. Hi, Mr. and Mrs. Calabasas."

They both nodded and managed tight smiles.

"We were just talking about this semester's *Cornucopia*, and if Renaldo had been participating," Ms. Ziller said, sending a message with her eyes that Dara read as *Don't talk about our trip to the library*.

"We are wondering because René won't tell us anything since . . . since the accident," said Mrs. Calabasas. "He isn't sharing his poetry with us. He hasn't even replaced his big blank book and—"

"We wanted to know if he was participating," said Mr. Calabasas firmly.

"I wish I had news for you," Ms. Ziller said, "but since his return, no, he hasn't been here."

"Maybe you could remind him?" asked Mrs. Calabasas. "He seems . . . forgetful. Like he doesn't recall some things from his life. We are just worried his brain is somehow—" She gripped the edges of the desk.

"Certainly," said Ms. Ziller.

"And please don't tell him we came here? We don't want him to know we are here. In fact, I hope he doesn't see us."

"If it's any help, I just saw him leaving with one of his *new* friends," Dara said, trying but failing to hold back the sarcasm.

"Have you been spending time together?" asked Mrs. Calabasas.

"Honestly, no. But René looked absolutely fine," she spat, making herself angry again, "like he's having a good time."

"But . . . I want him here. He needs to write. It's good for him," Mr. Calabasas said.

Dara watched Mrs. Calabasas sigh. Ms. Ziller grabbed their hands awkwardly.

"I wish more parents were like you," she whispered.

They stood up, and Ms. Ziller escorted them out of the room, assuring them she would do her best to encourage René to return to Poetry Club. She shut the door and sighed. She seemed exhausted.

Dara felt like she needed to just say it. "Ms. Ziller, I was just following René. Well, spying on him, to be honest. I watched him do this weird thing."

"What?"

"He blew kisses at himself in a mirror, and then took his fingernail and . . . Tommy is right. Renaldo is not himself."

Ms. Ziller's face twitched, but she didn't say anything.

Dara glanced out the window and pointed. "There's Tommy!"

Ms. Ziller came up beside her. Tommy was standing by his bike at the crowded rack, unlocking the chain, when a crowd of popular kids passed by him. They saw Renaldo buried amid the cluster of layered hair and pegged jeans and polo shirts. Dara watched Renaldo ducking into Welsh Walsh's Camaro. Tommy stood there looking at them.

"Ew! It's Gay! Don't give me AIDS, Gay!" someone said. The car sped off. Dara saw Renaldo in the back seat laughing. She watched Tommy looking wooden, like he had been splashed with ice water. Dara wanted to call out to him, but she was speechless. It was so horrible. Tommy quickly unlocked his bike and rode off furiously.

Behind her, Dara saw Ms. Ziller clutching her desk. "Ms. Ziller, are you okay?"

Ms. Ziller brought her hand to her mouth, holding back tears.

TOMMY

Tommy tried not to sob as he pumped his pedals down the road. He wouldn't ever know love. Maybe that was why his skin was so bad. Because his pores were all clogged with love. They were oily, like him. He had blown his one chance at it. Soon he would die. He was gay, and apparently everyone gay died. Or he would have to be a virgin forever. Maybe he would live if he never did it.

That didn't even matter as much as losing René as a friend. The person who introduced him to a whole world of poetry seemed to just give it all up like it was a childish game.

He rode to the library. If there was a trace of the old René, it would be there, in the library. He had to go back and see if there was any kind of message from him, from the *old* him. If he couldn't find *The Scared Art of Astral Projection*, he would find any other book René touched. He prayed that he could get a message from them.

He walked in, and the same woman was behind the desk, the

one that Ms. Ziller seemed to be friendly with. Tommy didn't want her to notice him, so he quickly turned left into the stacks. He made his way to the poetry section, where he had spent that afternoon last summer with René, sitting on the floor.

Tommy found his way to the occult section. The modest shelf sat there, undisturbed as before, the astral projection book gone. Then, as if he were being tickled with a feather, he felt someone behind him. He wasn't afraid, just aware, and when he turned, there stood the new girl, Oona Lustrada. She was wearing her same strangely woolly outfit. It was a humid summer day, but she didn't seem hot at all.

"Hi," Tommy said carefully. "I saw you in history, right? And I also think I saw you at the library the other day, too?"

Oona coughed loudly into her handkerchief. "Pardon me, interdimensional traveling brings up a lot of mucus," she said in her unplaceable accent.

Tommy reeled. "Interdimensional?"

"I didn't want this to be so abrupt, but there is an issue that needs to be taken care of. Your colleague, Renaldo."

"We're not colleagues. Or *friends*. He isn't part of the Poetry Club anymore," Tommy snapped.

"Exactly," said Oona. "He is being held hostage. We need to go get him."

A woman walked down the aisle and gave them a puzzling glance. Oona tugged on Tommy's sleeve.

"Let's walk this way," she said nervously. She pulled him to a table in the rear, amid the medical reference titles and wartime history. She was tiny, but her grip was firm. Her skin was pale, almost purple.

Up close, Tommy could see that veins ran across her face like a complicated road map.

"I think this is maybe the book you are looking for?"

Oona reached into her bag and pulled out an old, crudely bound book. It was yellowed and musty, the pages tied together with rough twine, the cover a thin piece of wood. On the cover, scratched away in carefully etched letters, was the title *The Sacred Art of Astral Projection*.

"Wait, you have the book?" Tommy asked, dizzy with shock. Where had she found it? Had Renaldo somehow dropped it and she picked it up?

"Oh, this is my copy. I made it myself, a long time ago. I take it with me everywhere. It needs to be with someone very honest to protect it from misuse. The one that was in the library is . . . with someone else. It is being misused."

"Someone?" Tommy pressed. "Renaldo?"

"No. But it's with him. The book is in the hands of the wrong being."

Tommy shook his head. He didn't understand. "What are you taking about?"

"Didn't you read it? There was a whole section on Consumers." Oona stared at Tommy with a haughty glare.

"Well, I only read parts of it," Tommy replied sheepishly.

Oona sighed, and then wheezed out another cough. She sounded very ill. "You people here are so much . . . faster. It's like you all talk faster than you think—before you can actually read and get the information." She slid the book over to him. "Open it up anywhere."

He obeyed. "'How to travel through the astral plane,'" he read.

Tommy flipped through the pages. Each one was written in careful script, as if concertedly scrawled to look like typeface by a human hand. Tommy landed on a chapter header: *Dream Travel.*

"That's the one you are good at," Oona declared. "The book knows. That's why I'm here."

Tommy felt sick to his stomach. He needed to get away. Minutes ago, on his bike, he had prayed for news, for messages from René. Now, here was this strange girl telling him René was trapped and Tommy could travel through dreams. Despite once suggesting that the astral projection book had something to do with René's coma, he felt like this was some elaborate joke, like the popular kids were trying to fool him into saying he was gay, and everyone would laugh at him.

"I'm think I am going to step away now," he said shakily.

"No!" Oona shouted.

People in the library looked up from their tables. Oona gripped Tommy's arm with force. "Don't you want to see your friend again? That person he became after the accident isn't him. I know you know that. I also know where he is."

"Where, then?" asked Tommy. He was getting angry at this twisted, strange girl.

She opened the book and flipped to a page. "Here."

The page had an illustration of a swirling landscape, with a dark cave like a hole on one side. A figure, drawn clumsily, floated above the hole. The title, in tiny, carefully painted italics under it, said: *The entrance into the higher astral plane.*

"Interesting what it's showing you."

"Showing me?"

"The book. It shows different things to different people.

It knows you can travel by way of dreams. It will show other methods to other people."

Tommy couldn't take it. He quickly ran for the door. Oona called after him, not caring that the librarian kept shushing her.

He got to his bike and quickly tried to unlock it. He felt Oona get closer, limping over to him like she was decades older.

"Please, Mr. Gaye. You must listen to me or this will go very badly."

"No, thanks!" said Tommy in a friendly manner like she was offering him Girl Scout Cookies.

His fingers fumbled over the bike lock as Oona stepped behind him.

He stood up. "Please, Oona, just leave me alone. You're scaring me, and I don't know what you are trying to tell me, and—"

She lifted her hands to her face. He watched her crumple to the ground, sobbing.

"This was a mistake. I told them you weren't ready. I'm sorry. I should never have made you follow me."

Follow me. Tommy stopped. He knew that voice. He turned to Oona in disbelief.

"You! You were in my dreams! You told me to follow you. Right?"

Oona Lustrada looked at him and nodded. "I was trying to help you, get you used to traveling. But I didn't want to take you too far. Not yet. Not until you were ready. That was stupid of me. I thought I had the luxury of time. But you aren't ready."

Tommy felt his face burn. He remembered René going on and on about how someone was trying to lure him in further.

"What am I not ready for?"

"The journey you will have to take to save your friend. We have to travel . . . to connect . . . to the Akashic Records. That's the only way to save him, Renaldo."

"The Akash . . ."

"Akashic Records. It's where every soul and act is recorded. It's like a huge, endless library. Like tree rings, it goes around and around. But it's a way for you to find your friend, before the demon plucks him from there."

Tommy felt terrified. This strange, awful girl was telling him about a whole world, full of deep evil and ancient energies. It was the way René talked all the time. But if he trusted René, the *old* René, then she was telling the truth. He took a deep breath and stared at Oona. Despite how fantastical and unimaginable Oona's words were, he had to believe them. He had to get the old René back. The one he loved.

"It will not be easy, Mr. Gaye," Oona warned, coughing violently. She doubled over like her body was shrinking.

"Are you okay?"

"I shouldn't have exerted myself. Flesh bodies are so fragile." Oona bent over and spit up blood and teeth, which jangled in her hands.

"Shit," she whispered.

"Oh my god!" Tommy gasped. "Can I take you to the hospital?"

"No, no, no, no, no," she breathed shallowly, "we don't have much time. I can only remain in this body a bit longer. Mr. Gaye, I can't reiterate this enough. Renaldo Calabasas is lost in the astral plane. There is a . . . demon . . . that is using his body, enjoying it while he is lost there. It has him trapped in a maze of delusion. We don't have much time to retrieve him."

Tommy watched Oona as she feverishly swooned and faltered. She managed to hold steady as she held up her withered purple hand and stroked his face. No one had ever touched his acne-ridden face like that.

"You are such a brave boy, Mr. Gaye," she said.

"I—I don't think so," Tommy stammered. "I'm terrified."

"No. You are brave. You *will* be. You will protect your friend." Oona let out watery air from her lungs. "We need to go to the place where you feel René the most. Where you connect with him. Can you take us there?"

Tommy slowly nodded, reminding himself of Renaldo—the *old* Renaldo that he loved so much, and like his heart was a weather vane, he knew exactly where to go. "Yes, I think so."

Oona wrapped her arms around his shoulders.

"Lift me up. I'm not very heavy," she said, and he obeyed, gathering her small body in his hands.

She was as bony and light as a sparrow. He felt her spine as if it were a fish's, brittle and barely covered with skin. Afraid he might break her, he took the jacket from around his waist and made a little bed for her in the front basket of his bike.

"Please hurry," Oona cried. "We're running out of time."

They rode through the streets and across two neighborhoods to get to Hollow Pond Park. Oona was propped up in the front basket of his bike, head of wiry, messy hair bobbing in front of him. In the dusk, car headlights turned on and glared as they rode down boulevards. They hit a pothole, and her body lurched to the side, hanging over the basket as if she were a Raggedy Ann doll. He stopped the bike and heaved her upright again, adjusting her head, a clump of her hair coming out when he did.

He wasn't sure how, but he found the park. Gently, he wedged the bike in the rack and pulled Oona into his arms.

"Let's go to the park, then," she said. She coughed again, lifting her thin arm to keep from hacking up any more teeth and blood.

The sunset was swiftly darkening the landscape. Autumn was making itself permanent, driving away all the promise and warmth of summer. The violets in the field had shed their petals and were receding back into the earth.

"Trees, leaves, breeze," she said. "I forgot how sweet Earth is."

Tommy was barely listening as he carried the small, sickly girl. He still didn't believe what was happening, but his body seemed to understand more than his brain did. He trudged through the field, following his heart, his irrational, trusting heart, his head doubting with every step.

A breeze blew and leaves scattered across the browning grass. Tommy saw a huge black feather blow across the field from the grotto of trees to his left.

"The feathers," Oona said. "Collect them, please? They will be helpful."

Carrying Oona, Tommy ran after them. Walking into the overgrowth, he pushed past the branches into a small clearing. At Tommy's feet was the body of a huge black bird. As big as a hawk, but black, decaying, and covered with flies.

"I thought so," Oona said as Tommy set her down. Limping, she walked around the perimeter of the clearing carefully. "It came into this plane through the Harbinger Birds. This was its previous body before pouring itself into Renaldo."

Oona let out a wheeze, like her lungs were collapsing. Before Tommy could move, she crept into the dark thatches of underbrush.

"Oona?"

"Stay there," she said weakly.

"Are you okay?"

"It's not a good idea for you to see me like this. I, um, am not very presentable at the moment, I'm afraid to say. You should prepare to travel."

"Travel where?"

"To the astral plane, Mr. Gaye. You will go, a spirit guide of yours will show up, and they will bring you to where we can meet, and then we will find René."

He carefully followed the sound of her voice. She was behind a large oak.

"Please don't come any closer, Mr. Gaye."

"But maybe I can help call you an ambulance or something? Or your parents?" As the words came out of his mouth, he suspected that she probably didn't have parents. At least, not here.

"Ha!" Oona shouted, as if confirming his thoughts. "My parents."

He lunged toward her and grabbed her wrist, pulling her out from behind the tree. She let out a surge of air that would have been a scream in a more composed body. Oona's face had caved in, her skin now completely purple. Her lips receded, exposing a row of blackened gums. Her eyes sank into her face until they were gray and milky beads.

"Don't look at me," she hissed.

Tommy fell back, stunned.

Oona hobbled deeper into the woods. "This body. It's some poor girl who must have just been killed."

"Murdered?"

"Not by me! I found it when I emerged in your reality."

"This body you are in . . ." Tommy could hardly believe what he was saying. "Is dead?"

"I hate doing it. I hate it."

"How did she die?

"I do not know. I slipped into her after her death. She was lying there."

"Where?"

"On the shore. I think she had been on a boat, escaping. A refugee."

"She was killed?"

"She drowned."

"Her family must be looking for her."

"Mr. Gaye. I think they died, too." Oona was quiet. "No one is looking for her. In my travels, I have found so many bodies like this. Ones that were tossed aside, forgotten, left for dead. Even in your reality, which purports to be so upstanding and equitable, there are so many forgotten people. The ones no one cares about. There are so many forgotten stories."

"We need to find out what happened to her."

"Mr. Gaye. It is my pledge to you. I will find a way to honor this body. I will be sure it rests. That's how I've traveled. I inhabit dead bodies. I would never steal a living body like . . . like what . . . it . . . is doing to your friend. Now, please, go back to the tree. We must get you on your way."

Tommy crouched to the ground. His face felt warm again. "What . . . is it? The thing that has taken Renaldo?"

"I guess, in this case, what we are dealing with is both a 'who' and a 'what.' A demon, you would say. But at one point it was a person I knew."

Oona sighed. She was exhausting herself.

"I've been chasing it for years and years. Trying to stop it. It's not easy. He's fast. I mean, it . . . is . . ."

"What does he . . . it . . . want with René?"

"It sits in the depths of the astral plane and waits for people like René. For the rare beautiful ones. It wants everything that *is* Renaldo because Renaldo is young and handsome. It wants carnal life. And Renaldo Calabasas is full of life. It stole his body and now it can feel breezes, the seasons, the touch of someone, kisses . . . everything that a body on Earth can do."

Tommy felt like he was being stabbed.

"It's killed scores of people. It killed my family. It is a Consumer."

"Consumer. You keep mentioning Consumers."

"Look in the book! Consumers are criminals. They use and abuse bodies and then throw them away like wrappers. Like what you do with that fast food you people eat."

"René will be thrown away?" Tommy gasped.

"Like garbage. Consumers don't care what they do to a body. They'll leave it battered and dying when they are done. You must find René and fight to get him back into his body."

"How do I do that?"

Oona was silent. The wind picked up and the trees rustled their leaves overhead.

"You have to listen. You can hear him, can't you?"

He realized he could, faintly. Now that he was paying attention. It was like there was a radio dial, and he was trying to tune in to Renaldo, and barely, through the static and snow of distance, he could hear him or, rather, feel him.

"That's why you are the one who can do it. You are pulled to him. And he is to you. He's calling to you. I know it's hard to believe. That's because you have been told to not believe—in yourself. This age you are in is so . . . material. But what if," Oona wheezed, "what if you let yourself trust in your connection? What if, for even just a moment, you stepped outside of everything that keeps you inferior? What if you let go?"

Tommy stood there in the darkness, with the leaves rustling around him, and for once, he tried to allow himself to feel confident. It was hard. All the years of doubt weighed down on him in layers like heavy coats.

"All those thoughts are just thoughts," Oona insisted.

Tommy felt his mind widen, and the edges of his body, his skin, soften until there was no surface. And somewhere out there, like a gleaming gem in a vast shoreline of sand, he felt René shimmering, signaling, vibrating inside of him.

"Go to the tree," Oona said gently, "and take the feathers. Lay them out in a semicircle around you."

Tommy tried to pick her up. Oona shrank back. She coughed again. "I don't have time, Mr. Gaye. Leave me here and go to the tree."

"But I don't know how!"

"Open the book and see what it wants to tell you. The book will explain, Tommy Gaye."

"But what about you?"

"I will meet you in the Higher Plane. Please, go to the tree? Thank you."

Tommy ran toward the tree, tears in his eyes. *Maybe this is all a dream,* he thought. He slumped down into the charred ground, into the crook of the tree. He had the book in his backpack. He opened it. The page was blank except for two words at the top.

Write here, it said.

He had his pen in his back pocket. He pulled it out and looked down at the page.

Write about him here, the page said.

He swore he hadn't seen that before on the page.

Renaldo. He tried to write about him, to him.

You are like smoke, a dark dance in the air.

No.

You are a storm cloud, weightlessly heavy.

No.

You are as mysteriously beautiful as black smoke.

No.

A crow.

No.

A raven?

Ugh, it was all useless. Metaphors were useless. All he wanted to really write was how he should have kissed him when he had the chance.

Don't stop. Keep writing about him, the book said.

Tommy wrote. *If only I had kissed him, if only I had kissed him. If only I had held him, if only we had kissed. If only the storm stayed away, if only we weren't afraid. If only he had slept better, if only I had the bravery of a magpie picking up what I wanted, stealing, being selfish not scared, if only I had the tenacity of a tree root to grab ahold of him and not let go. If only he were here. If only there was a call I could make to him. A call. A call. A call. A chord. A chorus. A chorus of calls that surrounds. A mist of wants. I want to mist my wants. A mist of Renaldo Calabasas.*

He was writing and reading at the same time, looking down at the words and tracing them with his fingers. He closed his eyes and felt himself getting drowsy. As if his skin had no edge anymore. His body floating, unlocking from its bones. He was lifting. He rose out of himself. He looked back to see himself there, curled into the tree like a hibernating animal. In front of him, he saw an entirely different landscape. It was barren, full of strange new buildings and colorful animated balloons covered with advertisements. His body fell past them, almost hitting one. He heard that irritating jingle: *Lollipop Cereal! Come along! Come along!* Then he saw a neighborhood of abandoned houses, crumbling roofs in a cul-de-sac, and like he was falling in a dream, he fell through the air. The only thing that felt solid was his heart, as sure as a compass.

2044
PRIS

I'm sure Jayde will be fine, Pris thought. She kept throwing the disk around the Black Tree and repeating Jayde was okay, while inside, she grew more and more concerned and regretful that she hadn't put her foot down with them. Now Jayde was in a hover sedan with a total stranger.

Thunder rumbled again. Pris pulled out the stack of pages— the 3D book she copied—to try and find the poem she wedged in it. The stack loosened in a gust of wind and flew through the field. She madly dashed around the park to capture the flying wad of pages. It fluttered wildly but landed, lodged into the field of dried weeds, as if the dead plants had grasped them. Pris grabbed the book until the wrinkled stack was back in her grasp.

The poem fell out and fluttered across the park. Pris dove through the air and captured it and tumbled to the ground, out of breath. The book was creased and bent backward, exposing its inside. It was dark now, and she couldn't read the page number.

She heard a screech.

A huge black bird, larger than she had ever seen, landed on the dead tree. Pris was amazed. The only birds she had seen were dirt birds—vultures and pigeons and other scavengers. This bird was grand, terrifyingly big. She suddenly remembered her dream, and how the bird appeared there, too, curling its beak down into the hair of that beautiful boy.

Feathers fell from its body and sprinkled on the ground. It looked sick.

Rain began. Fat pelting drops. Pris hastily wrapped the bundle under her shirt and covered it with her disk for protection and ducked under the tree. It was too stormy for her to run, so she flattened herself against the Black Tree. The smell of the char came off it, pungent as if it had burned yesterday. She felt along its surface and found a deep impression in the tree, not noticeable from far away. It offered shelter. The storm grew closer, the rain coming down in sheets, the thunder cracking overhead. She heard the bird screech again, painfully, and then suddenly it fell and landed in front of her, dead.

Pris pressed herself farther into the shallow cave. She took out the mangled book. She opened it up.

Beware of the Consumer, it said.

Suddenly there was lightning overhead. Pris looked down at the page.

Consumer.

The lightning flashed again. The page was partially obscured in the leaves.

Consumer.

The rain kept coming, and she curled farther into the hollow of the tree. What was the Consumer? Where were they? When would they appear? Pris kept churning it over and over in her mind. She laid her head on the side of the tree. It was surprisingly warm, and she felt herself weighted, like her body had been given a sleep-trigger pill, all that walking and worrying and disk throwing. It was all catching up to her.

She felt drowsy, and she nodded off.

TOMMY AND PRIS, THE ASTRAL PLANE

Tommy sat up. He was in René's room. It was empty, smelling stale as a shack, as if it hadn't been occupied in years. The room was covered in dust, and there were no sheets on the bed, just a filthy mattress that Tommy jumped off of quickly.

He looked down at his body. It was airy, shimmering like it was made of fine quartz dust. A thin line trailed from his belly button, like an umbilical cord of steam.

Through the window, Tommy saw that the ground had no grass. The earth looked baked, the world somehow browner. The closet, to his right, had its door removed, and inside dangled a few of René's white shirts, now yellowed and stained and moth-eaten. The floor, where he and René had sat cross-legged listening to music in the dark, was now just warped, rotted floorboards.

In dreamlike certainty, Tommy walked to the door and opened it. At the end of the hall was a large mirror, ornately framed. He didn't remember seeing it in René's house before. Walking down the hall, he passed the other rooms, also dusty and forgotten, empty but for cobwebs and some rusted bed frames or mottled chairs.

"René?" he called out.

When he got to the mirror, he didn't see his reflection. Instead, through the glass, he saw a yellow room.

A figure walked up to it. That girl, the one with the striped skin, holding that Frisbee. She looked at him with curious recognition. Then, her expression changed. She looked behind him with alarm. There was a screeching sound. Tommy turned to see a black bird diving toward his face. Tommy felt himself tugged into the mirror, through its water-like surface. The girl grabbed him, and he tumbled through. He landed on top of the girl, their limbs tangling, both of them trying to get away from each other quickly.

They stood up and brushed off dust.

"It's you! You were in my dreams," said Tommy.

"You were in *my* dreams."

Tommy examined the brightly lit porch they were standing on. The floorboards at their feet creaked with every step. He could hear the ocean, and wind chimes tinkling. Through a doorway, Tommy saw a wide living room that had wood floors and ornate furniture and mirrors everywhere, along every wall.

There was a faint milky trail coming off the girl's body, too.

"Um, hello," Tommy said as the girl glared at him. "I'm Tommy."

"I'm Pris."

"Pris?"

"Yeah. Priscilla. Pris."

"Wow. Like from *Blade Runner*?"

"You are the only other person who has said that to me."

"Who else?"

"My uncle."

Pris looked around and narrowed her eyes. "I've been here before."

"It looks really old."

"I think it is. I don't know why, but this is where I keep ending up."

"Wait . . . are you, like . . . some kind of . . ."

"Some kind of what?"

"Like, a ghost? Like, this is the house you haunt?"

"No! I'm not a ghost."

"Okay, no! I'm sorry. I'm sorry. I just don't know who is who or when is when."

Tommy waved at himself like he was swatting away a shameful fly. They were silent for a while.

"What school do you go to?" Tommy asked.

"Herron High."

"Herron? Wait, so do I. I've never seen you there."

"I've never seen *you* there," Pris said angrily. She was getting a little annoyed at Tommy's assumptions. She looked around. The house had many hallways. She started walking, and to her irritation, Tommy followed.

Pris stopped for a moment and looked at Tommy. "What year is it?"

"I'm not mad, if that's what you are trying to . . ." Tommy paused. "It's 1986."

Pris took a step back in shock. "It's 2044. I mean, that's the year I'm in."

"You mean, you are . . ." Tommy counted on his fingers. "Sixty years older?"

"I'm fifteen, but in 2044," Pris said.

Tommy started piecing the jumbled facts together in his head. "You are from the same neighborhood as me but, like, the future?" he sputtered.

"*You're* from the past," she insisted. "I'm from the present."

Neither could believe what was happening. They stared at each other, trying to make sure the other was real. Tommy kept his arms hugging his backpack, and Pris clutched her disk in her satchel.

"You are one of the . . . one of the boys I saw under the tree in Hell Park. In my dream," she finally whispered.

"Hell Park?"

"That night when that bird was coming for you. I saw it above you coming down and trying to get to your friend."

"Yes! And you threw your Frisbee at it!"

"My what?"

"Frisbee."

"My disk, you mean."

"Sure. I think you scared it off. At least, in that moment. It came back. And the Consumer took him."

"The Consumer." Pris tried out the words on her tongue.

"Yes. Do you know about him? And about astral projection? Let me see if I have the book."

Tommy grabbed the straps of his backpack and groped around until he found Oona's crude hardbound book. "It traveled with me!" he said with relief.

Pris slowly pulled out her copy. "I have it, too. Or at least a copy. I gave the original back to Jayde." She showed it to Tommy.

"You copied the whole thing? Wow, that must be a powerful mimeograph they have in 2044."

"Mimeograph?"

"Oh my god! It even has the missing corner. Where did you find it?"

"We found it in the Murder House."

"The Murder House?"

"The house. The one I just pulled you from."

"Murder House? That's René's home."

"That's where your boyfriend lives?"

"He's *not* my boyfriend."

"Sure looks like he was."

"He isn't! I don't know what you are talking about. And that's not the Murder House."

"Okay, okay, chill," Pris said. The boy was fragile, she could tell. "It's been called the Murder House since forever."

"It's just where René and his family live. He was struck by lightning. And then he became someone else. And I think he is stuck here. Or somewhere. The Consumer took his body."

Tommy flipped through the pages. He read:

Consumers can create traps for their victims. They will often lure their victims with a precious object. Like THIS VERY BOOK. And then they will take it away quickly to COVER THEIR TRACKS. Next will come the HARBINGER BIRDS (see glossary) to create a sacred area for the arrival. Travel from the astral realm into the earth plane is difficult. The Consumer needs to cross gradually into the earth realm. It will either do so by first inhabiting the Harbinger Bird or it will inhabit a newly deceased body before passing into the body of the desired human.

"Oona says this is what happened to my friend René," Tommy explained. "And that to save him we need to travel through the astral plane to this library and—"

"Wait. So we are astral projecting now?"

"I guess so. Last thing I remember I was under the tree."

"Me too."

"That must be where our bodies are right now, and these are our astral bodies. Wow, I can't believe it actually worked."

Pris was barely listening. She was coming to a realization of her own. "I think . . . I think this Consumer wants *my* friend, too!"

"But what do we do now? Where are we?"

They looked around the parlor full of mirrors. Tommy tried not to stare at Pris's striped skin. He wondered if this was normal in the future. Suddenly Pris pointed, eyes widening.

"Jayde!" she yelled.

Pris ran to a mirror. In the glass, Tommy saw someone sleeping in a bed. He assumed this was Jayde. The room was decorated with posters of pop stars Tommy didn't recognize. A woman—Jayde's mother, perhaps—was leaning over the bed, looking worried. Jayde's father entered, along with a strange object, which scanned Jayde's body as their parents held each other in distress. Pris looked at Jayde and reached her hand to the mirror. She tried to push her fingers through, but the surface remained hard.

"Why can't I travel through this mirror like the others?" Pris muttered, continuing to push on the glass.

"Is that your friend?"

"Yes. I'm worried. Last time I saw them they were getting in a sedan and going on a date, and then there was this huge lightning storm."

"Lightning? That's how it got René! And then he was in a coma for a couple days, and then he changed."

"Oh my god." Pris gasped. "The Consumer *definitely* has Jayde. It must have used the book to lure them. That Nomed guy, he was just a trap. I knew something was up with him."

"When René was taken, he was in a coma for two days. Do you think she's in a coma, too?"

"Jayde's not a she."

Tommy peered down at Jayde, whose long, thick hair cascaded around the pillow like a storybook princess cursed to sleep by a witch.

"Oh, gosh, I'm sorry. Okay. He."

"They."

"What?"

"Jayde goes by *they*. They are gender nonbinary."

"What does that mean? Does she, sorry, *they* want to be a girl?"

"Jayde doesn't want to be anything. They just want to be themselves."

"I'm so confused."

"Didn't you have a gender freedom unit in your sexuality education classes in, like, fifth grade?"

"Gender what? We barely *had* sex education."

Pris shook Tommy off and once again tried to reach through the mirror, her hand pounding at the surface. "I have to get to Jayde."

"Maybe the book has something to say," said Tommy. They each rummaged through their own book. "What do we look under?"

"Yellow house?"

"House of mirrors?"

"House of old, tacky furniture."

"Just look under *house*. House, house, house . . ." Tommy flipped quickly. He stopped and read one entry. "Oh! Maybe . . ." He pointed down and read aloud. "The House of Mirrors. It's, like, a depot that has access to other realms and times. And only certain special people are able to walk through them. Like you."

"Are you kidding me? I hate mirrors."

"Well, you're good at passing through them."

They bent over and read the entry.

Pris thought of the woman she saw. The one who looked like her, who beckoned to her and helped her pass through the mirror.

"Shh!" said Tommy, grabbing Pris by the arm and cocking his head. "Do you hear that?"

It was faint music coming from upstairs, a familiar jingle that sounded cheery but mechanical, like an ice-cream truck's tune repeating over and over.

Tommy grabbed Pris's arm and pulled her alongside him. Pris was surprised at first that he was touching her when they were basically strangers, but she could tell Tommy was frightened. She was, too. The sound emanated down the hall, from the top of a big wooden staircase. They walked through the hallway of mirrors, listening to the song getting closer.

On their way, Tommy passed by another mirror and paused. Through the glass he saw what looked like the bland hallway of a hotel. Someone stepped up to it and checked his hair. It was Tommy's father.

"Dad?" Tommy asked, watching as his father flicked out a poppy seed from between his teeth. Straightening his tie, Tommy's father turned around and knocked on a hotel door. A woman answered and embraced him. They started kissing passionately before he shut the door.

"What the fuck?" Tommy reached out to the mirror, aghast. "Who's that with him?"

"Not my mother, that's who," Tommy spat. "All those late nights working. No one works till midnight." He shook his head. "I'm such a fool. No wonder my mother is so upset all the time."

He turned away from the mirror and suddenly realized he was speaking to no one. Pris had walked down the hall. He ran to catch up.

She was standing in front of a large mirror at the top of the stairs. Tommy climbed the steps until he was beside her. In the mirror, he saw a vast expanse of colorful terrain. The ground glowed in a patchwork of bright colors.

Over the horizon, Pris and Tommy watched a slipshod wagon approach, its wheels warped and large. The song was loud now. They both recognized it.

"Come along, come along, crunchy colors tasty song, come along, come along."

They saw now that there was a figure inside the wagon. He looked like a cartoon with rainbow overalls under a multicolored suit coat; big, blinking bright eyes; and lollipops sprouting out of his head and jangling around him like hair.

"Is that . . . ," Tommy asked, dazed.

"The Lollipop Crunch guy?" finished Pris.

The animated character motioned to them.

"Are you ready to come in?" he asked in a cheery, sugary voice. "If you are, just step forward."

When Pris and Tommy didn't immediately respond, the cartoon lost his smile and snapped. "Hurry up. We don't have much time!"

TOMMY AND PRIS

"Jeez, you're slow," the lollipop man chastised them, his braids of suckers tinkling. Annoyed, he pushed them away with his hand. "Listen, I'm doing my best here, but if you could just be even a *little* more agreeable, it would make this trip a lot easier."

"I'm not going with you anywhere until you tell me who you are," said Pris firmly.

"I'm your spirit guide."

Tommy and Pris flipped through their books.

"You're our spirit guide?" Pris repeated.

The character sat up and forced a grin onto his face. "I'm Lolly. I'm here to take you to the Higher Plane."

Tommy bent over his book. "Spirit guides, spirit guides. It says here that spirit guides can sometimes come to you in dreams as the embodiment of something familiar to you. It makes it easier to follow." Tommy stared at the character. "But I don't have any kind of attachment to you." He turned to Pris. "You?"

"No. I mean, I know it. That ad-dirigible that comes by . . . It hovers over the Glade all the time."

"The what?"

"The Glade. That's where I live."

"Oh. Well, I see ads for Lollipop Crunch on the TV all the time. But I can't even eat the cereal. My mom won't allow me."

"My uncle won't let it in the house, either," Pris echoed.

They stared at the lollipop man.

"Well, I'm sorry for existing!" Lolly whined. "We all can't choose our guides, now, can we? This isn't some kind of shopping mall." He scowled. "This is why I told Oona not to give you access to the book."

"Oona sent you?" Tommy asked.

Lolly threw his hands down and let out a dramatic exhale. "Yes, of course. I've been tasked by our mutual friend, Oona Lustrada, to bring you to the gateway." He tapped the seats of his wobbly wagon. "Come on. Stop lolly-gagging!"

Finally at a loss for words, Pris grabbed Tommy's hand and silently stepped through the mirror. They passed into the new realm and climbed into the wagon. Lolly jerked the reins. In front of the wagon were eight puffy cylinders of different pastel colors in riding harnesses. Pris realized they were the sugary marshmallows in Lollipop Crunch cereal. They bobbed and chattered and began moving forward, pulling the wagon along.

"Grape! Cherry! Lemon! Lime! Strawberry! Orange! Mango! Thimbleberry! Wake up!" the cartoon man shouted rather viciously.

"Those marshmallows . . . are your, um, horses?" Tommy asked.

"Yuppers. And they are as slow as slugs. Because as we know, marshmallows are related to the slug family."

"No, they aren't," Pris said.

"*Yes*, they are."

"No," Pris said with confidence. "Slugs are Pulmonata. They are in the snail family."

The cartoon waved her off. "No way. Snails are cupcakes. Scientifically they are cupcakes. Marshmallows are slugs. Everyone knows that! What are they teaching you kids in school?"

He shook the reins again and righted himself proudly. Pris and Tommy shared a look as they pushed forward.

"I hope my body is okay," Tommy said nervously.

"Me too," Pris replied. She examined the translucent line of smoke coming from her belly button. Where was her flesh and blood? Maybe lying, still, under the Black Tree, vulnerable to the elements. She supposed that if she did perish here that her body back on Earth would die, too. And maybe both bodies would die simultaneously. Like, she would get eaten here, and then on Earth, get shot by a random bullet or have an aneurysm? Pris cleared her throat to ask the strange animated mascot a question.

"What happens to us if our bodies are, like, tampered with?"

"Beats me," Lolly said. "I'm a cartoon. I don't know anything about you weird Earth flesh people and your problems."

"But this is a dream, right?" asked Pris.

Lolly laughed. "Yes! Well, that's what most people like to call it. Dreams. It helps them think that their Earth reality is somehow *realer*," Lolly said, making sarcastic air quotes.

"This is the astral plane, right?" Tommy asked, trying to get his bearings.

"Yuppers. Well, technically, you are in the Lower Plane."

The wagon wobbled along, rolling over translucent terrain. Above Lolly was a twisted path of striped, gooey color dripping down out of nowhere. It dribbled into a hole, and a pink effervescent liquid gushed down it, like one of the waterslides Tommy's parents took him to when he was younger.

"This is not what I expected," Tommy said.

"Next I bet you are going to ask if there is some kind of mystical beast that will appear. Like a big bear or a lion. Well, hate to break it to you, but nope. All you have is me to get you safely to your next destination. Apologies in advance if you don't!"

"And what is the next destination?" Tommy asked.

Lolly turned to him. "I have to get you to the Higher Plane. There's a lot of ground to cover."

* * * * * * *

Pris and Tommy didn't know how long they rolled along. They were too busy following the landscape—a tattered, teeming terrain of loudness and honks and glitter, like a confetti sandstorm. They saw magical unicorns; sloppy, dirty smiley faces; giant foreheads with hair; roaming rainbow mushrooms; and constantly popping balloons. Among all of them were Legos and blocks and figurines and dolls and stuffed animals, writhing and running and bucking into one another like aggressive rams locking horns. Tommy nervously realized that this was the stuff of his twisted, incomprehensible dreams.

Lolly whistled. "We have to rest my critters for a bit. They need to enjoy a nutritious breakfast."

He bounced out and pulled gummy worms from his satchel and threw them at the marshmallows. Pris and Tommy watched the marshmallows' soft mouths become fang-filled chompers as they growled for more.

Pris bit her lip. Now that they were settled, she looked down at the trashy terrain that surrounded them. "There sure are a lot of children's toys around."

"Yup. The Lower Plane is lousy with toys. It's like a messy kid's room. That's because you humans—well, most of you—stop being able to travel when you grow up. So all your weird shit gets buried inside you, swallowed up and then thrown into the Lower Plane because you can't deal with it. Oona said it best: 'The Lower Plane is where imagination comes to die.'"

Lolly snapped his reins and the marshmallows continued. Pris and Tommy grasped onto the sides of the wagon as they lurched forward, moving through the chaotic confetti.

A rainbow kite fluttered close to the wagon. Pris reached out to touch it, and the cartoon man whirled around in a burst of anger.

"Don't touch anything!" he said. "You don't want any of these lower creatures attaching to your psyche."

At that moment, a small, cooing purple swatch of fur landed on Tommy's wrist. It made baby noises and snuggled into the crook of Tommy's arm. He reached down to pet it, and it leapt around his fingers. The coos became screeches. Tommy tried to pry it off, but it fastened itself like glue. Lolly stopped and rolled his giant dinner-plate eyes.

"See? I told you." He grabbed Tommy's hand and placed his comically giant hand on top of it.

"We do not want you here," he said to the creature. It quieted, and Lolly rolled the furry creature off Tommy's body, flicking it away like a wad of gum.

"How did you do that?"

"You have to be clear and firm. You'll get the hang of it."

They spent the rest of the time (an hour? a minute? who knew?) riding on the lumpy back seats of the wagon, listening to Lolly sing his jingle over and over. As they traveled, they saw unimaginable things: huge, towering beanstalks, like the kind in fairy tales, except these were ringed with balloon monkeys, gathered around each stalk three by three. A rabbit-headed creature with one human foot sat on a pile of oversize Magic Markers while a strange scarf-like thing flowed about and then formed a mouth out of itself and then vomited a deluge of capsule-like pills all over the ground.

Every now and then, something would land on their shoulder or arm and try to clamp on. At first it was scary, but both Pris and Tommy got used to it. "We do not want you here," they would say, before plucking them off like harmless rose beetles.

The wagon kept moving forward.

The air around Tommy and Pris was becoming murky and dark. The pair bobbed in their seats as something roared over the colored horizon. The wagon got closer, and Lolly yelled at his marshmallows.

"Turn! Turn! Hyaa, hyaa!" His voice sounded nervous.

"What is it?"

"The edge. The edge of the plane. We can't get too close."

The wagon lurched to the left, and Pris and Tommy looked out over the rim of a dark expanse. They saw a cascade of spheres—bubbles. Each bubble contained a moment of life. They passed by quickly: a boy burning himself on a stove, the sublime moment of the birth of a child, an old woman crying in a bedroom.

"We can't fall into that, or we will become a lost memory," Lolly warned.

The wagon righted itself and kept rolling along. They sat there, gazing out at the tumbling waterfall as it cascaded with event bubbles. Pris's eyes glistened in the pearly light.

"So," Tommy said, turning to Pris and trying to break the tension in this unimaginable situation, "you are from, like, the future?" he repeated.

"I already told you. *You're* from the past. I'm from the present."

"Well, for you."

"Maybe. You could be part of my dream."

"But I'm not. I'm awake. You could be part of MY dream."

"But I'm not. I'm awake, too," Pris said.

"Where were you before this, um, traveling?" Tommy asked.

"I was at the base of the burned tree at Hell Park."

"I was also at the base of a burned tree, except it was at Hollow Pond Park."

"Okay, maybe same tree, different times?"

"I hope our bodies are okay," Tommy said again.

"Maybe this is only, like, a second in our Earth time and we are just asleep for a moment?" Pris suggested, trying to comfort him. Tommy smiled. Pris saw, just then, how nice he was, and how hard he tried to stay hopeful.

"Well, whatever we are, you are in the future to me. Tell me what's going to happen."

"Hell if I know."

"No, I mean from between my time and yours."

Pris studied him carefully. "Do you really want to know?" she said. "Since 1986? Well. There have been a lot of storms and floods. Climate change has erased several cities and wiped out whole populations."

"Go on," Tommy said. He didn't know what climate change was but pretended to so Pris would keep talking.

"There was a big sickness. It came in and killed a lot of people. Our government wasn't ready for it and neglected helping people it didn't like, and a lot of people died because of it."

"I think I know about that sickness," said Tommy, with dread.

"Now we have to get tested every time we walk in the school. Or go anywhere."

"Um. When you say certain people, so you mean that, um, homosexuals?"

"Homosexuals? Oh yeah, I think I remember Mr. Richards using that term. Wait. You think that the virus only affects LGBTQIA+ people?"

"What? I'm sorry, was that a word?"

"Lesbian, gay, bisexual, transgender, queer, intersex, asexual, and plus. LGBTQIA+. It's like this term that my uncle uses, so I thought you may know it. We don't use it anymore. People just define their gender and their sexuality for themselves now, I guess."

"Like your friend Jayde."

"Yes, exactly."

"Well, what about you. What are you, then?" Tommy asked.

Pris said, shyly, "Well, I'm just a lesbian."

"Lesbian? Wow! You are?" Tommy asked in awe.

"Yeah."

"That's so cool," Tommy exclaimed. "I mean, I never met someone who just said who they were like that."

Pris turned to look at him. He was being genuine. A lesbian?

That wasn't cool at all. Pris needed to change the subject. She craned her neck toward the lollipop man. "Excuse me, sir?"

"It's Lolly. I am NOT answering you until you call me Lolly!" the character said insolently.

"Okay. Lolly. Sir? How much longer until we reach this Higher Plane?"

Lolly shrugged. "It's hard to say. The Higher Plane has a few entrances. It honestly just depends on you two."

"What do you mean?"

Lolly exhaled like Pris had asked the most obvious question. "This is all transmuted through your perception of the plane, duh," he said. Pris heard a crunching noise and looked down to see thousands of Completia Meal Boxes, crushed under the wheels of the wagon, stretching on for what seemed like miles and miles.

"So we'll see how long it takes. Hopefully not too much time before we reach Oona."

"Oona is on the Higher Plane?" Tommy straightened up. "She told me we need to get to the Akashic Records to save René. But why can't she just come here and take us there?"

"Higher Plane beings can't dwell in the lower planes. For very long at least. All the beings will attack her and try to glom on to her. I mean, look what happened to you, and we've been here just moments. She told me she was going to possess a body down on the earthly plane, and I was like, Oona, is your head screwed on straight? Especially a dead human—that does tons of damage to your astral body. It's all karmic, kids, the mystic law of the universe, cause and effect!"

Lolly prattled on and on as Tommy tried to digest what he was saying. A feather landed on Pris's head. It whispered a song that sounded like a soap commercial.

"You have something in your hair," said Tommy.

But it stayed locked in her locks.

"We don't want you here," Pris said. But the feather grew, its hairs turning into tendrils.

"We don't want you here!" Pris repeated, a little more panicked this time, tugging at her hair with both her hands. The feather grew snakelike arms that wrapped around Pris's hands, lodging them in her hair as if she were grabbing her own scalp. Then its body ballooned above her, expanding into flat wings attached to a bulbous body. The wings, in moments, stretched outward and began to flap.

"Pris!" Tommy yelled, watching the feathery creature pull Pris up out of her seat and into the air. Before they could do anything, Pris was high above the wagon, out of reach.

"We don't want you here!" screamed Tommy in a last-ditch effort.

Lolly turned around. "Oh, poop farts!"

Pris tried to wrestle herself free, grabbing onto the base of the wings. But the creature formed itself over her hands until they were encased inside a lumpy, feather-covered flesh-blob pulsing over her arms. The being gurgled, bloated with fluid. The wings were dirty, as if they had been run over by farm tractors. It smelled like manure.

Pris flew higher. The beast hoisted her up far enough that there was no way Tommy and Lolly could reach her. But it strained from her weight and wobbled as it flew, like an overstuffed dragonfly.

"I don't want you here, I don't want you here," Pris kept repeating.

"Oh, I'm afraid that won't work for this particular being," Lolly yelled out to her.

"Then what do we do?" Tommy demanded.

"We have to follow it. This is putting us behind schedule," sighed Lolly, disappointed.

"Where is it taking me?" she called down.

"Probably to its nest, I'm guessing." He turned upward and yelled out again. "Just one thing, don't let it eat your face!"

"Eat my face?" Pris yelled.

"It's desperate for a face!"

With a heave, the beast gathered strength and pulled Pris up farther. She held on to its feet (or what looked like feet) as she ascended.

"Um, don't worry, Pris! We'll get it off you, I promise!" said Tommy.

The beast fluttered off, its wings frantically flapping as Pris kept trying to wriggle free.

Lolly snorted. "Ha. You *promise*. You humans are always making promises you can't actually keep. It's so funny. No wonder you keep obsessing over these people known as 'politicians' . . . All you talk about over and over are these people with their empty promises."

Lolly stopped the wagon. He untied the reins from the wagon and, with an expert flick of his arms, unharnessed the marshmallows in front of him. They squealed and scurried off.

"What are you doing? We need to go get Pris."

"I know! But now we are off the beaten path, so to speak, so we will need to off-road." The cartoon mascot removed a cozy from the dashboard in front of him, revealing a giant cinnamon bun. "Luckily I just refilled the tank with finger-licking fluffernutter!" He squeezed the bun, and an engine deep inside the wagon began sputtering.

"Oh!" Lolly said, perking up his ears.

Tommy heard, far off, a series of wails through the air.

"Oh dear, oh dear, oh dear."

"What?"

"I think the beasts are converging."

"What do you mean."

"It seems that Pris is a great prize for them." He honked his horn and stepped on the gas pedal of his wagon. It rolled forward, even slower than before.

"Can't we go any faster?" asked Tommy.

"I'm trying!" Lolly snapped. Tommy let out an exasperated sigh. He looked up to see the creature and Pris far up in the air, like an errant birthday balloon.

"What kind of creature is that?"

"It's a Memory Thief. It eats up forgotten things. It survives on all those lost buttons, all those lost items . . . Grandmothers' keepsakes no one remembers anymore. Cast-off worn-down dolls. It has no head or heart, and it is always searching for them. It's basically jealous, all the time. And hungry."

"I'm sure glad those aren't on Earth. Or, I mean, in our plane."

"Oh, Tommy Gaye. There isn't a difference. Every plane exists everywhere. These beings are in your plane, too. You've seen them before. Those people who try to swallow up anything good. Who can never be satisfied because they have nothing inside themselves. Some of them even become presidents."

"Is that what has Renaldo?"

"Oh. Um. No. What has your friend is a demon. A Consumer. Something worse. Something much more powerful. That's why I need to get you to Oona."

"Well, please, Mr. Lolly, we have to hurry."

There was another wail that echoed through the air. Lolly stood up from his cramped chair, leaning on his balloon wheel, and held up his finger as if he could catch the sound.

"Ah! I think I found its nest." Then the little character adjusted his multicolored overcoat and ducked back into his seat. The wagon, finally, started speeding up, and Tommy gripped the side, almost getting thrown from the seat.

They came upon a series of hills that looked like pink, fluffy gumdrops.

"Hold on!" Lolly said, heading straight up one of the hills.

The ground beneath the tires rippled behind the wagon like it was awakened and surprised. Lolly turned back to Tommy. "You have to do it fast or the hills will turn into mouths, and the mouths will get lips, and the lips will get teeth, and the teeth will try to chew, chew, chew you!"

They moved swiftly up the hill and over the other side, into a shallow valley filled with stalks of bright green grass. The blades were as big as Tommy, as if he had suddenly shrunk and the world around him had enlarged. Lolly parked the wagon and unfolded himself from the seat.

"Come on," he said to Tommy, and walked into the tall grass. Tommy hesitated but looked behind him at the hills. The tire tracks from the wagon were undulating, forming into a long mouth filled with fangs.

Lolly darted forward, his rainbow wardrobe and shiny lollipop hair speeding past Tommy.

"Lolly, wait up!"

"Shh!" Lolly chastised him. "We don't want to startle our airplane."

The two reached a clearing in the center of the tall stalks. There, nestled in a bower of drooping blades of grass, was a large toy airplane. It was cocked on its side, plastic and worn-in. It was like a giant version of a toy boys half Tommy's age played with, though he never had because he didn't really enjoy playing with guns or planes or soldiers, unless he was making them little homes where they could cook and make out. Tommy remembered how many times he had his soldiers lying on top of one another having fake sex. It was a sudden memory that embarrassed him.

He reached in his backpack and pulled out the book. He opened it up, trusting it to tell him what he needed to know. In an entry entitled "The Lower Plane and You," it said that the astral plane often included emanations of your life, ways that you might translate deeper truths into your own mind. But here he was with a mascot of a sugary cereal he never ate and a toy plane he never played with. And if this was a joint illusion with Pris, he could probably conclude that she never played with this toy, either. Whose psyche were they in, then? *Who am I?* Tommy wondered with a startling fear. *If this is all from me, then why don't I know it?*

They approached the fuselage, and Tommy realized the plane was snoring. It was alive. The exterior was moist, like snake skin, though it was white and shiny like Tommy knew airplanes to be. Tommy watched as Lolly ducked down behind the body of the sleeping plane and then reemerged.

"Okay," Lolly whispered. "I just unlocked the door on your side. On the count of three we are both going to duck, open the door at the bottom of the plane, and quickly hop inside. Are you ready?"

"Um. Okay."

"One. Two. Three!"

Tommy ducked and found an oval hatch at his feet. He climbed in, squeezing his body through the hole. Lolly was already there, excitedly coaxing him through the opening. He continued to hold a finger to his lips.

"We want to be sure we are secure before we wake it up."

Tommy looked around. The inside of the plane was ringed with ribs like the inside of a chicken. It smelled like a barnyard, too. Lolly tiptoed to the cockpit and motioned to Tommy to join him up front. The two chairs for the pilots were drooped over, as if they were deflated. Lolly held on to the doorframe.

"Grab on," he whispered.

Then, he reached deep into one of his many patchwork pockets and pulled out a bright pink whistle.

"Buckle up!" Lolly said. "Well, don't actually, because there are no seatbelts. And if we experience turbulence, please don't locate oxygen masks because there aren't any of those, either. Ha!" Lolly blew the whistle, and the entire plane jerked. The two pilot chairs sprang to life, suddenly inflating. They swiveled toward the two travelers, and Tommy saw that they were eyes, not chairs. The eyes looked at them, startled.

Lolly waved back. The plane rocked back and forth, growling, as if it was trying to shake them out of itself.

"Please, calm yourself!" Lolly half begged, half demanded. "We aren't here to capture you. We just need you to take us somewhere. Up to a Memory Thief nest."

The plane whined like it was tired.

"I know, I know. You're exhausted," Lolly said, rolling his eyes to Tommy.

"My friend was kidnapped by a Memory Thief, and it's going to eat her face if we don't get to her," said Tommy.

The plane sighed and grunted. It seemed resigned.

"Thank you so much, we really appreciate your time," said Lolly, with a deferent tone that Tommy could tell was fake.

The plane's eyes moved back around toward the front. The console before it sprouted all kinds of knobs and switches. They were wet and slimy with saliva and moved up and down, clicking and adjusting on their own. The steering wheel emerged from the center of the console, and in a burst, the plane began to rev up. Lights turned on and the body of the plane began to vibrate, shaking Tommy until his teeth hurt. The plane rolled through the thicket faster and faster, the blades of grass slapping the front and sides of the plane as it barreled through. Finally, it lifted into the air.

Tommy gripped the side of the fuselage and looked out the cockpit window. He was struck by what he saw. It was as if a patch of suburban lawn, a perfect square, had been cut out of the earth and transferred here. Strewn in the lawn were wet, soiled, weathered toys—the wand of a bubble blower, two plastic soldiers, an old tricycle tire. It looked familiar.

The plane chugged along, and the view opened up. Below, he saw various squares and spaces, extending for miles and miles. It reminded him of that trip his family took to California when his dad had a business meeting and his mom made him bring the family, and how the land below them, when they were over the Midwest, was parceled out into squares and shapes, borders and discolorations. Except here they were multicolored, some bright red squares, some green, orange, purple. It should have been beautiful, but it wasn't. There was a feeling to it that made Tommy ache. He understood: These were patches of memory. The Lower Plane was a graveyard of them, of different shards of memory from billions and billions of souls, all heaped up and mangled and unorganized.

Tommy remembered a poem Renaldo loved—"The Waste Land" by T. S. Eliot. He remembered René reading it out loud. They were sitting in Tommy's room.

> What are the roots that clutch,
> what branches grow . . .
> You cannot say, or guess, for you know only
> a heap of broken images. . . .

"It's so sad," was all Tommy could say.

"It's about how lost people felt after World War I," said René, "how their faith in God and the hope of mankind achieving something beautiful had been taken away."

But I have you, René, and we can build something together, Tommy thought then.

But not now. René was not here next to him, and Tommy was high above a wasteland. How were they going to rescue Pris? How was he going to find Renaldo in all this?

PRIS

Pris didn't look down. She was high up, she knew that. She could tell because the air was thinner. Even in the astral plane, it seemed, there was atmosphere.

Pris tried to wriggle free from the feathered bird, but her hands were bound above her head. Pris would have tried to reach down into her satchel for her disk, but her hands were lodged inside the beast. She wasn't terrified. First, she convinced herself that this was a dream. And second, she could tell the thing wasn't entirely formidable.

It grunted and gasped. It worked desperately hard to hold on to her, as if it couldn't believe what it had caught. She began swinging, trying to create enough momentum to kick the side of the beast. But she couldn't do it. So she hung there below the flying ugly thing, like a twig for its nest, high above the rainbow terrain. She gathered the courage to look down. Far below she could see the wagon following her. As much as she would have liked to believe Tommy would find her, she knew she was in this alone. It was always up to her.

The creature headed upward, wobbling as it flew. She saw a floating island in the distance. It was brown and tangled, hanging in the air. As they got closer, she saw it was riddled with litter, like a landfill in the sky, speckled with objects and wrappers and debris.

Once they were above it, the thing let go of her, and she fell through the air, landing on a pile of trash.

She coughed—it was dusty and smelled old. The beast landed in front of Pris with a farty plop. Now as tall as a man, but still headless, it waddled close to her like a plucked turkey. It grew shoulders that poked out of the top of its wings. The shoulders each grew mouths, and the mouths let out a horrible wail. Far off, she heard its call answered through the pink, misty sky. There were more of this thing out there, and she got the feeling they were coming.

Pris needed to figure out where it could be harmed. The bird changed again. It folded over itself until it resembled a kind of fleshy taco. The two sides of it began thickening, and the center of it softened and turned red. A tongue unraveled out of the slit. Pris looked for a throat. That's where it would be vulnerable. She did not want this thing to eat her face.

It wailed again. She concentrated on where the sound was coming from. A stomach formed, and a diaphragm, and what seemed to be a chest. Then she saw it. A protrusion up above the temporary stomach. She reached in her satchel and pulled out her disk and threw it with all her strength. The disk struck the thinner section of the beast and then bounced back into Pris's hand. It stopped wailing immediately. Hot pink blood spewed out of its mouth.

Pris watched it writhe.

She remembered when she was eight years old, and was in the small yard outside of her house but still in the Glade, and she found some worms crawling in the earth median between the Smiley Sales shopping centers and Arcademonium. There had been a rare rain that had soaked the grass patch as well as the plots of synthetically grown tree systems meant to clarify the air. Earthworms, these wriggly things she had never seen before, suddenly were washed out of the earth and onto the smooth eco-pavement. She watched one wriggle and, like now, wondered where its mouth was, and how something so different could be on this planet. She remembered taking a plastic stick and squishing it, before watching it die. She felt guilty but also powerful.

For weeks afterward she would search for worms in the grass and torture them, fascinated by seeing them writhe and die. Day after day she did this, like a calculated, cold dictator. Then, one day, as she lay in her bed, she closed her eyes and saw the worms in the darkness of her eyes. She couldn't avoid the images. All the murders she had committed were playing out under her eyelids.

She stopped torturing animals after that. It was like a rite of passage at eight years old, that either you become a sociopath or you realize life is precious and stop destroying things around you.

But this thing wasn't a harmless bug. It was a beast that was going to eat her face. She flung her disk at it again. And again, the disk bounced off its skin and boomeranged back into her hand each time. The creature stopped wriggling and began flattening into a white outline, like the stencil they drew of dead bodies in detective holo-shows. She walked over carefully and poked at it with her disk.

She moved across the mound, past the beast. She noticed little pieces of paper here and there. She bent down to pick one up. A photograph—she hadn't touched them before, only seen ones in frames, like the photos on her wall at home that her uncle kept of his disk team. It felt strange to actually hold an image in her hands, on paper. This photo was old, faded, of a family, smiling, in puffy jackets in front of a snowy house. She picked up another. This one was of a couple—a man and woman—kissing on a hill. The woman was wearing an outfit that looked like it might have been from the last century. Pris estimated that it was probably from the 1940s. Other photos were strewn around, poking out of the matted mounds of hair.

Pris could have sat there all day (was there "day" here?) looking at these things. But soon she remembered that she was high up on this floating island of hair and memories. The ground was far below her. She tried to find Lolly's wagon. She yelled out, but her voice was muffled in the cloudy air. She looked down at the tangle of hair. Tangled deeper within were other objects she hadn't caught before. Rings, snow globes, letters, charm bracelets, brooches. This thing was a thief.

Pris quickly pulled out her book from the front pocket of her satchel and flipped to the back to look for an index. The index was there, but it seemed much longer than it was before, as if it encompassed the whole book, suddenly. She wasn't sure what she was looking for, but she tried her best. She looked for *feather creature, beast, hair nest, beast that grows*. Then she thought to look for the word *thief* and found an entry for *Lower Plane Thieves*. Underneath was a long list: Apple Thief, Card Thief, Energy Thief, Love Thief.

Memory Thief.

She quickly turned to the page, and there was an entry.

A Memory Thief, the book explained, *steals everything that can help create the memory of someone—photos, letters, bracelets, pendants, paintings—and brings it to the Lower Plane, where it builds nests out of it and subsists off the desperate longing energy of dying memory.*

Pris froze. A Memory Thief—this one, or one like it—if it had taken her, it must have stolen *her* own past. Perhaps her entire lineage. Maybe that's why she was a zero. Maybe her entire ancestry had been stolen, snatched away by some hideous, faceless creature like this one. It stole her past in this plane, and somehow it reverberated through time and space, and now she had no history, no parents, no ancestors back on Earth. She convinced herself of this and beat down at the hair with her disk, screaming and crying until she crumpled into a thatch of trash.

Something stuck out of the hair. A photo. It was that of a small girl, in a lumpy sweater and plaid skirt. She was smiling, holding a little backpack. Behind her was an ocean. She looked like she was going on a trip. Pris stopped her furious thrashing and stared at the photo. Something about the girl made Pris feel an ache inside, a sadness. She took the photo and slipped it in her satchel.

TOMMY

Tommy saw a giant brownish cloud, far off in the distance. As they got closer, he saw it was more mangy and solid. Like a hairball that was swept up after a haircut. And then he realized that was what it was.

"Is that, like, a giant ball of hair?"

"Yuppers," Lolly confirmed. "It's the beast's nest. Technically it's hair and nails, plus a bunch of other things. Lost objects."

Tommy was reminded of René's many diatribes about spirits, how one poor soul was cursed to walk the earth after death, and had to gather all the nails and hair it had shed in its lifetime before it rested.

They came closer and flew over the island. It was exactly as Lolly said, filled with tatters and trash and objects.

There was Pris, waving. Tommy waved back and screamed, "We will get you out of there!" But he wasn't sure if she heard him.

He also wasn't sure how they were going to get her down. They were in a plane.

"Lolly, what are we going to do?"

"Hm. You know, I hadn't thought about that. Ha! Hm. Rapunzel, let down your hair!" he said, laughing.

Lolly steered the plane around, arcing so that it would pass over the floating pile again. The plane was sighing. Its cartoon eyes drooped. "Oh dear. We better hurry, too, because it looks like Mr. Plane is losing steam."

Tommy inspected the fuselage. He moved quickly to the back of the plane, as if he knew what he was looking for, and there, behind some plastic cubes made to look like cargo, was a large heap of fabric as tall as him, looking worn-in, colored sunset orange and yellow.

He knew this fabric.

The memory came back to him. This plane was a toy of his brother's. That patch of grass was from his front lawn, and that heap of fabric was a toy parachute. He remembered playing with the parachute, throwing it up in the air and watching it float down. Tommy always waited on the front porch for Charley to join him. Charley was his hero, everything he had wanted to be.

What happened to them? How had they drifted so far apart? Tommy knew this parachute was a part of it. They were both children, Charley yelling at him to *stop running like a sissy, stop throwing that ball like a girl*. The memory flashed back to him in moments, to their neighbor, a girl his age, who had let Tommy "borrow" one of her Barbie dolls. Tommy took it home and cherished it, playing with the doll's hair for hours, combing it and making a store for her with little acorn tops as bowls and leaves as tablecloths. Then, there was a shadow overhead—his brother grabbing the doll out of Tommy's hands. *Why are you playing with a Barbie doll? What are you, queer?*

Tommy grabbed the pile of nylon and wadded it into a huge ball three times as large as himself. It wrapped loosely around something large and round that, for its size, was still light enough for him to yank out from the back of the plane and roll over to the wide cargo door on the side of the plane. He unlatched it and rolled the door open. The air whipped past, and Tommy had to grip onto the side of the plane to stabilize himself. He looked down at the huge floating nest. Fortunately, the cloud of hair was big enough that he wouldn't really miss it if he jumped out the side when it passed over. Tommy kept telling himself this was his astral body, it was all a dream, and that whatever happened, he would be fine.

"Lolly, can you get the plane to fly over the cloud super low? I'm going to jump out. I found a parachute."

"Wow, major! Okay, but just so you know, if you fall? Then your physical body back on Earth will, like, have a heart attack!"

"Thanks for the support, Lolly."

"No, but you totally got this. Just wanted to let ya know," Lolly said.

Tommy still couldn't believe Lolly was their spirit guide. But maybe in the Lower Plane, full of dangerous fluff and traumatic toys, this was the best guide you could find.

Lolly tapped the plane on the eyelid and asked it to arc back around and fly low over the mass of hair floating in the sky. The plane whined, and Lolly put his hands together in prayer and pleaded silently.

The plane, wobbling, aimed downward toward the island, and Tommy readied himself at the window, holding tightly on to the mass of fabric. As the plane dipped downward, he threw himself out of the window, pulling the giant mound of fabric with him.

He landed with a thud on a mound of hair, kicking up dander and dust. He looked down at his belly button—the faint trail was still there. After coughing and sneezing, he noticed the pile wasn't just hair, but all sorts of little baubles and necklaces and rings and tattered photos and notes and cards.

Pris ran up to him. "Tommy! Are you okay?"

"Yeah, I think so."

She hugged him, and Tommy found himself hugging her back.

"This thing stole memories," Pris said, pulling back, looking angry. "I think it stole mine, too."

"Stole?"

"Yeah past tense, I got rid of it."

"You . . . killed it?"

"It was going to eat my face! I hit it with my disk and it disintegrated."

She brought him over to the spot where the creature used to be. An outline remained, like a dusting of chalk. They stood there silently for a moment.

"Help me unravel this parachute?" Tommy said.

Tommy and Pris tugged at the pile, finding a corner, and began to unroll the faded nylon fabric. Inside was what Tommy expected: the head of a Barbie doll, with its eyes gouged out and its hair tangled and tied into the harness of the parachute.

"This is an old toy I used to play with. With my brother."

"This was your toy? What were you, some kind of psycho child?"

"No, my brother did this. He saw me playing with a Barbie doll and ripped the head off and tied it to this and then threw it up and down in front of me. It wasn't even my doll. It was the worst day. I'm just remembering it now."

Tommy had to stop himself, because the fright and sadness of that moment was washing through him in waves. He remembered crying and begging his brother to stop.

"I feel like this entire Lower Plane is just a trash heap of memories that have all been thrown away."

"Like a junk folder."

"A what folder?"

"Never mind."

Tommy and Pris grabbed the huge doll head, its hair like plastic straw, and heaved it on its side. Through the round base of the neck, they could see inside the hollow head. "There's enough room for us to climb inside," said Tommy. "We can throw it off the side of the island and float down to the ground."

"May as well. I mean, it's not like anything could happen to us here on the astral plane, anyway."

"Uh, yeah," Tommy lied.

Tommy remembered that the best way for the parachute to open was to fold it vertically in thirds and then roll it from the top downward, so that it unfurled easily. His brother taught him that.

The two peered over the edge of the hair cloud. Far below like a speck, they saw Lolly's bright orange wagon.

"I know where we can launch ourselves," said Pris. They took turns dragging the head over the surface while the other carefully held the parachute, and they climbed over the bushy, spongy ground to a small round area that jutted out over the side of the cloud. When they got there, Tommy rested, out of breath.

"Okay, give me a sec," he said.

Pris got up, adjusted her satchel, and walked around.

"What are you looking for?" Tommy asked as Pris scanned the ground.

Far off, they heard a screech.

"The other beasts are coming," Tommy said. "We gotta go!"

Pris kept searching.

"Pris! Now, please?"

She didn't seem to hear him. Tommy walked up to her. She was down on her hands and knees, rummaging through the hair and tatters and junk, grasping and sifting through it as if she had lost a ring. He watched as she picked up items to see if they could be hers. She pulled up a long silver necklace with a pendant on the end, flipping it over in her fingers for clues.

"Somewhere here, there has to be some token, some memory of my mom or dad. I can't go until I find something. But it also could be in some other nest somewhere else. My whole past—stolen! Some hungry creature took my past away. They left me with nothing. I'm a zero!"

"Pris, we don't have time," Tommy said softly.

"I don't even know what I'm looking for."

"Pris—"

"Why am I like this?" Pris yelled, her voice wavering. "Where did I come from? No one looks like me anymore! Why am I so . . . strange looking?"

"It's okay," Tommy said, crouching down next to her.

Tommy put his hand on her shoulder. "I don't think you are weird looking at all," he said genuinely. "Actually, I like how you look. No one I have ever met looks like you."

Pris rolled her eyes, but he could tell she was choked up. Tommy took the necklace from her hands.

"Listen, we have to get off this thing. We need to get to the Higher Plane so we can find Renaldo. And make sure your friend Jayde isn't next. But, Pris, when we do, we can come back here, and you and me can look for every island of lost memories and try to find your past for as long as it takes. Where all your memories and your parents' memories are all being held. I promise, okay?" He pulled her up on her feet. He put the necklace around her neck. "Here. This will be my promise to you."

There were more screeches. They were getting closer. They watched as a feather floated down in front of them. Before their eyes, it started expanding, plumping, turning into another creature.

Tommy tugged her sleeve and they ran to the parachute, diving into its head. They tried to push it from the inside to make it tip over the edge, but it wasn't budging. So together, they rocked and rocked, back and forth, turning the shell of the plastic over like a big barrel with all their might. Finally, it began to move, but it teetered on the edge of the island, still stuck. Right then, another creature flew into the plastic opening of the head, hitting the side of the parachute. They both screamed as the head rolled over the edge. Down they fell, with a beast fluttering around inside like a panicked bird. They knew they had to get it out before the parachute unfurled. The beast was small, but growing. Pris pulled the necklace from around her neck and swung it at the creature, which attached itself greedily, trying to get to her hand.

"Duck!" she told Tommy, who crawled into the protruding space of Barbie's nose as Pris swung the necklace with the creature attached around and around above her head, aiming it for the opening above them and pitching it out into the sky.

They didn't have any time to rest as the head tumbled through the air. Tommy and Pris clutched onto the sides of the plastic, flattening themselves along the wall as they fell quickly through the pink air. Then, they heard the fabric whip and unfurl. The head suddenly jerked up, and both of them were thrown violently onto the cranium of the doll head, into the straw-like knots of synthetic hair.

The head slowed, floating gently.

"Are you okay?"

"Yeah. You?"

"I think so. I think it's working?"

They reached for each other's hands and lay there as the head of the Barbie doll bobbed through the air. Above them, they watched the pink sky move past.

"Do you think it's better that we are here in the body when it lands, or should we climb up to the neck?"

"I don't know. I got a C in physics," said Tommy.

"Me too," said Pris.

They heard a whooping. "Hey, hey, hey!"

It was Lolly. They were getting close to the ground, and soon they hit it with a jolt that pushed the air out of their lungs like a bad cough. The parachute flipped to its side. The wind blew, and the chute, still inflated, careened above them, dragging the head along the ground.

"Wait! Wait!" they heard Lolly screech.

Pris and Tommy crawled toward the opening and watched as the parachute propelled them across the flat, dry landscape of the Lower Plane. The ground was as dry as desert, hard and caked. The wind didn't let up, and they accelerated, now racing at a wildly fast clip.

Something large was emerging in the distance, getting closer. On the horizon they saw a giant jawbone, lined with sharp protrusions. At first Tommy thought they were skyscrapers, but he soon realized that they were the huge fangs of a skeletal mouth.

The terrain got rougher, and they heard the ground cracking and crunching under them. Something broke off and flew into the head, striking Pris's shoulder, cutting it.

"Ow!" she yelled.

She pulled it out and found a small tooth. The parachute, tipped above them, kept speeding through the terrain. There was no way to even climb up to the lip of the head and jump out.

Pris grabbed her disk and, with one quick volley, threw it with all her strength out of the opening. The disk struck the chute, causing it to bunch and buckle. The parachute fabric tangled around the disk, stopping, sending the head rolling around it in an arc. Pris and Tommy gripped onto the sides as it rolled over itself, until it finally stopped. The two of them lay there, out of breath.

Tommy looked down at his navel. The faint line of smoke, the tether to his earth body, was still there, as was Pris's.

"We're alive," he said aloud.

Pris groaned as she sat up. "Ow, well, it sure feels like it."

"That was good aim. You are really good with that disk."

They stepped outside of the head. On the ground around them were thousands of teeth, up to their shins. Lolly's wagon approached.

"Holy cachongas, that was nuts! I thought you guys were goners."

Pris crunched through the teeth to the ragged parachute, retrieving her disk. Tommy looked out in front of him. They were on a flat pink plain, in the middle of a field of sharp teeth. Farther out, the teeth grew bigger and bigger, until they lifted up and into the sky over their heads along a giant bone-white arc.

"Is this, like, a shark mouth?"

"A shark? No," Lolly said, "it's the remains of a World Eater. They used to roam the Lower Plane, long ago. At least that's what the records say."

"The records," Tommy repeated. "The Akashic Records?"

"Yes, very good, Tommy. Look at you doing your homework. Now, we better get moving if we are going to get there."

Pris rummaged in her pack to find her roll of papers, but Tommy was already flipping through his book. He read it out loud. "'*The Akashic Records exist on the top of a parapet on top of a mountain on the highest height of an alpine peak on a teetering boulder on a rock on a smaller rock on a cairn in the clouds.*'"

"Is that where we are going?" Pris asked. "To see the Akashic Records?"

"Yes. As Oona said, it's the only way to get them safely away from the Consumer. Lucky for us, you carved a path through the teeth, so we can just make our way out of this without getting a flat tire. Right, wagon?" The wagon tooted, and Lolly winked.

Pris and Tommy looked at each other and smiled. They dusted themselves off and climbed back into Lolly's wagon, which began its incessant song again. The wagon jerked forward.

Come along, come along, crunchy colors, tasty song.

Come along, come along, crunchy colors, tasty song.

"That song," Tommy said.

"I know. It's almost comforting now, to be honest," Pris said.

Lolly's wagon continued upward. Tommy began to feel drowsy. He looked over at Pris, who also couldn't keep her eyes open. She moved her head toward the side of the wagon and tried to rest it, but it was too hard. She angrily craned her head back on the seat. Tommy watched as she fell asleep quickly, her head sagging and nodding, until it slipped, and her head was on his shoulder. Tommy's heart bloomed.

He took off his backpack and opened the book, turning to the Akashic Records.

PRIS AND TOMMY

The wagon continued rolling. Gradually, the sky grew cloudier, as if a mist were descending into the valley. It felt wet. Soon, the three were in a fog. It seemed to absorb sound. Even the incessant wagon song was muffled.

"Ah, we are getting close to the passage," yelled Lolly from the driver's seat.

"Passage to the Higher Plane?"

"Yuppers."

"How can you tell?" said Pris.

"Feel the air? It's tingly!"

Lolly stretched out his clown hands, and his hair jangled. He coughed afterward like he was coming down with a cold.

He was right. The air was agitated, full of energy. Like being near an ocean, on the edge of something powerful. The sky grew dark. Lolly clicked his tongue and stuck his thumb in his mouth, making a popping noise, and the lollipops in his hair lit up like lamps, beaming around them.

"It just gets less visible the closer you are to it, to ward off simpler beings. There's a few hurdles to getting through the gateway."

Pris tossed her disk back and forth between her hands.

"Hey," Tommy said tentatively. "Are you okay?"

Pris looked at him and watched him flinch, as if he was waiting for her to snap again. Her face softened. He was a nice person, and she felt bad for making him nervous around her. Perhaps the fog in the air made it easier to talk, because it felt insular and concealed, like a confessional booth.

"I'm so worried about Jayde," Pris finally said. "I don't know what I'll do if I lose them."

Tommy bit his lip. "Do you . . . like . . . like her? Them, I mean. Sorry."

"Oh, you mean am I, like, attracted to them? No, no. I love Jayde. But not that way. Just because we're both queer doesn't mean—"

"Wait. You call yourself queer?"

"Yeah. Why?"

Tommy laughed, the absurdity dawning on him. "Wow. So in the future it becomes okay to say you are queer?"

"Yep."

"That's what you call yourself? That's the term you use in your time?" Tommy laughed again.

"What's so funny?"

"It's just that is, like . . . in *my* time, it's the worst thing you can call someone. Besides, um, well, this other word."

"Oh yes, that one. That word's still a big one."

"But *queer*. That's okay."

"Uh-huh. It's a compliment, I guess in a way now."

"Well, where I am from, *queer* is used to mean somebody who is weak. Like the game 'Smear the Queer' on the playground. My brother used to play it with the other kids."

"What's the game?"

"You know, I'm not sure. Someone is picked and then everyone has to tackle them while they run around and try to escape being tackled."

"That's awful."

"But I guess in a way it's hopeful? Because look how much life can change."

Tommy looked down at his legs. Pris noticed his eyes were tearing up.

"I miss René . . . He is like Jayde to me."

"But more than that. You like him."

Pris watched Tommy's face clench.

"I mean, as a friend, but also maybe I—"

"You like-*like* him. You're queer."

"No, I'm not!" he shot back defensively, as if he wasn't even thinking, just reacting.

Pris saw his face in the dim colorful light. The anger and hurt in his eyes. She tried to remember what Mr. Richards told her about that time. That people felt shame for who they loved. She couldn't understand it. Not entirely. She felt a stab of guilt. She turned to Tommy and put her hand on his shoulder.

"It's cool. You don't have to be ashamed. Not with me, not now."

Tommy was shivering. "It's just so hard."

"Go ahead and say it. I bet you will feel better."

"Say . . . what?"

"You know."

She watched as Tommy held his breath and bit his lip. He glanced around the plane, as if he was checking for police or someone who would immediately kill him. "I'm . . . um."

"It's okay, Tommy. It's not going to hurt you."

"I'm, um. I'm queer?" Tommy exhaled. "I'm queer."

His lower lip curled into a cry, as if his face had stored the words in his mouth for so long they were cramping.

Overhead they heard creaking, like wooden boats were bobbing above their heads. In the mist, they couldn't see anything, but it sounded like trees were surrounding them. Giant oaks croaking and bending in a powerful wind.

"Are we in a forest?"

"I can't tell. Honestly I've never taken this path to the Higher Plane," Lolly said, puzzled.

Over the creaks was another sound—sipping and inhaling, as if there was a giant bathtub, and the drain was sucking in water. Dark figures started coming into view around them. The mist gave way. They saw they were indeed surrounded by trees. But there were no leaves on the ground, no branches overhead, just these massive croaking trunks.

"Wow, this place is so isolated. Hello!" Pris yelled. The echo took a longer time to come back.

"Hello!" called Tommy. "Guess what? I'm queer! I'm queer!" He giggled while he said it.

"Wait!" said Lolly.

"I'm queer!" said Tommy, delighting himself.

"Shh!" Lolly scolded, grabbing Tommy by the shoulder. Lolly looked deeply into his eyes. "These aren't trees. They are ghosts."

The sipping sound grew louder, and the trees seemed to be moving closer to the wagon. The drain-like sucking noise, Pris and Tommy realized, wasn't coming from the trees. Because the trees weren't trees. Like moving buildings, the massive shadows heaved toward them in the darkness. As one emerged from the shadows, Pris and Tommy finally made out its shape. It was about twenty feet tall, a body, shuffling on short legs and flat feet, above which was a big, protruding belly, leading up to a narrow chest and a spindly neck on which sat a pale face with red eyes and a strangely small mouth. It was surrounded by several others. The giants seemed frantic, craning their thin necks, their sticklike hands grabbing the air around them furtively.

The three sat completely still.

"Who are they?" Tommy whispered.

"I don't know," said Lolly.

Pris grabbed her book and flipped to the back, to the index. It took up the whole book again. "Big, tall . . ."

"*Creatures*?"

"*Dangerous*?"

"Maybe *Suckers*?"

"Oh God, hurry up, they're getting closer!"

The legs of the beings shuffled toward them, their immense duck feet flapping down on the flat, arid ground without care or concern.

Lolly revved the wagon engine.

They can step on us in seconds, thought Pris as she flipped frantically, finding a page.

"Long bobbling beings with glazed eyes as if they are starved, but with giant bodies . . ."

She tried to concentrate.

"Hurry!" Lolly cried. "What does it say?"

Pris burst out an answer. "Hungry Ghosts. They are Hungry Ghosts!"

"Oh no!" Lolly whimpered. "They are terrible. My friend KooKoo the Chocolate Crispy Mouse was eaten by them. Oh God, they love cereal. I'm done for!"

Lolly ducked into the bucket seat. He tried to cover his glowing lantern hair lollipops, but they beamed unashamedly.

"Lolly!" Tommy whispered angrily.

Pris scrambled to the wheel and righted the wagon. She grabbed the cinnamon bun that she had seen Lolly squeeze to turn on the engine, and pressed on it with all her strength. The engine sputtered on.

A large, flat foot stamped in front of them, but just in time, Pris hit the gas pedal and swerved right to dodge it.

"How do we get rid of them?" she whispered to Tommy. He looked at the open page in Pris's copy of the book.

"We can't, I don't think," he said. "We just have to try and avoid them and stay quiet."

Pris cut the engine of the wagon and held out her finger to shush Lolly. They stationed themselves in the atmosphere as the tall, awkward beings lumbered around them.

One giant shuffled dangerously close. Instead of turning on the engine, they hopped out of the wagon and pushed it frantically, trying to get it out of the way of the awkward feet that puttered along the ground like a giant grandma in slippers.

While pushing, Pris slipped and accidentally honked the bulbous cartoon horn on the driver's side. A Hungry Ghost turned toward them. It dove down toward the wagon.

"Oh no, no, no," said Lolly. "I never should have taken this job. Damn Oona and her favors!"

Then something screeched above. It was a Memory Thief, flapping through the air. One of the ghosts heard it and began sucking air around it. And like the most interactive game they had ever experienced, Pris and Tommy watched the creature get sucked into the pinhole opening of the Hungry Ghost's mouth. It screeched, trying to escape, but the mouth held on like a powerful vacuum. Drawn by the sound of agony, the other ghosts gathered around, and they pointed their purple, swollen pin-mouths at the trapped creature.

"Quick! While they're distracted, let's get out of here," Lolly whispered.

Pris kicked on the wagon's engine, and it jerked forward. She sped as fast as she could away from the melee of Hungry Ghosts. It wasn't too long before they were on an empty stretch again, flat as a desert. The wagon's wheels began to echo. Lolly crawled out from under the bucket seat. It was dark, pitch-black, and the only light was from the multicolored beams from his lollipop hair.

*   *   *

"Where are we?" Lolly said.

"Hell if I know," Pris said.

Lolly peeked over the console.

"Oh!" he whispered. "See that hole?"

Tommy and Pris peered through the mist. Ahead of them was a dark cave-like entrance.

"Go toward that. I think it's the gate to the Higher Plane. Wait, hold on." Lolly got up on the back of the wagon. He licked his giant thumb and held it up in the air. "*Brr!* Yes, go that direction."

"How do you know?"

"The Higher Plane is very cold. I can't stand it. It's like a refrigerator."

Tommy steered the wagon toward the blurry, dark mass.

The mist was still thick. But they could tell something was in front of them. It felt like they were reaching the end of a wide valley, like the edge of a great cliff was emerging. A glow shimmered, a semicircle, the mouth of a cave with a fire lit in it.

It smelled like home to Tommy—the rich earth of the humid woods, the healthy dark soil made from layers and layers of fresh rain and decaying leaves. It was the same smell from when he'd held René under the tree in the rain. He wished he was there right now. He wished he could have kept René safe.

"Do we know that this is the right passage?" Pris asked.

"Hell if I know!" Lolly mimicked.

It seemed like an eternity as they rolled toward the mountain, which eventually towered over them, a steep, almost sheer drop-off. The cave opening was more like the space between cracks of a canyon. As soon as they entered, a chilly wind blasted them.

"Ugh!" Lolly shuddered. His teeth began chattering in an exaggerated cartoony way. The wagon's jingle began echoing through the tall passageway. They had forgotten about it until now, and it sounded out ominously, distorting and reverberating back into their ears. It was mesmerizing.

Pris kept her eyes on the road. It helped to have something to do. That way she didn't have to think about how the Memory Thief had almost definitely stolen her past. Or about Jayde. Would she be able to save them at the Akashic Records, too? This Oona person that Tommy kept talking about—what if she didn't like Pris? What if she didn't want to help her?

In front of them was a cloaked figure in silhouette. It glowed in Lolly's multicolored light. It raised its face, and Pris saw half the face of a young girl, brown skin, with penetrating hazel eyes.

"Oona?" Tommy asked.

"Oh, I am so glad you made it," the figure said.

Tommy ran out of the cart and up to her. He wanted to hug her, but she backed away. Pris watched him stare up at the figure, which loomed over them, around seven feet tall.

"You are so much . . . taller . . . here in the astral plane."

"Yes, this is my true astral body, which I cannot change," she answered, a little wistfully. Her face remained half-hidden in the hood of the cloak.

Pris came up behind them.

"This is Pris. She's my friend from 2044."

Oona looked at her. "Yes. You," she said. Pris began to back away, but the cloaked figure's half-visible face smiled. "We are very fortunate to have you here."

Lolly shivered behind them. "Can I go now?" the mascot said, his knees knocking together.

"Yes," Oona said. "Thank you, you may go."

"Remember our deal!"

"Of course."

"When will I know it worked?"

"In time, Lolly. You can't rush memory like that."

"Okay, you promised!" he said, wagging his bulbous finger. Then he straightened and bowed quickly to Pris and Tommy. "Glad to do business with you."

"Well, thank you, Mr. Lolly, sir," said Tommy. "I guess we won't see you again."

"Oh no, you will. See you sooner rather than later!"

With that, Lolly boarded his wagon and was off. The jingle rang again through the vaulted canyon, lingering until it was a whisper.

"Well, I for sure don't want to see him again," Pris said.

"What did he mean?" Tommy asked Oona.

"I traded safe passage for you both with him for a tiny slice of your memory," Oona explained. "You may not see him again on the astral plane, but he will show up in your earthly lives. You will see his packaging often, or your future children may become obsessed with him as a toy. And that jingle? It will be stuck in your head."

"What? Forever?"

"Yes, I'm sorry to say. Follow me," Oona said, and they fell in step behind her surprisingly bulky body. "You probably came across a few creatures in the Lower Plane who subsist on memory."

"Pris had a run-in with one of the Memory Thieves," Tommy said.

"Well, memory is like food there. All creatures in the Lower Plane thrive on it. Lolly just wants to be remembered. He helps bring over humans, and in exchange, lodges himself in your minds. It was either him or Major Musket Tile Cleaner or the bear from Huggable Toilet Tissue. I tried to find a spirit guide who was the least irritating."

"But Lolly said that the Lower Plane is where memories go to die," Pris said.

"Well, I wouldn't call it a graveyard for memory. More like a landfill."

"That memory thing that kidnapped me had all sorts of objects and mementos."

"Yes. Those things. In a way they are an important part of the ecosystem—gathering all the loose, lost memories floating around and collecting them to make their nests."

"Like this," Pris said, remembering the photo she found. She pulled it out. Tommy snatched it from her.

"Oona! It's you! I mean, it's the little girl you . . . you put yourself in."

Oona stopped and turned to look down at the photo. "Yes. That's the girl I . . . inhabited briefly. It must have been taken the day she passed." Shadowed in her hood, neither Pris nor Tommy could see her reaction. She was silent for a while and then sighed. "Pris. You have extraordinary intuitive powers. It's why you are so important for what we are about to do. You have an exceptional ability to navigate this realm and find lost connections."

"Except for my own," Pris said under her breath. She placed the photo back in her satchel. They kept walking through the canyon. The walls began to widen, and Tommy could make out an opening, not too far away.

Oona walked ahead. Pris took advantage of her being out of earshot and whispered to Tommy.

"Who is this girl in the photo?"

"That's the body Oona, um, assumed when she came to Earth

to warn me. She was already dead. Oona didn't want to invade a living being like the demon does."

"Oona must be dead herself, right?"

"Yes. In Spain, in like the 1930s, I think? In Madrid. Her family was killed."

"During the Spanish Civil War?" Pris asked.

"Yeah, how did you know?"

"I have a really good history teacher." Then, Pris gasped. "Wait, do you see what I see?" she said suddenly, looking up. Tommy followed her gaze.

Above them were the stars, clear and crisp. It was as if they were in a mountain range, where they could make out all sorts of minor constellations. Everything was moonlight bright. They both exhaled, in awe.

"The stars. They're here, too," said Tommy.

There was something comforting about this to both Pris and Tommy. Under every realm, there was the universe, the stars, embracing them like the outer petals of a flower. They reached out and, without even hesitating, grabbed each other's hands.

Oona pulled out an object from under her voluminous cloak: a lantern that she held up with one hand while somehow striking a match with the other.

"Let's go to the records," she said abruptly.

Tommy and Pris saw that they were at the edge of a path. It dropped off below them into a dark valley. Oona shined the light to their left, where, in the flickered flame, an old, dingy platform was covered in dead ivy. They watched Oona quickly brush away the leaves, revealing a train of roller-coaster cars, like from an old, forgotten amusement park, and a track that turned upward, ascending the side of the cliff.

Tommy and Pris wedged themselves in the clunky two-person seat and pulled the rusty safety bar down over their laps. With that, the cars jerked forward and, clanging like an old carnival ride, began to move up the side of the mountain. Oona climbed the tracks behind them.

"Aren't you going to get in?" Tommy asked.

"I'm fine. There isn't enough room," she answered.

Tommy looked at the two empty cars behind him and was confused.

The car kept ascending, getting steeper and steeper until he and Pris were almost reclining in their seats. Up this high, they could see beyond the valley. The air felt cooler to Pris. She peered below and saw only a pinkish smoke like low-hanging clouds of cotton candy. A glimmering waterfall of light showered down, like the stars were sinking underneath them—a million balls of light descending downward in streaks.

"That's the event horizon," explained Oona. "All the moments that are set to happen lock in place, tumbling into one another, becoming actuality along with all their infinite possibilities." The event horizon cascaded with luminous moments, taking Pris's and Tommy's breaths away.

Oona walked behind them, buried in her cloak. She kept her face turned to its side, as if she was looking at a specific point out on the horizon. The cars jerked forward and sped up. Oona somehow clambered up steep grates to meet them again, her profile never turning.

"Oona, please, don't you want to get in with us?" Tommy begged.

"No, no. It's fine. I prefer to walk," she said politely.

Suddenly, not far away, Pris saw a stripe of bright color streaming downward, dwindling into a weak ember of light, blinking out. Then, another streaked across the sky in front of them, also diminishing into a spark, and then nothing.

"Look at that!" she said, grabbing Tommy's arm.

"What are they?" Tommy asked.

"Sacrifices," Oona said, in a sorrowful voice. "Events and people who have plucked themselves from continuing in any reality."

"What do you mean—they don't happen?"

"Some travelers to the astral plane choose to untether themselves from their earthly bodies, as well as from any other bodies on any other plane."

"Why?"

"Various reasons. Usually it's to prevent something from happening. They sacrifice themselves, their entire lives, so that they stop themselves from causing harm," Oona said, with sadness. She pointed forward. "We're almost there, to the Higher Plane. You should know what's next."

They both perked up.

"The Akashic Records are immense. It's where all souls' records are kept. Or should be," whispered Oona. "We are going to essentially prevent a theft."

While they climbed the cliff, Oona explained what they had to do. The only way to stop the Consumer was to find Renaldo's and Jayde's books in the Akashic Records. Once they located them, they would find their souls, floating in the astral plane. Once they were found and protected, the Consumer wouldn't be able to control their bodies anymore. It would force the demon to leave

Renaldo's body and block its passage into Jayde's body. Then it would be trapped, unable to leap from one body to the next.

"Otherwise it will pour right into Jayde's body," Oona said. "It's important for you to find Renaldo's and Jayde's records and hold on to them. That will help prevent the creature from leaping. We can catch it before it throws René's body away."

"Throws him away? What do you mean?" said Tommy.

Oona let out a serious exhale. "The demon. The demon travels from one body to the next on the earthly plane. It doesn't care about its vehicle as it moves from one to the next. Like the way you throw away soda cans."

"But where is René now?"

"And Jayde?"

"I hope somewhere safe," Oona said carefully.

"René!" Tommy cried. Pris grabbed his shoulder.

Tommy put his head in his hands. "I just don't know why it picked René. Why him? Why?"

Oona snaked an arm out of her material again. The hand reached for Tommy's knee. "Your bodies on Earth," she said, barely turning toward them in her hood as if she were embarrassed to look at them. "They beam light. We are all trying so hard to shine. But some just shine naturally. That's René. That's Jayde. That's why the creature is attracted to them."

"Don't worry, Tommy," said Pris. "We're gonna save him, okay?"

Tommy grabbed her hand, thanking her with his sorrowful eyes.

Oona quickly broke the moment and almost militantly spoke up. "Tommy. Pris. You have to stay clearheaded. You both have to be focused when you enter the records."

Pris turned to her. "Aren't you coming, too?"

"I will try. It may take me a bit. Your perception of the records will take some time for me to locate."

"What do you mean?" Pris asked, getting a little tired of Oona's secrecy.

"We all perceive the astral planes through our own bodies, our own eyes. So there are infinite interpretations of realities. I know you well enough now, Tommy, that I think I can find you."

"So everyone who has a record there is alive? Like, right now, alive?" asked Pris.

"Yes. Also those who have passed. Unfortunately some records have been lost. And some stolen."

"And what's in these records? Like, you can read about the person and who they are and where they are from?"

"Yes. It's all there."

"So . . . we go to this Akashic Records place," Pris said, "and we find the records of Jayde and René and take them. And then how do we get that thing out of René's body on . . . on Earth?"

"The earthly *plane*," Oona corrected Pris, a bit irritated. "We need to pull the . . . demon . . . back. Back to the astral plane."

"How?"

Oona sighed. "It won't be easy. This entity is strong. It's had a lot of experience going back and forth. It's a criminal."

Pris grabbed her disk, determined. "We *need* to get it," she said.

Oona stopped walking and lagged behind again. She doubled over, looking like she was about to faint.

"Oona!" Tommy said. He climbed out of his seat and hopped to the last car, clutching onto the side of it, trying to reach for Oona.

Pris grabbed onto the railing to try and slow the car's ascent. She lodged her disk under the wheel. Oona faltered and began falling backward. Tommy managed to hold her steady by snatching a fistful of her cloak.

"Don't touch me!" she screamed.

Tommy jumped back. Something moved in Oona's robe, and two hands squirreled out from under the thick material and through slits in the fabric. Two arms that were misshapen. One was hairy, muscular. The other was thinner, more delicate. Pris watched this happen from the wagon. *Oona is not just a tall girl*, she thought.

"I'm sorry for my outburst," Oona said, clamping her stronger arm on her knee and standing up again. The other arm's hand reached out to Tommy and placatingly patted him on the shoulder. Tommy could only silently nod as Oona grasped the sides of the wagon and climbed in. He knew better than to ask more questions.

"Maybe I can ride for a bit," Oona declared. "Please return to your seat. Let's continue."

Pris pulled her disk from under the wheel, and the cars resumed their ascent. But she kept her eye on Oona. At one point her hood gaped open, and Pris saw a scarred surface, something she couldn't quite make out.

Tommy sat next to Oona. "You still, um, have the face of the girl," he said tentatively. "The body you were in when you visited the earthly plane."

"Yes." Oona sighed. She looked down. "I'm sorry. This is another reason why we need to go to the Akashic Records. I need to find her. Hopefully that photograph you found, Pris, will help. Until then, I wear her."

"Wear her?"

Oona sighed in her hulking cloak. "I inhabited the body of a dying girl. Some poor soul. And now she is a part of me. I must help her rest. That is all I want. The demon is different. It doesn't care how many bodies it inhabits or what that means for its form here in the astral plane. It's destructive. It flouts all ancient edicts. It is a criminal. This is our chance to stop it."

"But we're just two humans," Tommy said, slightly panicking.

"You both are extraordinary. I wish you saw that," Oona said. "I've waited for people like you for a long time." Oona sat forward, as if readying for a speech. "Tommy, your imagination hasn't been weighted down by bitterness. And Pris, you're . . . exceptional. Someone like you comes along once a century. There are others, too, who can help. In fact, there's someone on the earthly plane now, a Protector, who has come into her own. She will be very important. It's all lining up." Oona, shadowed in her hood, turned to Tommy and looked at him with her one uncovered eye. "You love René. That's the most important thing. With your love, we'll stop the demon from ever hurting anyone again."

Tommy looked down, embarrassed. Everyone knew his feelings, everywhere, in every plane.

The roller-coaster car kept clanking upward and upward. The shimmering event horizon stretched as far as Tommy could see. He thought about René and felt a burning in his chest. From here, he could feel René more strongly. Warmth ran up his body.

"Hold tight," Oona said, interrupting his thoughts. She climbed out of the car and onto the track behind him. Tommy clambered over the cars and sat next to Pris. Like a carnival attendant, Oona leaned over them and secured the rusty safety bar.

"Why?" Pris asked. "Have we reached the top of the mountain? Are we at the gate of the Higher Plane?"

"It's not above," said Oona. "It's below."

Tommy felt the car dip.

He looked behind him to see Oona standing there at the crest of the track as he and Pris and the roller-coaster cars arced downward. For a moment his body felt suspended. Then the car plunged forward, his stomach and heart lurching, the air howling around him. He reached for Pris's hand, and they gripped the handlebar together. Then they closed their eyes and fell into a darkness that felt colder and colder with every scream.

1986
DARA

Dara brushed the leaves out of Tommy's hair and tried to wipe the soot from the burned tree off his cheeks. He was lying there on the couch in her basement. She watched as he sat slumped over, asleep but awake, sedate but fitful. He had been muttering words in his sleep—*pris, oona, lolly*—nonsense words. But then, suddenly he was quiet, and both Dara and Ms. Ziller thought he had stopped breathing. They crept in close to him when suddenly he burst out and screamed, "Watch out! Pris, Pris, Pris!"

After Mr. and Mrs. Calabasas left the classroom, Dara had tried to convince Ms. Ziller that René was possessed. Then, as if on cue, they saw René in the parking lot laughing at Tommy.

Dara watched Ms. Ziller's face fall into a kind of dazed seriousness. "I'll pick you up in the parking lot of McDonald's," she had said. Ms. Ziller had insisted on driving Dara to find Tommy after school.

Dara got a strawberry milkshake and sipped on it but felt like she was tasting chemicals and not food and that maybe this was bad for her. It was still baking hot in the air, like summer was insisting on being here. She could hear patches of wilderness in the distance whispering with life. She looked at a small sliver of woods between the McDonald's and the Home Realty building next door. She heard the cicadas hissing in the tall grass. She felt like something was beckoning to her there. Dara shuddered with energy. She stepped into the tiny patch of forest and felt the insects vibrating through her insides. It was as if they were whispering to her, saying, *Prepare . . . prepare . . .* She stood still and closed her eyes, getting lost in the clicking whispers.

Then she heard a honk. Shaking out of the trance, she saw Ms. Ziller wheeling up in her brown Duster. She motioned to Dara to get in, quickly, like they were doing something illegal. She had on big sunglasses and looked like Gloria Steinem.

"Did anyone see you?" Ms. Ziller asked sternly.

"No, why?"

"I can't socialize with students off campus," she said. "I got reprimanded for taking you to see René in the hospital." She jerked her car into reverse. "But I don't care. We have to find Tommy."

They drove to the library, and Dara watched again as Ms. Ziller was awkward and friendly with the woman behind the desk, who, after Ms. Ziller laughed and swished her hair, told them she had seen Tommy just an hour or so ago. He had left abruptly. She didn't know where.

"I have a hunch where he is," said Dara.

They drove through the maze of suburbs. It was 6:00 p.m. by the time they made it across town to the new developments.

The sun had plunged below the trees.

They snaked through the streets of the new constructions. The streetlights snapped on as they wound through the subdivision. By the time they got to Hollow Pond Park, it was already dark. They found Tommy under the willow tree. He was hunched over like he had drunk a six-pack of beer. Dara gasped, at first afraid that he had also been struck by lightning. They rushed up to him, but Tommy just seemed to be in a deep sleep.

"Thank God no one else was here," said Ms. Ziller, shaking him. "Tommy? Hello? Is he okay? We need to take him to a hospital!"

"No," said Dara. "Hold on."

Next to him was a worn-in book, its edges soiled and the cover faded—a practically ancient relic that Dara hadn't seen before. Tommy's finger was on a page. Dara bent down to read it.

You must protect him. Take him somewhere safe.

"Let's get him to my house," Dara said. "I don't think a hospital can help him."

"Dara, I can't just allow you to—"

"Listen to me!" Dara said, fully convinced as she spoke. "Something big is coming."

Ms. Ziller looked at her with wide eyes and breathed rapidly, nodding in half belief. Then Dara and Ms. Ziller managed to carry Tommy's catatonic body up from his spot under that tree in Hollow Pond Park. He was heavy, and it took all Dara's and Ms. Ziller's strength to move him. Tommy jerked in fits and spasms as if he was in a bad dream, clutching onto the old book like a stuffed animal.

"Lolly! Pris!"

They lifted him—Ms. Ziller carrying his feet as they weaved

through the field to her car. They lugged him over the withering violets and hoisted him into Ms. Ziller's hatchback, gently resting him in a fetal position, his head on a balled-up jacket. Then, they both leaned on the doors, exhausted. Dara looked back at that tree. *Something powerful happened there,* she repeated to herself. In the full moon light, the blackened branches rose like limbs of crying children. Ms. Ziller walked to the driver's seat and eyed the box of cigarettes in the console. Dara climbed in next to her.

"I'm telling you, I really don't think René is himself," Dara explained again. "He's someone else, somewhere else. And Tommy's looking for him," she said.

"And you are getting this all from that book?" Ms. Ziller said questioningly. "You know, another explanation could be that Tommy's having some kind of emotional episode, because of everything, because of how René is shunning him."

"Either way, do you think taking Tommy to a hospital and explaining that to a doctor right now will help him?" Dara responded.

"Well, maybe he's just fainted from stress," Ms. Ziller said halfheartedly. But she drove Dara through the sprawling suburbs all the same.

When they reached Dara's house, they lifted Tommy's body out of the car and across the clipped grass of the front yard to the basement door and the couch. Ms. Ziller clumsily deposited Tommy and then smoothed out her hair.

"Are your parents home?"

"No. It's Friday, and they have their roving dinner party."

Dara grabbed a plastic *Ghostbusters* tumbler and filled it with water from the downstairs bathroom faucet.

Ms. Ziller collapsed on the chair, catching her breath. "I shouldn't be here," she said, half to herself.

Dara returned with the water. Ms. Ziller kept getting up and sitting down, on edge, like she couldn't believe what was happening.

"I shouldn't be here," she repeated. "I could get in trouble."

"I mean, I don't think you are going to kill me or anything."

"You just don't know how strict Mrs. George can get."

Tommy was still clutching that book and wouldn't let go of it. But finally, he seemed to relax a little in sleep. Dara carefully slipped it out of his hands. That damn book. Dara picked it up and flipped to a page. Like it knew what she wanted, it opened to an entry about *Protectors*.

But before she could begin reading, Ms. Ziller began crying.

"Are you all right?" Dara asked.

Ms. Ziller swallowed. "I . . . I have to go. I need to take care of something. Be sure Tommy is safe."

And then, abruptly, she left. Dara sat in silence and watched Tommy have another fit, whimpering. Whatever dream he was having, wherever he was, it was not a place that was peaceful. She grabbed the book. She wasn't sure why, but her hand reached out like it would give her lifesaving tips for someone in a catatonic state. Maybe there was something in it about helping to calm him?

She opened and read the first line.

Go outside.

She stepped out the basement door into the grass. She heard the hissing of insects getting louder and louder, surrounding her in sound.

Later in life, Dara would remember what happened next as a

dream. A long, vivid dream that haunted her. For years, she would work it out in therapy, about that terrible autumn in tenth grade and how, perhaps, this dream was a way for her to process grief, to come to terms with what happened to René, to cope with how distanced her parents were with their caregiving, to deal with her shame about her sexuality at the time. There were so many things to unpack with this dream. Regardless, she would remember herself as a kind of protector, watching over Tommy, watching over René, too. And she would remember the book—that astral projection book and how they were all obsessed with it. How they all thought it gave them answers. Her therapist would say it was normal for young people, especially young queer people back then, to seek answers in supernatural fictions since there weren't any resources or support out there for them. And that made sense. But still, Dara, for the rest of her life, could never let go of this dream, and the strange events that unfolded within it, events that were so vivid, they almost seemed as real as memory.

SALLY

Sally Ziller turned on Organza Boulevard. She knew the general area where Luke Smoshe lived. When you were popular, people were always yelling your address down the halls: "Dude! Luke is having a party tonight! Organza Boulevard!" She also knew he had a pool and that his parents were away and that Renaldo Calabasas was 100 percent at that party.

Sally had been popular, too, when she was in high school. She had the hair for it. It feathered perfectly. She became a cheerleader, but that was just to get closer to Marlena, the captain, who she had a crush on.

Sally parked near a wooded section of the neighborhood, some expanse of forest that hadn't yet been turned into houses. She got out of the car and looked at the woods. She realized then that these wet, smelly forests, the ones she ran through as a child barefoot, were disappearing. She turned to see new houses being built, much like the area where they found Tommy, and she sighed. *This is all going to be wiped away, isn't it?* she thought. *Like my friend Edward.*

It still chilled her bones the way Dara had repeated the phrase Edward—or the Edward in her dream—had said to her. *Something big is coming.* But she shook it off. She didn't want to believe in premonitions, or any kind of supernatural experience. She was a teacher—she was trained to help these kids, make them feel like they mattered in this world, not fuel their otherworldly fantasies. She was here to extract René from his unhealthy decisions and to return him to his authentic self—the passionate, maybe gay poet. And then Tommy would awaken from his strange slumber and everything would be fine again.

Sally wasn't sure which house was Luke's. She expected cars and crowds of people and music to guide her. But the block was quiet.

A woman marched by with her hair in a headband, purple leggings, carrying Heavyhands. Her Walkman was blasting some macho, pelvis-thrusting song about eyes and tigers. Sally waved to her, trying to be as friendly as possible. The woman looked at her, frightened.

"Can I help you?" the woman asked.

Sally tried to put on a personality that made her seem as feminine and cute as possible.

"Hiee! I am so sorry to, like, bother you, but I'm headed to a barbecue and I am sort of lost."

"A barbecue?"

"Do you know where the Smoshes live?"

"They're having a barbecue?" asked the woman. She swelled

with indignance. Sally couldn't tell if it was because they shouldn't be having a barbecue on a Friday night or because she wasn't invited.

"I mean, it's just a work thing. You know Luke's parents . . . um . . . they . . ." Sally struggled to remember their names. She'd met them at Parents' Night and had tried very hard to say something nice about Luke. Oh, their names were in her somewhere. *Oh, wait,* she thought, *here it comes, like a sneeze.*

"Marvin! Marvin and Davilla!" she said, bursting. "I volunteer with them, and we're all getting together to host a little writing campaign for the midterm elections."

She hoped that this woman would be thwarted by her little pro-Republican act, even though inside, she felt sick. The president of the United States was ignoring this virus, ignoring the people who were dying because they were not part of his heterosexual world vision.

"I'm just going there to write some letters to mail. And eat some burgers, of course. Isn't that all part of the fun?"

She felt even sicker as her baby voice rose higher and higher. She twisted her hair. It came out of her so naturally, this helpless girl act.

The woman smiled. "It's down the block, 3005." Then, mercifully, she jogged away.

Getting closer, Sally could see that the party was almost over. The lawn was littered with remnants of plastic cups, and a girl was patting her friend's back as she puked on the front lawn.

Sally took a big breath and walked up to the house, where three seniors were sitting cross-legged in the driveway, smoking. They barely noticed her. Avoiding the front door, she crept around the side of the house, peering into the backyard behind two leafy bushes. Through the slats of the freshly painted, expensive-looking fence, she saw Renaldo—shirtless, wet, dancing by the pool. The latest album by the Cars was playing. Welsh Walsh came up to him, dipping his key into a little baggie of white powder before putting it under Renaldo's nose.

Sally knew that kids did drugs—she wasn't stupid—but the ease and familiarity René had with snorting coke surprised her. Just as she feared: René was making poor choices, masking his trauma. If she didn't get him out of there, he was going to do something destructive to himself. She had to talk to him and make him see how important it was for him to remain creative, remain friends with Dara and Tommy. What he was doing now was tearing Tommy apart.

Renaldo turned to Stacey Divine and began pumping his pelvis into her backside. She scooted forward, pretending to be fine but looking clearly uncomfortable. Then, Welsh Walsh came around the girl's front, twirling her and pushing her toward Renaldo. Now, she was trapped between the boys as they high-fived over her head. Sally unlatched the gate.

"Stop!" she shouted.

"Ms. Ziller?" Stacey Divine said, sounding surprised.

"That English teacher?" Welsh Walsh echoed. "What are you doing here?"

"Both of you, get away from her."

"It's cool, it's cool," Stacey Divine said, arms crossed around her chest. She stepped away quickly and scampered back into the house.

Sally walked up to René. "Come on, Renaldo. This isn't where you want to be." She pulled at his arm.

"Unhand me, wench," Renaldo said with a strange haughtiness. Reflexively, Sally felt her grip on René's arm loosen.

Then, his face changed, and she watched as he plastered on a polite smile.

"I am sorry for the misunderstanding. I would like to end any kind of relations we had in the past." He said this in a rushed way as if he had said it countless times before, tossing it off like he was canceling an order of fries.

Sally blinked at him. There was nothing of René in his posture or demeanor.

"Renaldo, your parents are worried about you. We are all worried. You aren't well," she pleaded.

Renaldo laughed. "Parents," he said sarcastically. He was still wet from the pool, water glistening his body. He looked more muscular. *Or maybe that was how he looked all this time under his clothes,* Sally thought. But he carried himself proudly, like he was an ancient pharaoh. He moved across the poolside deck to where Welsh was now standing.

"What a funny concept. That there are these older people who are supposed to watch over you." He grabbed Welsh and pulled him into a hug. "Personally, I believe in brotherhood," he said. "Blood brothers."

He threw a beer bottle on the ground, smashed it, and grabbed Welsh's wrist with shocking speed. Welsh jumped, but Renaldo held on to him tightly.

"What are you doing, man?" said Welsh, laughing nervously. Welsh tried to break free, but couldn't, like René had superhuman strength.

"René, leave him alone," said Sally, trying to stay calm.

Welsh struggled to untangle himself from René's clutches, but he held tight.

"Don't you want me?" René taunted, staring at Welsh. "Isn't this what you wanted, secretly? To fulfill your desires for me? To be overcome by me?" He grabbed Welsh by the sides of his head and clutched him like he was a melon. Sally watched as René began squeezing.

"Ow, stop, René," he said, pleading.

Welsh's eyes began to bug out of his head from the pressure. Sally had no choice. She rushed up to them and, with her knee, kicked René in the crotch. René gasped, and then smiled.

"Pain, wow. Amazing. This is pain. *This* is pain."

He turned to her with a grin, tossing Welsh aside like a rag doll.

He crept closer. "You know, you could join me. I mean, you are very beautiful, despite the weird hairstyle that is so popular with this era."

Sally felt her body electrify in a strange way, like a trance had come over her. She dropped the bottle.

"Come join me. What's your name again?"

"René, you know me," she choked out. "It's Sally. Sally Ziller."

He grabbed her by the hips and bent over her, bowing them both so that her back arched over the pool.

"Come to me," he said. She felt a hand stroking her thigh. He was so close that she could feel his breath. And then his mouth was on hers. She felt the air being sucked out of her like a tornado between her lips. The bottoms of her lungs began to ache. Her lower ribs started to hurt, and she worried, wildly, that her lungs were collapsing.

It was then that she remembered one afternoon after school. René had come by. It was when she first thought that maybe he was too into these occult subjects and might be a little troubled. He walked in, tugging at his hair, more disheveled than usual, and he told her about how he was obsessed with possession. How different cultures all talked about it. And as if to speak to her, to her Baptist upbringing, he told the story of the Gerasenes in the New Testament. She couldn't help it; the Bible still enthralled her, no matter how far away she tried to get from it. She knew it well. A man was possessed by not one but multiple demons. "And then Jesus asks him his name, and he says, 'My name is Legion, for we are many,'" René had recited.

Now, dangling over the pool in his strong grip, as she felt him sucking the air out of her lungs like a cool vacuum, she realized Dara and Tommy were right. This wasn't René. He was as they said: possessed. She shuddered with biblical fear, terrified that this would be the last thing she felt before she died—

Suddenly René stopped. But he didn't reel backward. Instead, he was frozen in place, his arms stuck around her like a statue.

"Ms. Ziller? Are you okay?"

Sally opened her eyes and saw Dara standing behind Renaldo, peeking over his shoulder. "Can you get out of his grip? I think I, like, immobilized him, but I don't know for how long, so it might be a good idea if you moved sort of swiftly. Is that . . . Welsh Walsh? Why is he in a pink Speedo?"

Sally curved her head to the other end of the pool to see Welsh Walsh passed out, splayed over the diving board.

She crawled out slowly. She hung from René's arms and swung herself to the side of the pool, sticking her landing.

Dara looked impressed. "Nice."

"I was a gymnast when I was your age," Sally said sheepishly. "I was going to pursue the whole Olympics thing, but my coach was a fucking creep." She looked at Dara. Her hair was streaked with dust, slicked off her head as if she had been in a jet stream. She held the old book of Tommy's in her hands. "How did you do all that?"

Dara seemed confused, like she just woke up out of a dream. "I'm not sure. The book led me here. I know this doesn't make sense, but I'm pretty sure I *flew*. And then I saw you and I think the book helped me put René in a frozen state."

They stared at René, unmoving, hanging over the pool.

Sally shook her head. "I can't believe *I'm* saying this, but I think he was trying to suck out my soul. I . . ." She hesitated. "I don't even think that's René in there at all. You were right. He's possessed."

Dara reached into her hip bag and pulled out a book. "It's all in here. Whatever is possessing René . . . I think it *eats* life, like a gypsy moth in a tree or something. It's called a Consumer."

They stared at René. His arms, sinewy and pulsing with life even though he was frozen there.

And then he spoke. "Ahem," he said, clearing his throat.

Sally, instinctively, put her arm in front of Dara. Dara pulled it down. René, still paralyzed, somehow regained use of his face and neck. He, or it, turned to them. Curling like an eel, René's body slowly coiled back to life. He shook his head and wriggled his fingers.

"You did this to me?" he said, glaring at Dara.

"Yes. Yes, I did," answered Dara, trying to sound confident as she quickly turned to the book and flipped to a page. Sally watched as she searched for a solution.

"How . . . are you doing this?" Sally asked Dara, in awe.

"It's the book. It's telling me what to do," Dara explained. Landing on a page, she reached down and pulled out a feather from the book and then motioned over her head. "I . . . I call upon the west and east to banish you from this body!"

"How sweet. You're a Protector. It's nice to see you humans still have them around in this funny era. The way you worship is so watered down and superficial, I didn't think there would be Protectors anymore."

Dara continued reading from the book. "By Tituba, by Marie, by Yemaya, by Grimhilde, by . . ."

René began blinking and moving his arms. He seemed drowsy.

"That's not going to work with me, you insignificant, Earth-bound little girl," he said.

"Get the fuck away from us," said Sally. "Get out of our friend's body." She spoke like rage was boiling inside her. She picked up the broken bottle.

"Oh, please. You wouldn't hurt his beautiful body." He ran his hands over his torso.

"Sisters. I ask for your strength, to bind all Earth's Protectors," Dara read.

"You have to be more forceful," René said, patronizing.

He drew closer. Sally held the bottle in front of him. He grabbed her hand swiftly, before she could react.

"We both know *you* wouldn't cut this beautiful body. But me? I don't give a fuck."

He took the bottle and pressed it into his chest. It punctured his skin, blood pouring out in streaks down his stomach, into the hair creeping up from his low-slung swimsuit.

"You can't banish me," he said.

"I'm not. I'm locating you," said Dara, skimming the pages of the book before declaring, "Powers of the Higher Plane, he is here! See him! See him!"

René backed away. He glowered at her. "You little fool."

"Your presence has been revealed to the Higher Plane," Dara said confidently.

René grabbed someone's pair of pants draped over a lawn chair, put them on, and with great agility, ran to the fence and vaulted over it.

Dara and Sally rushed out to follow him, watching him sprint barefoot down the street. They could hear the flesh of his feet smack the asphalt, like he was damaging the skin and bone but didn't care.

Sally fumbled for her keys to her car. "Come on!" she said, rushing out of the backyard onto the street.

They watched René dodge into someone's yard, leaping over another fence.

Sally jumped into the driver's seat. She motioned to Dara. "We are gonna lose him!"

Dara turned to her. "Roll up your window," she said commandingly, with dead, direct eyes. Sally obeyed. "Go back to my basement. Watch over Tommy. I will follow René."

Before Sally could say anything, she heard a buzzing noise, one that seemed to be getting louder and louder. Out the car window, a cloud of insects came circling around Dara. They were hissing, and Sally tried to open the door, but the insects flooded the exterior of the car in a thick, opaque, angry mass. A plague of wings smeared themselves across the window. Sally screamed and watched the brown cloud engulf Dara's body. They billowed under her long silk coat and into her sleeves, lifting her into the air. Dara looked at her and smiled. Sally screamed Dara's name as she turned away and floated off, through the wedge of forest between Organza Street and Nativity Boulevard.

JAYDE

Jayde was falling. It was like a roller coaster, where you felt it in your stomach, that drop. *I'm dreaming*, they decided, *because I'm not terrified by what will happen when I land like you are in real life.* Jayde never really had vivid dreams. Pris always made fun of them because their entire lives, Jayde would fall asleep halfway through whatever holo-show they were watching and then would snore like a beast, and invariably they would feel Pris jabbing them in the arm to turn over and shut up.

Then Jayde remembered. Their stomach lurched again, and it wasn't from falling.

Jayde remembered being in Nomed's car, his silence, his skin falling off like a flaky pastry. They remembered seeing his face that wasn't quite a face at all. It was more like a dead body that had been flattened by brute force. Then they had screamed, and now they were here, falling and falling in a dream.

Jayde closed their eyes and, at last, landed on something. Or, rather, they felt something flat under them, a shiny, smooth, reflective floor, as if glass had slipped quietly beneath them as they descended. When they opened their eyes, they saw an endless blue sky and a purple horizon line, as if the sun was about to set in a dense fog. In the distance, they could hear music—a beat echoing through the gloom. They stood up on the glass floor to follow the sound and almost fell over. Jayde looked down. They were wearing shiny, cobalt-blue stiletto heels. They felt the tight, slick dress they had on. Delightful—they were wearing cute clothes in this dream. They smiled and walked toward the light.

Figures emerged. All standing, leaning against a bar. There was a dance floor and steam rose from it, in the center a halo of warm light. Jayde approached a bar and saw a tall man with broad shoulders. He was wearing a tweed jacket and trousers, but no shirt. He was beautiful. His skin was blue-black, his face chiseled and perfect. Next to him was another man with short hair and an angular face, with a nose like a Greek statue's. And next to *him* was a beautiful woman, like a model on *LOOQ*. Jayde could tell everyone was staring at them. *Maybe I'm at the party Nomed was supposed to bring me to,* Jayde thought, *and I fell asleep.* If this was true, the party was perfect—rich and chic, like the way they heard Manhattan or Miami was before the Virus and the Fires.

"Hello," someone said behind them. Jayde turned to see a tall figure in a silver shimmering catsuit. Their body was muscular, like a gymnast, as if they had just come from a rigorous floor routine. "I'm Almood."

"Hello," Jayde said. This person was everything Jayde wanted to be. And wanted.

"You just arrived?"

"Yes. And you?"

Almood was about to say something but stopped. They looked at themselves with puzzlement. "I don't remember." They wandered off in the smoke. People hovered there, behind the mist, dancing, talking, almost like shadow puppets.

Jayde walked into the mist. They weren't afraid, really. They credited that to the stilettos and this dream, because in dreams you could do anything. On the smoky dance floor, they found a man and a woman lounging on giant pillows shaped like dollops of whipped cream.

"Excuse me," they said. "I hope this doesn't sound too ridiculous, but can you tell me where I am? Like, what the name of this club is?"

"That's so interesting," the gorgeous woman said. She had a long neck and what looked like butterflies tattooed along her neck and into her clavicle. "Did you hear that, Antoine?"

The man, rosy-cheeked, with cornflower-blue eyes and a floppy curl of hair coming down his forehead, cocked his head at Jayde.

"So amazing."

"Sorry, maybe you didn't hear me. Do you know where I am?"

"Fascinating."

"I'm intrigued."

Jayde gave up on the couple and kept walking, bumping into people. They were all beautiful and busy. Occupied. Everyone was occupied.

They saw an exit. There were two large men standing there at the entrance with sunglasses and blazers on, built like wrapped mattresses. One held a stiff black wand that looked like it could shock you. Jayde approached and tried to slip by.

"Excuse me."

The man with the wand grabbed Jayde's arm tightly. "You can't leave."

"Yes, I can."

"No. Please go back to the dance floor."

"I can do what I want."

"Turn away from the exit," the man demanded, before grunting to the other bodyguard. "A new one. See how angry they get? They're all like this at first, so keep your wand handy."

Jayde backed away. This dream was getting more belligerent. *Belligerent.* Another word they had recently learned. They ran past the dance floor and looked for other doors before tripping over two girls making out on the floor.

"I feel like I've met you before," Jayde heard one girl say to the other between kisses.

"Me too."

Jayde rushed through the crowd and heard similar conversations.

"Do I know you?"

"Maybe—you look really familiar."

"It's so weird, you remind me of someone I know."

"Oh, I get that all the time, who?"

Jayde ducked into the hall. A door swung open and a professional woman walked out, adjusting her pantsuit. She looked like a TV executive. Maybe she was? Jayde entered the room. Inside, the lights were low, and a hallway of black tiles stretched in front of them. They heard a flush. It was a bathroom. The club music thumped through the walls. Jayde walked down the row of mirrors and sinks and saw a female figure bent over the counter, frantically combing through long honey-colored hair.

They gasped. "Contessa?"

Contessa shook her head as she fumbled with some lip gloss. "You aren't real," she said without turning.

"What?"

"You aren't real. Stay away."

"I'm sorry, Contessa, but I *am* real. I mean, I think I'm dreaming, but in real life I'm—"

She gasped. "Oh my god. You're actually making full sentences."

"Well, yeah."

"Did—did you just get here?"

"Yes. Where is here? Where am I?"

"Crap. You have to leave, quickly."

"I tried but the guard wouldn't let me."

"No, up there," she said, pointing to an air-conditioning vent on the ceiling. "I tried, but I couldn't get there in time. But you haven't been swallowed yet. I can tell."

"Swallowed?"

"You can think for yourself."

"I'm so sorry, but you need to be clearer—"

"See? You have opinions! I used to. I have only one opinion now, and it's that I need to get out of here."

Contessa pulled over a heavy wooden chair sitting in the corner and then found a trash can and placed it on top. She looked at the door. "Make sure the guard doesn't come in," she said to Jayde.

"What are you doing?"

Jayde watched as their idol gripped the sides of the vent,

digging her fingers through the slots. Her nails bent backward, twisting with blood.

"Stop! You're hurting yourself!"

Contessa didn't listen. She tore off the vent, ripping off some of her nails. She motioned down to Jayde. "Come on, you have to go first. You'll know where to go."

"I don't know where I am! I don't know where to go!"

Jayde began to cry. This dream was getting very intense. Still, through tears, they obeyed their idol. They took off the stilettos and climbed up the wobbly metal canister. Jayde remembered climbing up a tree in the Glade with Pris, who was always much more athletic and stronger than they were. They missed Pris. They wished Pris was here. Determined, Jayde sniffled and squirreled their body through the small opening.

"Good job," Contessa said. "I'll follow you inside. Maybe I can make it this time before it comes."

"Before who comes?"

"Hurry!" Contessa yelled.

It was strange to see her so alarmed and panicked. Contessa was always effortlessly composed in her Ting videos. Or was before she died.

This is a dream. This is a dream, Jayde repeated in their head.

There was a sound coming from behind them. From the club. It was the sound of someone or some*thing* gulping, like they were swallowing a large pill whole. Jayde kept crawling through the ducts. They passed by another opening, out to the dance floor of the club. Through the slats, Jayde watched the crowd of people mashing into one another. With horror, they realized that some people were writhing and screaming for help. Others were silent.

One sat cross-legged, their eyes closed, as if they had given up completely. Another was laughing through their tears. Jayde heard the sound of crunching, as if the bodies in the club were snapping one another's bones.

Jayde whimpered, but kept crawling along. They glanced behind them. Contessa was there, trying to follow.

"Keep going! Don't look back at me!" she said. She was holding tightly on to the sides of the passage. Then, without warning, Contessa screamed and flew backward.

Jayde wanted to call out to her, but they felt voiceless. They had to keep going. They had to do what Contessa had wanted. So they continued crawling. They felt a suction behind them, like the opening was a vacuum. Jayde braced themselves along the sides of the air duct and pushed their way forward. They scampered deeper and deeper into the ducts—using all their strength to keep from being pulled backward like Contessa. They crawled toward a glow, a light gleaming along the sides of the tunnel. They crawled until they were so bruised and out of breath they had to stop. Below them was another opening. They peered in through the slats. It looked quiet, and smelled old, like not a club but some room from another time. Jayde grabbed onto the vent and wrenched it free. They cut their finger and thought of Contessa. Her abject fear. What was that thing that came into the club?

They heard a throaty gargle behind them, and the suction got stronger. Without looking, Jayde dove through the opening and fell, landing with a thud. This time it wasn't a soft, dreamlike descent.

Jayde rolled on their side. They opened their eyes and saw an ugly orange carpet. They were in a bright room, dusty, with shelves and shelves of old books stacked between them. This was a library. Like the old kinds Jayde has seen in movies about magicians and detectives. *Oh Goddess. I'm having the weirdest dream right now. Why would I ever be in a library?*

Jayde stood up. They were still bruised, and their ankle hurt. They peered down at their body. Something was coming off them—this milky tornado whooshing out of their navel. Jayde ran their hands through it like it was smoke from a candle flame.

Backing up, they bumped into a wooden stand while they walked. On it was a book. A thick book. Jayde had never really been near a physical book. They had seen them in cartoons about old people and in photographs of their abuelita in school. But here was a real book. Solid, its pages so thin. Gossamer pages. (*Gossamer*, another word they loved.) And on it, Jayde saw a long list of words. All sorts of words. It was a dictionary, they realized. Soon they were poring over words: *anent, gnomon, illumine, skyey.*

They could have stood there for an eternity, trying to find all the words they wanted to know. But then they saw something out of the corner of their eye. Something ran across the floor, down one of the hallways full of books. It was wearing something white. Like a ghost.

Jayde darted between the shelves to hide. They grabbed a book from the shelf, ready to use it as a weapon. They so wished Pris were here, because Pris could hit a target with that disk like no one else they knew. Jayde could hear the thing breathing, and possibly whimpering. It sounded human.

The figure scampered past Jayde through the next hall of books, so close it made Jayde gasp. Then, the figure ran past the reading tables and ducked behind the waist-high shelves of encyclopedias, where it was darkest. Jayde sighed with relief. This person was also afraid.

"Hello?" they called out. "Don't worry, I'm not going to do anything. I just got here. I just would love to talk to someone real."

"You aren't real! Get away!" the person said.

He stood up, clutching the sides of the table. He was wearing all white. A baggy white shirt and white pants. Jayde recognized the shirt. It was the same one they had taken from the Murder House. He had curly, beautifully thick hair. His face was sweet and delicate, with a strangely long nose. He had brown eyes and a warm presence. He was about Jayde's age. But he looked hurt. Jayde glanced down at his stomach. Something was coming off it—a faint, cloudy line thinning into the air, just like Jayde's.

"Are you okay?" Jayde asked the boy.

"Why should I tell you? You aren't real! You are just another illusion trying to get to me," the boy screeched.

Then, he grabbed a book from the shelf and threw it at Jayde.

PRIS AND TOMMY, THE RECORDS

Pris opened her eyes, her head resting against a bony shoulder. Somewhere in their journey, she must have fallen asleep. She looked up to see Tommy and sat up, embarrassed she had used him as a pillow. He was still peacefully asleep. How was it that they had drifted off? They were already asleep on Earth. She looked at him, his bumpy face and pursed lips.

She got out of the roller-coaster-like contraption they were still sitting in, and saw that Oona was gone. And that they were in a library. It was dingy, with orange carpeting that looked like it was from the last century. There were wooden shelves full of books. She had never been in an actual library before—just seen them in old photographs of the suburbs, where the Murder House was, where the houses all stood in rickety rows, many burned down from the Fires.

Tommy woke up with a snort.

"Ow!" he yelped. His eyes darted around the room. "What's going on? Where's Oona?"

"I think we're in a library, Tommy," Pris said, kneeling down to soothe him.

"But why are we back?"

"Back where?"

"Oh, sorry. This is the library René and I went to all the time. The one behind the Kmart, not the school one."

"Behind the Kmart?" Pris repeated.

"Yeah," Tommy said, "it's also where I met Oona."

"Maybe this is where the Akashic Records are," Pris conjectured.

"Really? Here?"

"You know what Oona said. The astral plane takes the shape of the strongest tethers to the earth for us. This must be a strong one."

"Yes," Tommy agreed.

"Well, then, we have to find René's records. And Jayde's. Like, right now."

"Right!" Tommy said. He stumbled out of the seat and ran across the floor to a cabinet of small drawers. Pris watched as he traced his fingers over the front until he found a drawer and pulled it open.

"What's that?" she asked.

"The card catalog."

"The what?"

Tommy looked at her, confused, then realized. "Oh, this must be another thing you don't have. All the books have an associated card. You can flip through and look for them by author or subject or title."

"How?"

"This thing called the Dewey decimal system? Different numbers group different subjects, and then you go from there." Tommy rifled through the box of cards. "Do you want to help look? We're looking for Renaldo Calabasas. *C-A—*"

"I know, I know. It's like you think I haven't had Latinx classmates or something," Pris said. "This is going to take forever. How did you ever find things in, like, a day?"

"I don't know. Somehow it works. This summer, we did get a computer. But the librarian had it at her desk and you had to ask her and I . . ."

Pris heard typing behind her. The clacking sound of fingers on an old computer keyboard. It was coming from behind the curved wooden partition of the librarian desk. She motioned to Tommy to stop talking.

Carefully, they inched toward the desk and peeked over the large console. There was the hunched figure of a woman, with short black hair and glasses. Tommy recognized her—the librarian that Sally knew. Except instead of wearing her polyester turtleneck, she was in a long flannel nightgown.

"That's the librarian!" Tommy whispered. "But in a nightgown. So weird."

"She must be asleep," Pris said, jumping over the counter. In one leap, she landed on the other side and unlatched the door for Tommy to get in.

"Hello?" Tommy said.

The woman jumped. "Oh! Jeez!"

"Sorry!" Tommy apologized.

"You," the woman said. "Tommy? The little gay boy . . ."

Tommy bowed his head and flushed.

"But why are you here? My, my, this is such a random dream."

"We're looking for someone. Or . . . a book of someone's. His name is Renaldo Calabasas. Can you look it up?"

"Well, sure! That makes sense," she said, bowing over the computer. "This is a weird dream I'm having. Maybe this is what they call a work stress dream. Because these new computers are so complicated, and I feel like I am falling behind in technology and won't be a viable employee. They are talking of getting rid of a third of the staff, but the union says our pensions will be fine, but I'll have to be employed another fifteen years for that to matter, and . . ."

Pris interrupted. "It's C-A-L . . ."

She watched the librarian type the letters into the computer. The typeface, so foggy and amber, blinked.

"Found him!" the librarian said.

Pris peered into the screen. "There's a weird row of numbers."

Tommy got excited. He looked around and found a pencil. Pulling out the book, he opened the front jacket. "Can you read the number aloud?"

"911.324. What's that?" Pris asked.

"That's the number in the stacks. Now look up Jayde!"

"To get their number, too?"

"Yes."

She spelled *Jayde Gonzalez* to the librarian, who dutifully typed it into the computer. Jayde's number came up, too, along with their address.

"Wow, this is really direct," Pris said, impressed. "Usually you have to go through tons of filters to get someone's home address on the Hub."

"What?"

"Never mind. Write this down: 911.372."

Tommy scribbled it down.

Pris looked at him. "Now what?"

"We get the books."

Pris jumped over the desk again. Tommy turned to the librarian to thank her. She beamed at him.

"Tommy Gaye. You became such a nice man, such a wonderful man. Sally was so proud of you," she said, touching his arm.

Before Tommy could ask what she meant, she yawned and made a pillow with her hands on the keyboard.

"This is just the weirdest dream . . . ," she said, and then as she fell asleep, she disappeared.

Tommy gasped.

"Tommy, hurry up! I have no idea what I'm looking for!" Pris said. She was already deep in one of the stacks, motioning to him vigorously. He followed her voice until he found her.

"What *are* we looking for?" she asked.

"911. History section."

They moved through the narrow aisle. There were so many books. Tommy walked ahead of her. She was glad that at least his version of the Akashic Records worked for him, because this was too confusing. Pris noticed labels on the edges of spines. 920.03, 920.04, 920.04 again. The titles were emblazoned on the spines: *The Trials of Penelope Bright, Mavis Cordelia: Unstoppable Woman.* The rows seemed to expand and contract as she neared them, as if there were hundreds more volumes, thousands, millions, but just by looking at a section, the spines multiplied and the shelves expanded.

"I should look for Jayde!" she said. "How do I—"

"Just look at the numbers. You see how there's a load of numbers after the decimal point? That's where it gets more specific."

There, between *Jayde Gonzalez: A Short Life* and *Jayde Gonzalez: Disappeared*, she found *Jayde Gonzalez: Future Model*. Pris grasped the book and held it to her chest. Jayde was still here. They were okay.

She watched Tommy scamper farther down the aisle.

"Caku . . . Caku-u . . . Cakzz . . . Cal, Cal, Cal, Cal."

He scrambled over to find a stepping stool and perched himself up on it, peering at the top row. "It's here! I found it! Between *Renaldo Calabaras* and *Relando Calabatas. Renaldo Calabasas: Prodigal Poet.*"

He clutched the book and exhaled. She stood up and ran toward him in case he was about to fall over.

"It's here," he repeated breathlessly. "He's here."

Pris reached up to him. Then, peering over the shelves, Tommy stared at something and gasped.

"What is it?"

He looked as if he had seen a ghost. Pris watched as he climbed off the stool and began running down the aisle. Pris darted after him. She followed him past the stacks, which seemed to grow taller and taller. The air seemed to solidify and darken, as if the library had become a huge planetarium and the roof had been removed to reveal the depth of space.

Tommy scurried around a corner, clutching René's records. He was fast for a kid who looked like he hated sports. She found him down a long hallway, standing there in a large sitting area. The air cleared up again, and the space was as it was before, dingy and yellow with bright overhead lights and a musty smell.

Tommy was staring at something. No, not something—*someone*. Sitting in a chair was a boy about Tommy's age. His back was facing them, but Pris could see that he had on a white shirt that was soiled with what looked like soot.

"René?" Tommy whispered.

He hesitated. Pris put her hand on his shoulder, gently pushing him to go to his friend. Instinctively, he grabbed her hand, and they walked toward the boy. "René?"

"Go away," the boy grumbled. "You aren't real."

"No! René, I swear it's me. Tommy, your friend? We've come to find you. To take you out of here."

Tommy carefully rested his hand on René's back. René jerked away from his touch and crouched under the chair.

"I don't believe you! You did this before! You take people I love and pretend they're here and then you bury me even deeper in this library!"

"René, I swear! I'm not anyone else!"

"No, no, no!"

"René," Pris said, her voice sounding firmer than she felt. "Stop."

Miraculously, it worked. René slowly turned around. Pris saw his face. His skin: dirty and beautiful, his eyes exhausted but bright. No wonder Tommy loved him.

"Who are you?"

"I'm a friend of Tommy's," she slowly explained. "I'm helping my friend, too. We want to get that thing out of your body and make sure it doesn't go anywhere else."

"I don't know you."

"No, but I swear I'm not, um, trying to hurt you."

"I haven't seen two people together yet," René said. Pris watched his face warm. "That's a good sign, I guess." And then he stood up and grabbed Tommy's shoulders. "Tommy? Is that really you?"

"Um, yeah, it's me," Tommy said.

So shy and genuine it would be impossible, Pris thought, *for René to doubt he wasn't real.* René began to cry. Tommy pulled him in and they embraced.

Pris backed away, still clutching Jayde's records.

"I'll be up by the computer," she said, trying to make herself scarce. She walked through the stacks, hoping that Jayde was all right. At least she had their records. Holding on to their records meant that they were not in danger.

Pris walked by shelf after shelf of books. So many stories. So many lives. And there she was, so unconnected that she didn't even know where she was from. Then it hit her. She should look up her own record.

She glanced back at the two boys. They were sitting there talking energetically to each other. Tommy was showing him the book. "And then I sat under the tree and read how I could come to you and then I guess I fell asleep. But the weird thing is that I met Pris in this house and then we met this lollipop person and he took us up this hill and then we fell asleep again so this is—"

"A dream within dream," said René. "Just like Edgar Allan Poe says. That makes sense. The planes aren't like separate realities, they are dreams, dreams within dreams."

Pris walked over to the computer. She typed in her own name. Priscilla Cherry Devrees. Cherry was supposedly her mom's name, according to Uncle Myles. Pris thought he likely made up that fact, but it was still her middle name, all the same. There was the number. 911.889. She walked over to the stack.

The row of 911.888s seemed to go on forever. Then suddenly, she saw 911.810. Her record was somewhere above, high up between the two other sections. She backed up and realized she needed a stool to get to the top shelf. There wasn't one around, so she ran and jumped up, her fingers grasping the higher shelf. A few books tumbled onto the ground. *Oh God,* she thought, *I hope I'm not destroying someone's life right now.* She kept climbing, the dust from the shelves and the must of the books making her sneeze and almost lose her grip. She made it to a shelf that said .888. As she inched across, she looked at the titles. *Priru, Prirv, Prirz* . . . there it was. Priscilla Cherry Devrees. It had no subtitle. She grabbed the volume, and crooking her arm onto the shelf, one leg dangling off the ledge, she opened it. The first page was blank. As was the second. She kept flipping through. Blank, blank, blank.

She didn't know what to say. Even her record was blank. Here she was, in the hallowed Akashic Records, where every single person's life was documented, and hers—her past, her future—was completely empty. Her assumptions were right. The Memory Thief *had* somehow stolen her past and her future, too. She was a zero, officially, just like everyone at school had said. Just like she thought. She buried her head in her hands, and balancing up there, perched on the shelf, she felt tears brim in her eyes. She didn't want to cry, and tried to suppress it, but the lump of emotion emerged from her chest like a scream.

"Pris? What are you doing?" she heard someone say. She recognized that voice. And when she looked down, she saw Jayde wearing a tight-fitting dress that Pris had never seen them in. It was torn, and Jayde was barefoot.

"How did you get here?"

Pris jumped down from the shelf. "Jayde!" she said, running toward them and throwing them into an embrace.

"What are you doing here?" Jayde said again, their face muffled in Pris's shoulder. "This is the most florid dream."

"Are you okay? Did, um, anything try to attack you?" Pris tried to compose herself, wiping away tears.

"What? What are you talking about? Wow, in my dream, you are so real. This is unbelievable."

"How did you get here?" Pris asked. She was so relieved to see Jayde, standing before her, away from the grip of the demon, away from the terrible image she saw in the mirror of Jayde comatose in bed. Maybe she still had a chance to save them from being possessed. All thoughts of her feeling like a zero seemed to dissipate as she held Jayde in her arms.

"I woke up in a club," Jayde explained. "I think Nomed brought me there? It was full of people, and then I tried to get out, so I went to the bathroom and found Contessa. THE Contessa. We crawled through the air duct, but only I made it. Something took her."

Pris grabbed Jayde's hand. "Don't let go of me. Okay?"

"Honestly, you feel so real!"

Pris pulled Jayde through the stacks, to the center, where she found Tommy and René. The two boys were sitting, crouched together, laughing and chattering, like they had a secret language. She wondered if she would ever find a connection like that.

"Oh wow. It's that beautiful boy."

"René? You've seen him?"

"Oh yeah. He's really going through it. I think he's being chased?"

Pris held on to Jayde's hand. "Tommy?" she whispered.

Tommy looked up. "Jayde! Pris found you!" He ran up and, without thinking, hugged them.

"This is Tommy. We've been, um, traveling together. We're here to bring you and René back down to Earth."

Jayde looked at Tommy and then at Pris. "Back to Earth? Where am I, then? Heaven?"

Before they could answer, René reached out and grabbed onto Tommy's shoulder, tightly. He looked up at the ceiling.

"It's coming back!" René said. "We can't be here."

"What do you mean?" Pris asked. "What's coming back?"

But Tommy and René didn't respond. They were looking behind Pris's head.

PRIS

Something was echoing through the vent above Pris's head. There was a shriek, far off. Then an arm emerged.

"Contessa?" said Jayde excitedly.

Another arm reached out. Jayde got a chair and reached up toward the hand.

"Jayde, wait a second," said Pris.

"It's Contessa! The Ting megastar! We were in the bathroom together at the club, and she tried to escape but got pulled back. She must have broken free!"

Jayde grabbed the hand, and it gripped onto their arm. "Ow! It's okay, Contessa. You don't need to squeeze. Ow!"

Another arm emerged, pulling Jayde up by their hair, lifting them up into the vent. Jayde screamed.

Pris quickly threw her disk at the two arms, while Tommy grabbed a large hardback atlas and climbed up on the chair. He pinned the arm wrapping itself in Jayde's hair and, with his other hand, pried its fingers off them.

"We. Don't. Want. You. Here," he yelled.

Jayde tumbled to the ground. "I . . . I felt that. This isn't a dream, is it?"

René scrambled over to Tommy.

"Are you okay? Wow, I've never seen you so . . . angry," he said, helping Tommy up.

"We've been through a lot," said Pris. Tommy looked at her, and they smiled privately, grabbing each other's hands.

Another arm emerged above them. They heard a growl, closer, that sounded like a giant stomach.

"Oh Goddess," said Jayde. "It's the thing."

"The thing? What thing?" asked Pris.

"When I was in the club. I saw all these people. They were . . . growing into one another. Becoming something else."

"It's trying to get me, too," René said. "It's been chasing me around the library."

"It's the demon," Pris said, helping them up. "And it is trying to take over your body."

"What? Why?"

"Because you are both beautiful and smart, with promising futures. It wants to be you," Pris said bluntly. René blushed.

"And what about Contessa?"

"I think it already got to her," said Tommy. "I'm sorry, Jayde."

Another vent banged open above them, and more arms poked out, grasping the air. René tripped and fell, screaming as an arm emerged at his feet through a drain on the floor. It latched onto his ankle, pulling his leg into the hole. René tried to yank his leg away, but the arm yanked at it again and again, tearing his white pants and digging its nails into his calf.

"Ah! No! No!" Tommy hammered at the arm with his book, over and over. "Stay away from him! Stay away!"

Pris and Jayde ran to beat at the arm while other arms emerged. Finally they wrenched René free and pried his records from the emerging hands.

Behind them, at the entrance, the doors rattled.

"It's coming!" Pris screamed.

The doors burst open as if a hurricane was outside, blowing the books around the library like litter.

"Get your records!" yelled Tommy. René and Jayde grabbed their volumes and clutched them with all their might.

A figure appeared in the doorway, in a hood.

"Oona!" Pris and Tommy said in unison.

"Quickly, we must go. Follow me," she said.

Pris and Tommy took their friends' hands and raced after her. The mist subsided, and through the doors they saw the familiar hallways of Herron High School. But as Oona kept leading them, the hallways changed, becoming longer and dimmer. It was like a maze, lit by candles.

"Where are we going?" asked Pris.

"Your Protector did her job. She located the creature on Earth. But now the creature knows we are after it. We have to go somewhere away from the records, a more level playing field," she explained, moving swiftly as her cloak fluttered behind her. Pris swore she saw four legs gallop under the fabric, as if Oona were riding a horse.

Finally, they emerged onto a vast plain. In front of them was another bleached giant skull, intact with white teeth. Pink dotted the sky, like it was sunset, though there was no sun.

They all ran to Oona, who turned away from them to obscure her face, hunching into her hood. "We must wait here and hope that the Protector on the earth plane has fulfilled her mission to pull the creature out of René's body. I just pray that she hurries. He will figure out where we are soon."

Pris stared at her. She was getting tired of how cryptic Oona was being.

"How do you know all this?" she asked, marching up to the cloaked figure. "And why won't you look at us?"

"Stay away!" Oona demanded. "It's just best. I have an allergy to light, and I—"

Pris threw her disk through the air, aiming it for the billow of the cloak that fluttered behind Oona in the breeze. Like a magician at a tablecloth, the entire cloak flew off Oona and into the air, revealing her body: a human spider. Eight legs, eight arms, and a head with four faces. Pris saw an eye and a face in profile look at her in alarm, the profile turned to reveal another profile. The eyes all looked at her, whimpering, tears pouring down their cheeks. The figure turned around and revealed another face, a man with long dark hair.

"Don't look at me!" it said, turning to expose another face. "Don't touch me! I told you," the face screamed. "I told you we carry our bodies with us . . . ," they all said, their mouths moving in unison.

Like a deer on slippery ice, Oona scrambled for her cloak and ran off, crouching farther away from them. Pris and Tommy glanced guiltily at each other, René and Jayde hiding behind them in fear. They walked over to her. Pris put her hand on Oona's hulking, sobbing back.

"Oona. I'm sorry I didn't know. I thought maybe you were an impostor."

"I hate how I look. I hate it."

"We don't care," Tommy said. "We understand."

"I want to help these souls find their home. But it . . . my brother . . . keeps changing and stealing other bodies, and I don't have time, trying to prevent him from . . . I keep having to inhabit bodies . . . these poor dead souls. I'm so sorry!"

"Brother?" said Tommy.

"It's your brother? The demon?"

Oona's four faces sobbed. "Yes," it said in unison, "that's why I've been so desperate to stop him. We were so young. Your age. In Madrid. 1938. Just like you, we found the book and learned how to project. But he—he got greedy, addicted. We were so poor."

As if a window had opened up in their minds, Pris, Tommy, René, and Jayde all saw Oona's memory.

A war-ravaged tenement in Lavapiés, the working-class neighborhood of Madrid. The stairway to Oona's apartment torn off by a bomb so that she and her brother have to climb up and down from a mangled pipe onto the street. Oona holds out her arms for Sebastian to catch her as she jumps down off the hanging gap of steps. The dark alley in front of their house strewn with people, starved, with nowhere to go. A recent bombing left their neighborhood a blasted landscape.

At a destroyed church. Oona's mother, after waiting in a long line for her family's small ration of black bread and lentils, walks up to her children empty-handed. Trying hard to smile, she sends a young Oona with Sebastian, a strikingly handsome young man, to play "scavenger hunt" amid the rubble for anything they can find. Oona and Sebastian clamber over the dust and rubble. And then, Oona finds a cast-off orange peel and, jubilant, calls out to her brother. It rests on top of a book that has a colorful cover, like melting stained glass. Sebastian snatches it up and stares at it.

They bring the rind to their mother, who quickly hides it in her skirt. At home she boils the peel in water, and they all sit down to have their one luxury: hot orange-peel tea. Then Sebastian grabs the book and huddles on top of the chair pillows in the corner, where his bed is.

After fighting and bombs and terror, Franco and his army come marching into the city, with their fascist bird on all their banners and flags. They even have a little propagandistic magazine for children. Pelayos—all to try and twist the minds of young people to turn against reform. Sebastian drinks up every word.

A book lies on Sebastian's bed. When he isn't looking, Oona picks it up and flips through the pages, too. She is drawn to it but can't read a thing. She finds a scrap of paper and pulls out a sewing needle. She dips it in an inkwell and begins painstakingly transcribing the letters.

After she etches her last letters, she finds two thin pieces of board. She carefully carves holes in the pages and binds them. Her brother walks in, wearing knee-high boots, a dark blue shirt, and matching beret on his head, haughty, a different look in his eyes, almost like they are lighter in color. He snatches the original book from the table.

"And just like that," Oona explained, "my brother changed. He joined the FET. I begged him not to. Back then, I don't think the demon had entered a body yet. I think Sebastian was its first. It was waiting for the right vulnerable moment. I think it's easy for the demon to get to Earth during a time of genocide or plague. A doorway opens. It inhabited Sebastian and grew inside him. And Sebastian welcomed it. Soon, there was no telling where he ended and the demon began. He joined the fascists. He became something monstrous.

"And then, one night, he walked into our apartment and killed my parents . . . saying they were traitors. He was about to kill me, too, but I had my copy of the book. All I remember is that I held it up to him, I heard a gunshot, and somehow, that's when I left my body. I stepped into the astral plane. I just entered into it, like, like I was a gust of air."

Standing there in the astral plane, the travelers bowed their heads in sadness, reeling from the most intense history lesson they had ever had.

Behind them, the wind picked up. Oona's faces grew stark and stern. She crouched to the floor, the eight arms clutching the ground. The legs gathered at the rear, steadying her body as if readying for a tidal wave.

"He's arrived," she said.

Pris looked out at where Oona's many eyes were piercing the air. Something dangerous was coming.

It was huge, moving in giant undulations like a shadowy ocean was arriving. As it got closer, the friends could see it was a fleshy beast as big as a city block, all eyes and heads and legs. Like Oona's body but a hundred times bigger. A squirming, wriggling landfill of bodies. It snorted through a thousand mouths. All of them were pulsing and red, warbling in some strange collective anger, snarling at the same time, then laughing, then crying, hundreds of faces moving and speaking in unison.

"Oh, my brother," Oona wailed. Her four faces looked out with a plaintive cry. "Sebastian! Sebastian! Listen to me," they said.

The thousands of mouths stopped howling. They mumbled, quieted, hummed.

"It's listening," whispered Jayde.

Oona carefully stepped over to her brother and touched his pulsing skin. She stroked the bumpy flesh between six eyes.

Pris felt Tommy grip her hand firmly, as if he was finding strength. He held René at his waist, and Pris tugged Jayde closer, too. The four of them stood there, holding one another as if they were trying to become one body themselves.

"Is that . . . the thing that took over my body?" said René.

"Yeah, I think so," Tommy murmured. René fell into Tommy's shoulder and started crying. Pris watched Tommy's face, a mixture of love and sorrow. He cautiously reached his hand up toward René's head, and brought René into his arms.

Oona spoke again. "Sebastian, it's me. Please listen."

The body shivered, and all the faces fluttered. At once, the hundreds of eyes blinked sleepily.

"Yes, Sebastian. Don't worry. We'll get you out of there. We can still release all those people, and you can come back," she said.

Pris noticed Oona was acting more like a hostage negotiator than a sister. The shape rippled again, as if a belch was forming.

"No!" it said, snapping awake. "This is a trap. I won't be stopped!"

Pris watched as a rumble moved through its body, undulating through the top of the creature, sending its thousands of bodies into a wave, as if they were a stadium of howling fans. The wave of arms and faces jumped up in the air, except in place of joy was horror.

The wave thundered toward them like a stampede. Pris and Tommy braced themselves as the blob stood on its legs—the legs of hundreds of humans, some bare, some thick, some shapely, some in torn skirts, some in shredded business pants, some in dingy sweats, tumbling over themselves. They were all screaming endlessly. A bloodcurdling chord of screams.

DARA

Dara opened her eyes. She felt the delicate legs and wings of insects fluttering off her body.

Beware, beware, beware, the hissing insects whispered.

She was standing in front of René's home. The lights were on inside, but the house was quiet. A panic grew inside her chest. She walked through the front door.

"René?" she called out.

She could tell something terrible had happened. Something smelled . . . sinister. A mixture of flamed-out candles and expired meat. Then she saw what was on the floor and gasped. Lying on the ground was the body of a dog ripped open—its guts bulging out of it like a bowl of wet, rancid fruit. Trembling, she moved through the doorway and into the bedroom. There she saw the legs of a human body. It was René's mother, lying on the floor, a spray of blood spattered over the white comforter.

Before she could run out of the house, someone sat up from the chair in the living room. René. Covered in blood, scratch marks down the sides of his torso like someone had clawed at him in desperation.

"You think you know what you are doing, don't you? But you have no idea," he said calmly, holding a letter opener.

Her heart leapt in her chest. She was terrified, but she could hear the insects whispering to her: *Protect. Protect. You hold the power of the earth.* Dara hadn't realized it, but she was still holding on to the book. She quickly flipped through the pages, trying to find the way to defend herself, her hands shaking.

Do not be deterred from your goal. Stand your ground. Claim space on the earth.

René smiled. "You're too late. Look around you. I've discarded every one of them."

Dara could not believe this was the body of the same boy who she had loved and cared for, who was her closest friend. His hair was caked in blood, his stained face grinning. Dara looked frantically down at the book.

"I, um, demand that you leave René's body," she said nervously.

"Ha! You are the worst Protector I have ever confronted in all my years," said the demon. "At least the others had elocution skills."

He circled around Dara like a predator. Dara tried her best to look formidable or, at the very least, calm. She convinced herself this was a dream. René—or the creature that possessed him— sensually glided his hands over his body.

"This body, it's so wonderful," René drawled. "I've been in so many. But this one is the most beautiful yet."

Dara stood there, trying not to move. Then she saw it—something descending over René's head. A spider. It landed on his head and crawled quickly through his hair. She watched as it combed through his locks, completely unnoticed. Then, it tossed a web out and clamped onto René's neck. René felt it at once.

"Ow!" he screeched, smacking and killing it.

Spiders—Dara realized at once—her closest friends, her obsession: now her saving grace. Maybe that was what froze René at the pool. It wasn't a spell. It was a spider. And this one, on René's neck, was a black widow. And another, and another, all descending on him, injecting him with venom all over his neck. He slapped at them frantically, smearing their bodies across his skin.

"Goodbye, brave ones," she whispered.

René gasped, rubbing at his neck. He swore and faltered, heaving for breath.

"You won't stop me from traveling," he said to Dara, looking at her with his sharp, strangely hazel eyes. He closed them and concentrated.

"Why isn't it working?" He became angry. "Oona!" he screamed through coughs and wheezes.

Dara rushed over to him as he lay there, splayed out on the bloody floor. She couldn't stop herself—this was René's body, still her René—she couldn't leave him there alone. She lifted his head into her lap as he foamed at the mouth.

"René! Are you . . . are you okay?"

She looked into his eyes. René, or not René, stared up at her. She stroked his hair.

"Please come back to us," she said as he choked with weak breath.

Then Dara heard the sound of insects again, of cicadas, crickets, getting louder and louder, and she closed her eyes, floating upward into a cloud of slumber.

TOMMY AND PRIS

Pris held on to Jayde as dozens of hands and eyes and mouths screamed over them, drool dripping from their mouths.

"No! Don't let it take me! I'm sorry! I want to go back to my body! To my bedroom!" screamed Jayde.

Pris's body took over, like she was built for this attack, her strong legs and arms gripping the ground angrily, unwaveringly. She looked for Tommy through the trample of body parts. He was clutching René, and also furiously shouldering them through the rush of legs like an angry linebacker.

"We don't want you here!" Tommy screamed. "We don't *want* you here!"

The faces kept coming in waves, the hands reaching out for them before rubbing their eyes and lips as if they were trying to find their old bodies, looking for an end to themselves but only finding more skin.

But the demon was woozy, as if it had been poisoned or drugged. The legs were beginning to falter and buckle, knees knocking onto the ground. Pris tried to wriggle toward Tommy as she held Jayde, dodging shadowy faces.

She pulled herself and Jayde toward the boys. The creature's many faces screamed at them. The mouths called Pris and Tommy fat. They called them ugly. They called them anything and everything Pris and Tommy had heard people call them all their lives. They even called them words that they had only called themselves, in those private, self-hating moments in the mirror.

The faces hung over them, eyes bugged and sarcastic, drool spilling out of their mouths. "Who do you think you are?" the mouths said.

Like a jolt had run through them at the same time, Pris and Tommy both understood. The demon was just like a bully. Afraid, not evil.

Pris looked to Tommy and grabbed his hand. "We have to get out from under here," she said.

Tommy nodded. Wrapping each of their friends in their arms, Pris and Tommy guided them between the sagging flesh and buckling legs to the open air.

Climbing out, tumbling onto the ground out of breath, they watched the massive blob begin to deflate. The faces all began to close their eyes. The body's pulse slowed. The beast groaned, and it echoed across the flat pink astral expanse.

Another hand emerged, and another, and then six more as Oona emerged from beneath the Consumer. She whimpered and reached out to touch its body. Her eyes, all eight of them, filled with tears. Then, four of her arms braced themselves and pushed her onto her legs. She stroked the demon's face.

"It's over," she said softly.

Jayde looked down at the little stream of smoke still floating out from their navel and flung their arms around Pris.

"We did it!" they screeched. "We're alive!"

They rushed up to Tommy. "You are the bravest person I have ever met," they declared.

René smiled hesitantly as Jayde continued cheering.

Tommy turned to look at Oona, still with her hand on the massive body. "What about all these souls? What will happen to them?" Tommy asked.

Oona's faces looked down in sadness. "I'm afraid I don't know. Sebastian will be resting now, forever, but these souls, the ones he abducted—it will be a long process for me to find them. To return each individual to their proper place in the Akashic Records and lead them to rest."

Tommy leapt to his feet. "What do you mean, rest? *Death?* You can't return these people back to their lives?"

René stiffened. He gently pulled Tommy's hands off his shoulders. He let out a whimper and, turning, ran around the side of the dying creature.

Tommy froze, struck with a realization that he refused to believe. "We have to save René. You told me we could!"

"I know," Oona replied, exhausted. "I wanted it to be true. That he had a chance to go back to his body, but . . ." She trailed off, her shoulders hunching.

"But what?" Tommy said. He swallowed a cry. When Oona did not speak, he ran after René.

The boy was huddled on his knees in front of the creature, almost as if he were in prayer. The bodies and faces towered over him in a tall wall of bodies in the peace of death. Tommy knelt down beside him, Pris and Jayde trailing behind.

There were familiar legs and arms embossed into the side of the creature. The legs were pale and strong, the arms nimble, and there were those distinctive calluses between his pointer and middle finger. A lefty. René's own body, his double, hung in midair.

Tommy stood behind René and watched his back convulse in grief.

Jayde gasped. "It's René!"

"Or it's his soul . . . trapped in the creature," Pris murmured.

The double looked at René, sobbing. "I killed them."

"No," René gasped, "no, you didn't."

"Who? Who did you kill?" Tommy asked shakily.

"I killed them," the double repeated. "They're all dead."

"The Murder House," Pris said, suddenly realizing. "That's René's house. His family was—"

Tommy felt his stomach turn. What Pris had told him was true. René's family was killed by René's own hand—by the *demon's* hand. His head was spinning.

René began sobbing. And soon both Renés were crying in sync, their wails doubling in a painful harmony. René reached out to his double trapped in the body of the creature, and they embraced.

René looked down at his navel. The milky trail coming off him wisped in the breeze, weakening.

"No!" Tommy said. "No, you have to come back."

René composed himself. So did the other René. They looked down and watched the wisp at René's navel sublimate in the air like cigarette smoke. René held his book, his Akashic Record, in his hands. And then he let go. Tommy, Pris, and Jayde watched as it crumbled into ash and flew off into the breeze.

"What . . . what are you doing?" Tommy asked.

"It has to happen, Tommy," René insisted. "You know it does."

Tommy could not listen—*would* not listen. He grabbed René by the arms, refusing to let him go.

"No," he said, "*no*. We're supposed to be together. We saved you. We're going to go home and—"

"I can't let that happen, Tommy," René interrupted. "You are going to be okay. You will have a beautiful life. I just know it. You have so much left to live for."

"You can't go! We can still put you back in your body!"

René cupped Tommy's chin, holding it like it was the most precious thing in the world. "I loved you," he said.

Tommy felt like he couldn't breathe. He had waited so many weeks, so many months, to hear those words. And now they were coming at the worst possible time.

"Loved?" he croaked.

"I know you will be loved in the future, too. If you don't remember anything, I hope you remember that. That you deserve to be loved. That you are beautiful."

René kept Tommy's face close to his, as if memorizing every pore, every bump, every freckle.

"I finally know what cerulean is," he declared. "It's the color of your eyes, Tommy. I can see into them." René sighed. "I wish I had time to write this out. But *you* are my poem."

"René!"

"Maybe . . . in another dimension . . . we'll meet. But in this one—I have to go."

Tommy could not speak. And then, René did what Tommy thought was impossible. He leaned over and kissed him.

Tommy felt the softness of his lips. *My first kiss,* he thought. *My first kiss is René Calabasas.*

René stepped back and walked to a spot on the flat terrain away from the others. Tommy would have followed him, but Oona placed four of her hands on his shoulders.

Through his tears, Tommy saw a column of pink light shoot up like a comet streak. A galactic cloud began forming. He watched as Renaldo closed his eyes, exhaled, and then disappeared into the column. As soon as he stepped inside, the pink streak narrowed into a tiny ember. The delicate pink flame floated up in the air and off into a star-streaked sky.

Tommy crumpled to his knees.

"I'm so sorry," Oona whispered.

He looked up at her, his fits of tears slowing as he stared into her many eyes. She stroked his head until he began to feel drowsy. Soon, he was falling into her massive frame.

With her four sets of lips, Oona whistled. In the distance, Tommy and Pris heard the familiar lollipop song, which sounded, this time, like a dirge.

Pris watched Oona lift Tommy's body into Lolly's wagon, which was now draped in black fabric. Jayde was growing sleepy, too. They stumbled over to the wagon and slumped in the seat beside

Tommy. Delicately, Oona pulled her book out of Tommy's backpack and held it as she stroked Tommy's hair.

Then, Pris heard screeching. Two giant headless beasts flew down and alighted onto the corners of Lolly's wagon. Memory Thieves. Pris jumped to defend her friends.

"No," said Oona, stopping her. "It's okay. This is their job, to help them forget."

They watched as Lolly's wagon rolled away. Now it was just Oona and Pris.

Pris swallowed hard. "Did René . . . did he . . . ?"

"Yes. He's gone now. He chose to stop his life before Sebastian could enter his body. He was poised between planes, between life and death. So he sacrificed himself to save his family. Now he will be a constant glimmer outside the event horizon." Oona's four faces smiled. "But look what you did. Jayde is safe. And so are you. You are a brave, brave girl."

"What about Tommy? Is he going to be all right?"

"Yes," Oona assured her. "This will all be a dream for him. Things will be different in his dimension now. René's home will never become a place of murder. For Tommy, René will be a tragic memory. And what happened here, in the astral plane, will all be a blurry dream to him. For Jayde, too."

"And for me?"

"You may not recall. But it will come back to you, someday. You will have moments of recognition. Hints."

"Will I remember you?"

"I don't think so. Not now at least. Maybe we will meet again when you are older and travel through the astral plane. For now, though, it's best for you to return to your life and just be who you are—a smart, brave girl," Oona said softly.

The wagon, with Tommy and Pris lying in it, was far away now. Pris could barely see it, Lolly's jingle faintly chiming.

"I'm going to miss Tommy."

"Oh. You will see him again, soon." Oona pointed to Pris's satchel. "In fact, there are a couple things I need you to take care of, in your bag. Just to help tie up some loose ends."

"But what if I don't remember? "

"You will, in your way. I wasn't exaggerating before. You have extraordinary intuitive powers. You're different, Pris."

"I am?"

Oona hesitated. "I was waiting for the right moment to tell you this, but I suppose it's now. You should know that one day, when you are older, you'll come into your own. Your ancestors will help you."

Pris crinkled her eyebrows. "That woman, the one in my dreams. She looked like a warrior."

"She was. You come from a long line of warriors. An ancient race that has been battling demons for centuries. They are Master Travelers, like yourself. But they slip through time and events. Your past, your parents, your ancestry—they weren't stolen. They were simply hidden. You'll realize one day."

Pris rushed through a mixture of emotions. Relief, from realizing that her past had not been stolen, joy from her warrior ancestry, anger because she knew she would not remember this conversation. *You'll realize one day.* She was sick of waiting. "Why does everyone keep me away from who I am? When? When will I know who I am?"

Oona sighed. "Your destiny is all your own. You get to decide when you're ready. That's why you have to return without memory of all this."

Oona's hand reached up and stroked Pris's cheek.

"A descendant of warriors," she confirmed.

Then she lifted another hand of hers and slapped Pris's face so hard, she blacked out.

1986
TOMMY

Tommy woke up feeling like he wanted to sob. And then, his radio alarm clicked on. "We Built This City" blasted through the speaker. The worst song ever written. It was going to be a terrible day, like always. He stretched, groggy, his sinuses stuffed. As he reached for a tissue to blow his nose, he tried to remember his dream. It seemed so vivid and detailed just seconds ago, but now he couldn't recall a single thing.

Was René there? In his dreams? Tommy lay there in bed trying to piece together the images he had just seen in sleep. Reality and dreams, in his slumbering state, were like loose mingling threads. Or better yet, like the lint you gathered from the dryer.

He would have to talk about it with René. René loved dreams— maybe if he described the colors to him, the bits and pieces of light, René could help Tommy make sense of it all.

Yes, now he remembered, the night before last, he and René

had gone to the park. They had almost kissed. René seemed troubled. Then there was a terrible storm and a blackout that lasted all day. He spent last night wondering if René was okay and must have fallen asleep.

He got out of bed and went to the bathroom to get ready for school. He washed his face without looking in the mirror. He didn't want to see what kind of breakout he would have to deal with today. But then, sighing, he finally did.

He gazed at himself, his skin. Yup, still broken out.

But this time, he stepped back. He gave himself a long look. He was tired of hating himself. This was his skin, his body, his wild and precious life. *Why not try accepting it, Tommy?* he thought. *You are fine. You are going to be fine.*

He heard the faint chime of the doorbell downstairs. That was odd. No one came by this early in the morning before school. Must be some church friend of his mom's. He finished drying his face and putting on clothes and walked downstairs. He entered the kitchen to see his mother and brother. They both had weird looks on their faces, as if they were apologetic about something. It was weird to see his brother this way, so concerned, like he actually cared about Tommy's existence instead of rolling his eyes at him all the time. He turned to his left and was surprised to see Dara— not in her usual pale foundation and dark eyeliner, but bare-faced and serious. He somehow knew what she was going to say.

"It's René," Dara said. "He was struck by lightning last night. He's dead."

Tommy let out a small laugh. This had to be an elaborate joke. Somehow, everyone had come together to create a terrible prank. But his heart sank when Dara's face remained stoic, his family shocked into place like statues. It was real. René was dead. He felt it. He bowed his head. Dara pulled him into a hug, and Tommy heard himself cry into her shoulder.

On the TV, he could hear that same annoying commercial playing. "Come along, come along . . ."

He knew there, his head buried in Dara's shoulder, that he would remember this moment, and that jingle, for his entire life.

2044
PRIS

Pris snapped awake. She heard the quiet tussling of leaves. It was a sound she hadn't heard often—just when she turned on the hologram forest option they had at home. She looked up to see long branches swaying overhead.

She was at the tree in Hell Park. It was morning. There was grass around her, brown and green in patches. The branches above her were bursting with leaves. She was confused—she remembered this tree being an old, burnt-out pile of charcoal. Or maybe that was a dream?

She tried to stand up but felt a weight on her shoulder. Jayde. They were fast asleep, snoring like an old beat-up hovercar. Pris's dream was fading from her, but she did remember that it involved protecting Jayde from something terrible. *Jayde's safe,* Pris thought. *I kept them safe.*

Jayde woke up with a lurch.

"What? Wait. Pris? Why am I here?"

"I guess we fell asleep." She tried to hide how happy she was.

"Wasn't I supposed to . . . wasn't I with . . . ?"

Pris sat forward, pulling Jayde upright as well.

"I think Nomed stood you up. We sat here for a while and then . . . ," Pris said. She didn't remember herself, though, how they ended up asleep under the tree.

Jayde shook off dirt from their legs and stumbled to their feet. "I don't remember at all. That's strange. And then you stayed here with me?"

"I guess I did. I didn't want anything bad to happen to you. So I waited with you here. We must have fallen asleep waiting for him to show up and he never did."

Jayde looked down, ashamed.

"I'm glad that guy didn't show up, Jayde. Promise me you won't meet up with strangers like that anymore? Promise?"

"Yes. Okay. I'm sorry." Jayde rubbed their face. Even though they had slept all night on Pris's shoulder, they still looked gorgeous. They ran their finger over their teeth. "I'm also sorry I was such a bitch to you last night."

"Yeah, you were."

"I know. I was just so excited, you know? I don't know. I guess I thought Nomed could have . . . taken me places."

"You'll go places, Jayde. And you don't need some guy to help you there." Pris picked at the grass. "Maybe just hold on a little longer. Like, three years. When we're eighteen."

"No way! That's way too long," they said, laughing.

Pris gazed out at the park. She noticed the violets, shaking delicately in the breeze, and looked up at the huge tree, its willow branches tumbling down overhead. "Can I ask a really weird question?"

"Of course."

"Has this tree always been here?"

"Pris. You come here all the time to throw your disk! Are you, like, sick or something?"

Pris recalculated. "No, sorry, what I meant was—this tree. It looks so much more leafy and alive today. Does it seem greener than usual?"

Jayde stared up at it. Then, they scrunched up their nose and shook their head. "Nope. Still the same skanky-ass Hell Park tree."

Pris shook her head and Jayde giggled, their eyes focused on their best friend's face. "What?" Pris asked.

"Nothing," Jayde said, smiling. "I don't know. You seem . . . different. Stronger. I think all that disk throwing is filling you out."

"Filling me out?" Pris felt exposed.

"Own it!" Jayde said. "But one thing we have to do is go shopping. No more of these raggedy sweatpants. And that big baggy satchel of yours! You wore it all night? Please."

Pris had forgotten she still had it on. She clutched the bag.

"I gotta pee," said Jayde. "Can you cover me while I go?"

Pris faced the field while Jayde squatted behind her and kept talking. "Oh Goddess, Pris, I had the weirdest dreams last night. I'm just remembering now. Something about a monster and running away and a library. It kept changing. It's that bony shoulder of yours probably; I mean, who knew what was put into my brain from your bony shoulder!"

Jayde kept chattering. Pris opened her bag. She was almost

afraid to look inside to see what she would find. Inside was her trusty disk. And in the front pocket was a stack of bound paper, the title torn off to read *The Sacred Art of As*—. Yes, that book. Pris remembered copying it the other night, and her and Jayde talking about it, but she didn't recall where the original book was, or how they even got interested in it. Maybe just another one of Jayde's incessant string of obsessions. As Pris pulled out the book, a paper, folded in a neat triangle, slipped out. Pris picked it up and unfolded the parcel. A poem. "Storm Omen." It was dedicated to someone. Pris was surprised to see whose initials were there.

They left the park, and Pris walked Jayde home. They stopped at the entrance of Jayde's compound so Jayde could check their wrist.

"Yup, no messages from my parents. It worked. Let's hang out next Friday, too. For real, this time," they added, "not as a cover." Then, they yawned. "I think I'm gonna sleep till Monday."

Pris nodded, watching as Jayde clomped up the front porch steps. The morning air was fragrant with the smell of dirt and earth. Maybe it was full of toxic carbons and trace metals, but it smelled fresher, realer—not like the purified air of the Glade. Pris felt more alive than ever.

As she walked home, she started to remember her own dream last night. She struggled to hold it in place, and soon, it receded like writing in the sand being washed away with the tide. She felt for the poem in her front satchel pocket and noticed something else had flattened, almost unnoticed, next to it. She pulled it out. A photo, of a young girl, standing alone, in a woolly, worn-in sweater in front of a beach. The photo brought with it all sorts of feelings that rushed into Pris's mind. She somehow knew that this girl disappeared, long ago, and that her body was somewhere close by, maybe even in this area. She needed to give this photo to someone.

Pris felt clearheaded. It was as if that dream last night, the one she couldn't remember, had motivated her, had pushed her forward. She also knew, suddenly, what she wanted to work on for her summer project.

When Pris got home, her uncle Myles was in the kitchen, bent over the stove. He was doing something odd—he was cooking.

"How are the Gonzalezes?" he asked.

"They're fine. Jayde sends hugs."

"Aw, Jayde. Tell them I would love to see them soon?"

"I will," Pris replied.

They didn't have school that day because it was a teacher work day for grading final papers, but Pris couldn't wait. She had someone to see.

"I forgot my history homework at school," she lied. "Can I take the scooter and go get it?"

Her uncle looked up from his simmering saucepan. "Oh, chickpea, you just got here!"

"I know. I'm sorry. Jayde reminded me. We're doing a section on forgotten names in history. And I just . . ."

Pris stopped and saw the expression on her uncle's face. He had been worried about her, she knew. He had missed her last night, but didn't want to say anything. It made her heart hurt.

"Promise me you'll be home by dinner?" Uncle Myles said softly. "I thought we could do dinner tonight, just you and me. Cammie is out with her friends. And I am making us mycelium sliders with my famous barbecue sauce. I was thinking about it all night when you were . . . gone."

"That sounds great, Uncle Myles. I promise I'll be home by then. I won't be long." She went over to him and hugged him hard.

"Whew, you smell like dirt and all kinds of wrong!" Uncle Myles laughed. "Take a shower first."

Pris locked the scooter on the hover cage and stepped down onto the airlock entrance. Inside, the roving blue eye moved over her and her bag, not sensing a thing. She walked through the halls. They were so much more echoey when no one was in them. But they also felt smaller, like miniature-golf versions of school. She felt like she was an older adult visiting her former classrooms, like she was inches taller.

On the way to the culture and history wing, she passed through the atrium. The projection screens were still at work, swashing the air with animations and announcements. Lists of winners in swimming and aero-gliding, pictures from Penguin Spirit Day. One of Jayde in their outfit kept cropping up, as if the algorithm was a model scout and could tell how hologenic Jayde was. One image showed Pris standing behind Jayde, looking frustrated and angry. Pris stared at herself and, for the first time, noticed how guarded she had made herself. How she had grown so used to being isolated and alone, she had forgotten how much people needed her—Jayde needed her, Uncle Myles needed her. *No more small self,* she thought.

On the opposite wall, she saw sign-up sheets for disk team.

Without thinking about it, she waved her palm in front of the tablet to sign her name for tryouts. She ran out before she could change her mind. Also, she didn't want to miss him.

She made it to the door and peered past his name emblazoned on the smoked glass. When she knocked, Thomas Richards beckoned her in, still bent over his desk with a pile of papers in front of him. He looked up at her, his eyebrows crinkling.

"Pris? What are you doing here? Do . . . do you know you don't have school today?"

"Yes. I'm sorry to bother you, Mr. Richards. You said you would be here today grading our projects. So, um. I wanted to talk to you about something."

"Oh, okay. Do you have permission? I don't want to get you in trouble for being here unregistered," he said.

"I'll only be a minute. I think I want to switch my summer project," Pris declared. "I want to do research on the tribes in Africa that fought off Dutch enslavers. I think there were some who were fierce. That fought off attacks. There aren't many records. But maybe I can try."

"That's a great subject, Pris. How did you come up with it?"

"I'm . . . not sure. I think I read it somewhere? I just woke up and it sprang into my head."

"Well, sure, Pris. It sounds like a great assignment. And please, if you need any help, let me know. I'll be here all summer." Mr. Richards sighed. "We were going to go to Madrid, but I'm afraid my partner isn't feeling too well."

"I'm sorry."

"No! It's all right. He'll pull through. Not the Virus, thankfully." He offered a tight smile. "Is that all you came here for? You could have just told me through Ting, you know."

"Yes, um, well, actually there's something else. I visited the library a few days ago and found this . . . this piece of paper. It's hard to explain. Anyway, I think you should have it."

She pulled out a piece of paper, folded into a triangle, and handed it to him. She watched Mr. Richards unfold it, shakily.

"'Storm Omen,'" he read. "'For T. G.' Tommy Gaye." He laughed then, like he'd forgotten Pris was in the room. Then he turned, with a bewildered look in his eyes.

"How did you know this was me? That Gaye was my last name?"

"You mentioned it once in class. You said people used to make fun of you."

"It's why I took Martin's name. I should change it back."

"Of course you should."

Mr. Richards smiled at her. And then, silently, he read the poem.

> I am naked, only in my skin,
> bare bark,
> listening for storms
> waiting for omens
> That never come
> Lightning strikes
> A jagged web
> Like roots brighten the sky.
> Maybe you will not remember.
> This night when clouds gathered
> And I became a blurry memory.
> But I will always be beside you

Stolid, silent.
A tree.

He carefully placed it on the desk and looked down.

"I found it in a book," Pris said softly. "Um, on astral projection?"

Mr. Richards's body started shaking. Pris thought he was laughing again, but she realized he was crying.

"René," he whispered.

* * * * * * *

Pris didn't expect to spend her afternoon this way—following Mr. Richards's car on her hover scooter. After he had wiped his tears, he told her that he wanted to show her a very important place. He'd also called someone to meet them there. If it were any other teacher taking her to an unknown location on their day off, Pris would have immediately gone home. But with Mr. Richards, Pris felt comfortable. She felt safe.

When they pulled up to Hell Park, Pris saw another car there. It looked like a black vintage vehicle—a hearse, painted with spider legs. A woman stood beside it, leaning against the door. Music was blasting out the window. She was wearing a long black coat, her hair swept up on top of her head like she had flown there, or at least had kept her hover sedan's windows open while she drove.

Mr. Richards waved to the woman as he parked. Pris pulled her scooter next to him, and he got out of the car and leaned toward her.

"Just a heads-up, that's my friend Dara. She's very smart, but she sometimes has wacky ideas. She is a very accomplished artist and scientist. An entomologist, to be exact. But she also says she is *intuitive*," Mr. Richards said, making air quotes and rolling his eyes. "Don't let her talk your ear off with all her supernatural hogwash."

But seconds later, he called out to the woman, joyfully waving to her.

"Well, hello there, Dr. Baura."

"Hello there, dear," said the woman. She turned to Pris. "I'm Dara. You must be Pris. I've heard a lot about you."

Pris was entranced. Dara was so striking. She wore deep brown eyeshadow, her dark eyes shining.

"So, Thomas," Dara said, "what brought me all the way from across the Chesapeake to see you? Not that I don't love seeing you."

"It's an auspicious day," said Mr. Richards. "Pris is one of my best students. She is an incredible researcher. And she found this."

He pulled out the poem and handed it to her. Pris watched Dara's face as she read the poem. Her expression shifted as if the sun had passed over into a sunset.

"René," was all she could say.

They all walked across the park to the tree. It was the second time Pris had been there that day, and she still couldn't get over how much greener it was—there was a thicket of violets surrounding the tree, like they had bloomed over the past few hours.

"It's so verdant here," Pris said, borrowing a word she learned from Jayde.

"It's an important tree," Mr. Richards agreed. "I like coming here. It's my special spot. Don't tell anyone! The last thing this place needs is people coming here. Oh! I almost forgot. Pris, I have something for you." He rummaged through his pockets and pulled out a gold pen.

"It's something that our teacher gave each of us, long ago. It's for you."

"Me? A pen? Wow, it's so old."

"Ha! Yes. It's to get you to write your thoughts on paper, where no one can monitor you. It's for big words, and small ones, too," he said. He patted her on the arm. "Keep writing!"

He rushed forward, like he was in a hurry.

"You go ahead, Tom," called Dara. "My knee is acting up, and Pris here can help me." Mr. Richards barely even listened and was already bounding up the hill to the tree.

Pris held out her arm to offer to Dara.

"Oh, I don't need your help, thank you," Dara said. "That was an excuse. Tom wants to be alone. But you can help me find the path up there. I don't want to step on Sally."

"Sally?"

"The violets. They were planted here after Sally died. Our teacher."

"Yes. Mr. Richards has spoken about her."

"This place is sort of a garden of memory for us. The tree was planted after our friend René died."

"You mean this is a grave site?"

"Yes. There was an old tree here. René and the tree—well, they were both struck by lightning here many years ago. We replanted a tree in his name. Sally raised the money and made it happen. Then when she died, we planted the violets. Her wife, Deb, scattered her ashes here. They are exceptionally hardy plants, aren't they?"

Pris walked beside her. They both looked up at Mr. Richards. He knelt under the tree, and then sat curled into it, as if it had its arm around him.

"René . . . meant so much to him. To me, too," Dara said to her. "Coming here brings it all back for him. That day we found out René died here. It was so painful."

"I'm sorry. I didn't mean to upset him. Maybe I shouldn't have given him that poem?"

"No. No. It's good for him to feel things. It's not healthy to bottle up everything. Martin is a good man. Tom is happy. But we all have loss in our lives. And anyway, the longing for love is love, right?" Dara said.

Pris was silenced by that. *Longing is love?* All that aching she felt for Taya, for someone, anyone, was a form of love? She had to think on that. Then she remembered something more important.

"Um, Dara, this is a strange question, but . . . there's something else I found. I was thinking you might help?"

Pris pulled out the photo she found in her bag, of a little girl in a beat-up wool sweater and skirt.

"Who is that?"

"I . . . I'm not sure, but I think she is somehow related to this park. I just sense she isn't far. I thought maybe you could help me search for her."

"Ha! Oh dear, what has Tom been telling you about me?" Dara chuckled.

"I mean, I wondered if you had expertise . . . in finding people." Pris realized how silly she sounded.

Dara did not seem fazed. "I do have access to pretty great forensics specialists. Are you sensing she is here? In this park?"

"Yes. I think maybe she went missing, a long time ago. I feel her presence here. Do you?" Pris asked Dara.

"I haven't tried this in a long time. I'm a little rusty." Dara touched the photo and closed her eyes. They fluttered as if she were sleeping, having active dreams. She opened them. "Yes. I think you're right. You have strong intuition."

"I think you do, too, don't you?" Pris said. "Well, that's what Mr. Richards tells me."

"Ha, but then he probably also says to not believe in that spiritual hogwash, right?" Dara said. Pris handed the photo to her. "I'll see what I can do."

Mr. Richards motioned for them to come over, and Dara paused.

"Oh! I forgot, I brought blueberry jam and biscuits. I thought we could have a little food. It's in the car." She started back, but Pris stopped her.

"Actually, I have to go soon," Pris said. "I told my uncle I'd have dinner with him."

"Oh. Okay. Well, in that case, let me give you my card."

She pulled out a lacquered piece of paper. A card. Pris had never seen one. It had her name: *Dara Baura. Forensic Entomologist, Artist, Creative* with a large spider drawing, its legs spanning all corners of the card.

"Thanks," Pris said.

"It's so good to finally meet you." Dara repeated, bringing her into an embrace.

* * *

That night, Pris and Uncle Myles had a long, indulgent dinner. He even bought marzipan and creamed gelatin for dessert. Cammie appeared to say hello. "But this is your night together," she said, and dissipated in a blue mist. Outside the window, the dirigibles sounded especially loud and numerous.

Jayde Tinged her. Going to sleep early! See? I'm being good :) :)

Let's go into the city tomorrow, Pris wrote. We can say we are going to the Terrarium.

Yessssss. Let's invite Benz and Knip? Especially Knip lol lol lol.

Pris chuckled and lay down in her bed. As long as she was with Jayde, they could explore.

Pris thought she wasn't tired, but it didn't take long for her to start dozing off. A thought came to her as she did: One day she would know all about her past, her parents. She could just feel it. She wasn't a zero; she was full of stories yet to be discovered.

She fell asleep, and had a dream. Nothing special, just her, flying through the sky, dipping up and down like a bird riding a current. But while she slept, she held on to her disk, tightly—ready for anything.

TOMMY

Tom Richards watched Dara walk with Pris across the park. His student reminded him a lot of himself as a teenager—her insecurities about her skin, her identity. He hoped she would continue to write. She was coming into her own.

He was embarrassed that he had cried in front of her. It just came out of him. Seeing that poem by René released a valve he didn't even know he had shut tight. He didn't even remember that René had dedicated it to him. How could he have forgotten?

He remembered loving René so much. Writing so much bad poetry about him. He wasn't afraid now. If he could go back in time, he would have just grabbed René and kissed him.

But then he died, out of nowhere, struck by lightning. Not even AIDS. Only recently, when he took up meditation, was he able to finally breathe through the memories from that horrible event. He got to a place of gratitude. Losing someone so young would be a training for the loss he experienced for the next three decades, as friends and mentors died from AIDS. And then, the Virus. His whole life of weathering loss. It was a wonder he was still alive.

He really had Sally to thank. At fifteen, after René's death, he was swallowed in darkness. Sally stayed by his side the rest of high school and into college. She introduced him to her friends in the city—her gay friends who had survived AIDS somehow and who were forming a group to protest the lack of health access and action by the government. Tommy and Sally and Dara joined in some of the protests. They chanted and marched, but never as furiously as the men in the front, the ones who were dying, howling, "ACT UP! Fight back! Fight AIDS!"

Then, so many years passed. Tom went to college for American studies (where he wrote a thesis on the potency of commercial jingles, centered on that irritating song for Lollipop Cereal he couldn't get out of his head). Then he got his master's in education. Traveled to Japan, Mexico. All the while, he stayed in touch with Dara, who went on to study entomology, moved in with her girlfriend, Maxine, and started drawing again, beautiful illustrations of insects that were getting some attention now from a blue chip gallery. But then she also lately started calling herself "intuitive," like she might be receiving messages from other dimensions. Tom just had to roll his eyes. But as much as he thought some of her beliefs were too woo-woo, he was so proud of her—and Sally, who went on to start the first gay and lesbian student union in Herron, later called the LGBTQ Union. By the time she retired, the union had its own wing in the school, and Sally was celebrated with a banquet dinner at the local hotel. Tom came back for it. It was the typical affair—a half-walled-off hall in a hotel, tureens of overcooked pasta and croquettes, but it was nice to see how many people showed up for her.

Including his brother, Charley, who had finally come out of the closet, after their mother died. He married Billy Major, the sleepy lunkhead who sat next to Tom in history class in high school. At one point, Charley came up and hugged him, a few free gin and tonics into the reception.

"You always knew who you were," he said, and then fumbled back to his husband. Once again, Tom marveled at how different he and his brother were. And yet, the same.

Tom looked above him at the swaying leaves and leaned back against the trunk. It wasn't as big as the tree from when he was a kid, but it was getting pretty big now. He couldn't believe the tree had survived the Fires, the Virus, the abandoned suburbs, and neglect from the enclosed, monitored communities.

It was what made this park so special. Somehow it still thrived. This little green patch of land. It was his secret. And now it was Pris's.

The violets shimmered in the breeze like sequins.

Yes, he would start Poetry Club again. These kids needed poetry now more than ever. He would announce the club on Monday. Maybe he would write some poetry, too.

He let out a long exhale.

Some nights, when Martin was peacefully asleep, Tommy was able to dream. Not often, but every now and then, in that blurry time between dreaming and waking, he had a vision.

It was always the same.

He would walk to the door of his bedroom and open it. On the other side was a giant parlor, filled with light, decorated in shades of yellow. He would drift across creaky floorboards, carrying a tray with a teapot and mugs on it. He could hear the surf in the distance. There were mirrors everywhere on the walls.

Out on the porch, sitting in a chair, old but still with sparkly eyes, was René, deep in a book. It was always a different book. Something lyrical, something as delicious and dense as peaches. It was *Thomas and Beulah,* it was *Speak, Memory,* it was *The Woman Warrior,* it was *Labyrinths.*

"So much to read," René always said, and Tom, in the dream, would always bend down and embrace him.

Then, combing back his crinkling, gray bush of hair, he would whisper back, "Yes. So much to read."

THE END

THE SACRED ART OF ASTRAL PROJECTION

A Primer for Beginners

Hello, student.

If you have found this book, it means you have been recognized as having the aptitude to successfully travel to the astral plane.

You may have already done so, in fact.

Have you flown in your dreams?

Have you had a dream where you "awakened" inside your own body and left it there in your bed as you rose up out of it?

Do you feel the places you have traveled in your dreams have an uncanny realness to them, like you can smell or taste or feel them?

Then you may have experienced initial contact with astral travel!

In fact, you may have been drawn to this book because of signals and signs that led you to it—perhaps it was left somewhere, and your eyes fell upon it. Perhaps it was given to you by a fellow traveler. Perhaps you found yourself "guided" toward it. All these are signs that beings from the astral plane are encouraging you to learn about this powerful practice because the Master Travelers see in you the potential of becoming one yourself.

It is unfortunate that you live in a sped-up world, raised with little patience and short attention spans. This primer is arranged in what you, in your reality, refer to as FAQs and an index so that you can quickly apprehend a breakdown of astral travel basics before moving forward.

WHAT IS THE ASTRAL PLANE?

It is essential to understand that your existence, standing there on the earth in a body of flesh and blood, is only a modicum of your real, true presence, and there are other planes where our energy exists.

This is not the only dimension in which your body lives. There are ethereal planes of existence that are parallel to our own physical plane and that interpenetrate our world.

The Astral Realm comprises two other main planes.

These are the Lower Plane and the Higher Plane.

The Lower Plane is vast and chaotic, full of beings and creatures far beyond human imagination. It is noisy and crowded. It is also how one can travel from place to place, reality to reality. Because it is a transit hub, it is also a dumping ground, littered with debris—memories, knots of the unconscious. It is where many beings live, unseen to the human eye but dangerous.

Think of it as a highway. Above this is the Higher Plane. It is here where grander achievements dwell. This is where only select travelers can enter, along with other creatures with higher vibrations. It is also the home of the Akashic Records, as well as the event horizon and other mystic engines that rule the universe. It's important for you to understand these engines, but we don't have time right now because as I said you are not built for patience.

WHAT MAKES A PERSON ABLE TO TRAVEL?

Like many psychic abilities, astral travel takes skill and intuition. To be able to "leave" the body takes a great deal of imagination and will. Some astral travelers have been handed down the ability from ancestors; it's in their blood. Others are simply born with the sensitivity. Astral travelers are highly sensitive people. They may have allergies or other sensitivities to their reality, like acne, rashes, or other skin issues. Their skin, in other words, is almost confused about its state in their physical reality.

ARE THERE DIFFERENT WAYS TO TRAVEL?

Entering the astral plane is very personal. Some travel through meditation, some through breathwork, some by dreams.

And within those methods, travelers also have specific tools that act as guides or gateways. Some pass in and out of the realm by way of mirrors, some use trees, some by dreams, some all three.

Some travelers contact the Astral Realm through their art or expression. They dance, draw, or incant their way into the realm through song, poetry, dance. These talented individuals may not even be aware that they are lifting themselves into higher planes and making contact.

Master Travelers are always searching for extraordinary talented individuals such as these.

IF I AM ASLEEP WHILE I AM TRAVELING, WHAT HAPPENS TO MY PHYSICAL BODY?

It's extremely important that you find a safe place for your physical body while you travel. Make sure you are in a secure chamber. If you are alone, this means double-bolting your door and locking any windows, shutting chimney flues, sealing off keyholes. If you are able to, find one or two trusted helpers to watch over your body.

WHAT ARE SPIRIT GUIDES?

These guides are benevolent, highly evolved beings whose job it is to assist you through your life journey. They have been called guardian angels. Almost everyone who astral projects is aware of at least one guide.

It is advisable to facilitate a meeting with your principal guide early in your astral projection experiments. Call out to it upon entering the astral plane. The being should appear to you almost immediately in a form that is pleasing or familiar.

So many of our altered state experiences have a surreal quality to them. It can sometimes seem difficult to understand what is real. It can be easy to discount the guide who appears to you as being just a product of your imagination. One of the best ways to tell the real from the unreal is to gauge your emotional state.

How do you feel when you see this guide? Nervous? Sad? Elated? Relaxed? These feelings will lead you to your guide.

HOW DO I BEGIN?

Because you also belong to an impatient era, I know you want to start quickly. It is not advisable to go far when you begin your astral journeys. Going too far into the astral planes may expose you to dangerous situations or harmful creatures before you have had a chance to know how to ward them off. There are some entities out there who are waiting for new travelers to arrive in the astral plane so that they can take advantage of them! So, for your first attempt, let's start slowly.

STATIONS

Travel takes a powerful imagination, and full control over your mind and your mind's perceptions.

STEP 1: Place markers at different spots along the path of your living space to the outdoors. For example, you may have a station at the foot of your bed. At the door of your room, at the top of the stairs. At the bottom of the stairs. In the foyer. By your shoes. At the front door. And so on. In your mind, try placing a familiar object at each of these stations: a marble or a colored handkerchief. These are your "stations" of travel.

STEP 2: Focus on a place you would like to visit. A friend, loved one, or even an environment you know well and have an emotional connection with.

STEP 3: Lie in your bed. Imagine moving from station to station: foot of the bed, door of your room, top of the stairs, etc. If your mind drifts off, simply return to your first station and begin again.

STEP 4: Close your eyes and become cognizant of your body. Feel the energy moving through your body, that tingling sensation all over your skin. Imagine the space of your body on top of your skin. Imagine the space above your head. Imagine the space between your ears. Imagine the space around your heart. Imagine the space around your body, growing larger and larger like a soft cloud. Now count down: five, four, three, two, one.

WHAT HAPPENS IN THE ASTRAL PLANE?

Other books may describe the astral plane as a glorious space full of vast wonder. This is only partially true. Yes, there are glorious beasts and angelic beings. (Classic mythical creatures such as unicorns and what you may refer to as "faeries" are there.)

But there are also lower beings who do not have peaceful intent.

WHAT ARE LOWER ASTRAL ENTITIES?

No one has adequately defined just what a lower astral entity really is or where they were created. But most of us who have projected have seen a few. Some could be called faeries or other types of discarnates like ghosts. Others are demons. And others could be described as fallen angels. Anytime you feel uncomfortable in the presence of someone you meet in the astral plane, or you find yourself being physically or psychologically attacked, it's a Lower Plane entity. Time to get away.

Try moving away quickly, in the hopes the demon doesn't follow you. But you can also visualize weapons or tools, or ask your spirit guide to help you.

WHO ARE THE MASTER TRAVELERS?

These are individuals who have reached the highest level of astral travel. They are able to navigate from the higher place to the lower and into various realities. Master Travelers can even incarnate into physical realities from the Etheric world. Though they must do so following the ethical code of all Master Travelers.

When visiting a physical plane, Master Travelers must strictly remain observant so as not to damage or interfere with the reality they are exploring. This means they can inhabit small animals, such as birds, woodland creatures, or sea animals, for example. It is NOT permitted to leap into human form. This can be dangerous for the body of your vehicle as it separates the human from his or her essence and may cause lasting damage to the body and to the people around them.

At the beginning of your journey, you may enter HOUSE OF MIRRORS. This is a depot of sorts. Where your body and mind are given a way to comprehend the endless variations and pathways of the astral plane. It is here you may see into other present lives as they are occurring in your reality. But it is also a way station for travelers to enter the astral plane, where many pass through on their way into the plane of death. And where those who are living and those who are dead can connect, briefly. But only the strongest travelers are able to do so, and only for a moment.

BEWARE OF CONSUMERS

Once you make contact with the astral plane, you have, in a sense, "debuted" into the other places of existence. It is extremely important to take precautions. There are some travelers who will take advantage of you.

There are dark forces in the Astral Realm. It is important to be extremely careful when traveling, lest you awaken a dark force or become trapped in its grip. It's very rare, but some forces will snatch your being, sever your astral body from its physical body.

Once someone is severed from their body, there is little they can do to recover. A Consumer may lure you toward them, offering grand, glittering riches, only to snip off your soul and enter your physical body while you remain trapped, floating in the Astral Realm with no way back to your earthly form.

On the exceedingly rare occasion that a Consumer may enter an earthly body, they may possess superhuman abilities: strength, quick reflexes, powers of hypnotism and pheromonal attraction. They "play" with and often misuse their victim's body, much like you may do with an avatar you are inhabiting in a video game. WARNING: Consumers can also inhabit books. In fact, they may even lure their victims by using this book itself!

MEMORY THIEF

A Memory Thief is a creature constructed out of envy. It is jealous of Earth dwellers who build narrative out of their lives, something that isn't possible or permitted in the Lower Plane. The creature steals objects and keepsakes from people, resulting in things being "lost" in the earth plane.

With enough energy built up, it enters the earth plane and can slip in and out of rooms like a small bit of fluff and is attracted to human beings and floats toward them like lint. Once there, it will attach itself onto a small object and transport it back to its nest. If you have lost something, it was probably a Memory Thief.

It does not have a face, as faces are distinctive, an aspect it longs for.

It creates large nests out of its objects, as well as by stealing strands of hair. Longer hair is best, because hair holds memory.

PROTECTORS

When there is a plague, or a large culling of humans in this plane, the opening between the worlds opens up, and creatures come through from the other side, all sorts of beings.

If you are reading this, then you have a calling.

You are among the earthly denizens who, though you may be locked to your plane, have the ability to sense and feel other planes around you. You may get messages from the dead, or signals from beings in the Astral Realm who are calling to you.

You hear voices.

You see signs.

You have weird dreams.

Some on your world may call you a witch or medium. In darker times in your world, you may be called crazy, and you may be hospitalized, drugged, or electroshocked into a dull submission. Or you could be persecuted, accused of serving Satan, and boiled alive.

You have access to other planes, but you cannot travel there.

Do not be distressed. We travelers depend on you.

Your job is not frivolous. Transporting yourself through the astral plane leaves your physical body vulnerable. Throughout history there have been important and very well-regarded people who have protected and guarded their beloveds from harm during their travel.

Many helpers are seen as witches. They are open to energies and can sometimes manipulate them, but they are relegated to the earthly realm, though their power over it is indomitable.

We travelers need you. You are our Protectors.

AKASHIC RECORDS

The records are a compendium of everything that has happened to every single soul from the time it was created until the present. It is a record of all past and future events organized by name; any person can look up the record of their soul.

There are many ways to view the records on the astral plane, many means by which they can appear. Some describe them conventionally as a giant book, some see the records as a library, some as a book on a pedestal in a guarded space on the higher astral plane.

The records may exist for you in an astral residence. Remember, thought forms live on in the astral plane. The repeated thought builds up and takes form.

They are the greatest source of spiritual wisdom you can access in your lifetime. Misusing the records can result in punishment. Some individuals, especially Master Travelers, guard their records with extremely strong defense mechanisms. If you go looking for someone's Akashic Records, you may find yourself confronting astral guard dogs.

HARBINGER BIRDS

These creatures, usually black oversize crows, are in allegiance with Consumers. Their provenance is unknown, but they have the ability to travel between worlds and often sacrifice their bodies to Consumers to prepare the way for their arrival. You can often find the remnants of Harbinger Birds on the ground near or at sites where a demonic transference has occurred. Their long, black, shiny feathers are inordinately large.

WRITING INTO TRAVEL

Let yourself write your way into travel. Write down everything you feel about someone, someplace, some object that is distant from you but that you feel most strongly about. Write it out. Write it here.

ACKNOWLEDGMENTS

This book would not exist on the earthly plane if it wasn't for my exceptional editor, Elizabeth Lee, whose skill, spirit, and punctiliousness are interdimensional.

Thank you to Kent Wolf at Neon Literary, a stellar agent in human form. Nathaniel Tabachnik for your early edits. Karl Jones for listening to my strange idea at a coffee shop and setting this on its way. I really owe the experience to you, and I am so grateful. And to Francesco Sedita, whose longtime encouragement has meant so much to me. After all these years, I'm so happy I finally get to work with you.

To everyone at Penguin Workshop, including Rob Valois, designers Sophie Erb and Julia Rosenfeld, proofreader Ana Deboo, copyeditor Vivian Kirklin, and production editor Kristen Head. I appreciate your hard work so much.

To Benjamin Currie, for your breathtaking cover art.

To my readers, Kathrene Binag, Clarence Haynes, and Cesar Guadamuz. Your important feedback made this a better book.

Thank you to Dr. Almudena Cros, for her impassioned, informative tour of Madrid at the time of the Spanish Civil War. To Paul Preston and his work on the subject. Charisse Noche for her insight in growing up in the Philippines and Virginia. Dr. Pedro Giron for his medical advice. James Brezina and Judy Sutel for their invaluable insight on education and what it's like to be a teacher today. Erin Clarke for meeting me at a subway food court and giving me a pep talk early on in this project. Celeste Lecesne, who, one day in September of 2016, drew the Ten Worlds on a piece of paper for me.

To Jodie Capes Fogler, my incredible coach. To Betsy Capes and

The Path. And to Jill Pangallo, the best accountability partner and even better friend.

To William Johnson, for his indispensable advice. Tim Murphy for always being around to vent about our dingbat career choice to be writers. Brianna Snyder for reading an early draft and giving me good vibes. Intuitive energy healer Scott Clover for his immensely helpful notes on exploring the astral plane.

I am very grateful to Erin Pavlina and her extraordinary book: *The Astral Projection Guidebook: Mastering the Art of Astral Travel*. Also, thanks to Edain McCoy for *Astral Projection for Beginners*.

I want to thank my English teachers in grade school, especially Genie Rosebrock, Jill Hilliard, and Kathryn Russell, as well as my high school's literary magazine, *The Symposium*. To the Hiller family and Mr. Jack E. Hiller, for bringing history to life in evening discussions during high school. The Richard Byrd Library in Springfield, Virginia, which provided the inspiration for the library in these pages. And to my lifelong friends from high school, especially "The Penta"—Elizabeth Hiller, Pam Lawrence, John Osthaus, and Karen Lawrence Swanson.

Thank you to Yaddo, where early pages were written in January 2020, right before the big shift. Thank you to Four Eleven Gallery and the Carney family, whose magical home in Provincetown is where many ideas and pages were conceived and written.

To the two most amazing parents: Suzanne Snider and Robin Vachal. To Will O'Bryan, Cary Curran, Lorraine Tobias, Nancy Balbirer, David Schweizer, and the Kusama-Hinte family for just being there.

Thank you to my family: Rita, Cathileen, Quinn, River, and Ben, as well as Dave and Steve—my brothers who are so much cooler than Charley. And to Mom and Dad, who commanded that I get back to work on this every night after we made dinner together at the lake. Those summer evenings will be some of my most cherished memories.

To all the poets and poetry lovers in my life, especially my great friend Virginia Heffernan.

To the late, great Bodhi Tree Used Bookstore in Los Angeles, where, one day in the '90s, the polychromatic cover of a curious book caught my eye. And, last but not least, to Ophiel, the late author of *The Art and Practice of Astral Projection*, the aforementioned curious book that continues to capture my imagination.